34/100:
An Edge of Almost

Lucky Tyagi

BLUEROSE PUBLISHERS
U.K.

Copyright © Lucky Tyagi 2025

All rights reserved by author. No part of this publication may be reproduced, stored in a retrieval system or transmitted in any form or by any means, electronic, mechanical, photocopying, recording or otherwise, without the prior permission of the author. Although every precaution has been taken to verify the accuracy of the information contained herein, the publisher assumes no responsibility for any errors or omissions. No liability is assumed for damages that may result from the use of information contained within.

BlueRose Publishers takes no responsibility for any damages, losses, or liabilities that may arise from the use or misuse of the information, products, or services provided in this publication.

For permissions requests or inquiries regarding this publication,
please contact:

BLUEROSE PUBLISHERS
www.BlueRoseONE.com
info@bluerosepublishers.com
+4407342408967

ISBN: 978-93-7018-997-3

Cover design: Daksh
Typesetting: Tanya Raj Upadhyay

First Edition: May 2025

TABLE OF CONTENTS

A BLANK PAGE 1

WHERE IT ALL BEGAN 7

FIRST IMPRESSION 14

THE FRESHMEN TRIALS 35

THE SPACE BETWEEN 57

MORE THEN WORDS 80

NO MORE FEAR 90

A NIGHT IN THE SHADOWS 104

A DANCE OF DOUBTS 126

FALLEN FOR THE FALLEN 149

BOTTOM OF THE GLASS 177

OF REGRET & RESOLVE 195

ONE STEP AT A TIME 219

WHISTLE BLOWS 237

THROUGH THE ALLEYWAYS 255

THE LAST LAP 279

THE LAST ROLL CALL 294

THE LAST WALK 303

A BLANK PAGE

"*Good* days are like grapes; gather them, crush them, and bottle the memories. They age like wine, to be sipped beside a fire."

When I look at myself now, compared to who I was in tenth grade, I see a complete transformation. I still haven't figured out what exactly led to this change. Was it someone else, was it me, or was it simply the circumstances and people around me? Every path leads to more paths, and I'm curious to see where this one will take me.

I've stopped over thinking. Now there's no path, no blocks—nothing holding me back. I'm free, though sometimes even freedom can be unsettling. I feel as if everything has been erased. I know I care about her, and she's aware of it too. Yet, despite knowing that we could never truly be together, we stay close, although not really close at all. What lengths do we go to in the name of desire?

I am just roaming around to find the reason why I want someone in every damn thing in life. When I go to a party, when I dress up for college, when I play something, when I write something good, when I do something good…why I always want that someone to watch me from a corner as I did and appreciate me for that.

Why when it rains, we miss someone. Why it makes a smell of a past moment when we see the weather changing. These questions linger, with no clear answers from either my heart or my mind.

Dreams have become like broken promises, shattered as easily as hearts in a Hindi movie. Yet I chase them in my mind, even if none have come true. I haven't figured out why every song seems like its written just for me, or why every movie plot seems to mirror my own story.

I was sitting in my room, seemingly at peace. The day has been usual expect for the fact that today I feel a little turmoil. I was not even sure whether it is a turmoil or just exertion after the end of the day. I took few deep breaths and try to calm myself, but it is of not much help.

Today felt like any other day, yet I sense a subtle unrest within me. I can't decide if it's actual turmoil or simply fatigue. I take deep breaths, trying to calm myself, but it doesn't help much. My mind floods with thoughts, and I struggle to contain them. Restlessly, I look outside at the encroaching darkness, searching for something elusive. Waves of emotion sweep over me, and I try to focus, but memories and names blur together. I fear being misunderstood or accused of seeking attention. What if I'm wrong? How would I explain?

I try to remember the day, looking for something that might explain my mood. But nothing stands out. Then it hits me: maybe it's the routine, the same thing every day, that's bothering me. But if it's always been like this, why does it bother me now? Why am I suddenly upset about something I've accepted for so long? The thought calms me a little, even though it doesn't fully make sense. I feel a bit better now and ready to move on.

I was holding a pen, with my elbow resting on the table. Under my elbow were some sheets of paper. My posture made it look like I was thinking deeply about something. But that was not true. The paper in front of me was completely blank.

My hand moved towards the paper a few times, almost on its own. The tip of the pen touched the paper lightly, leaving behind a small dot.

The truth is, I couldn't think of anything to write. I couldn't even form a proper idea in my mind. It's so ironic! Just moments ago, my mind was full of thoughts, overwhelming me so much that I decided to write them down to find some relief. Writing was supposed to help me feel better. But now, as soon as I sat down with my pen and paper, all those thoughts disappeared—without leaving a single trace.

A new challenge appears: a sudden change from having a lot to having nothing. Strangely, this emptiness makes me feel calm, washing away my past frustration. I try to remember what I was thinking about before... maybe boredom? But nothing feels clear.

As I sit quietly, I feel at peace. For a moment, I think about giving up, but since I have already started, I decide to continue. I feel calmer and more focused, with new energy as a writer. The past troubles don't bother me anymore. Instead, I feel a strong sense of purpose, which is exciting.

I have written a few words, maybe even sentences, but I am not sure if they are for a poem or a story. They could fit either one. Reading them again and again doesn't help me decide. I choose to stay true to my own thoughts, without letting others influence me.

Taking a deep breath, I feel a little more confident. Now, all I need is a good start. I look around, hoping for inspiration.

There was a clock on the wall... I think something in relation to time but find it difficult to write in entirety. It would require a lot of effort, thinking and ironically time!! Since my mood has become somewhat light, I decided against the subject. I see some books on the table and a painting hanging on the wall. It strikes me that I can write something on philosophy, something in general about how I feel... but as soon as I begin to write I realize that my knowledge is inadequate for such a subject and I abandon it on the fear of being shallow. Then I decide to write something out of imagination, a total fiction, start at random... but after a little while I find myself incapable of doing so. I establish that a story is not something I can write today, for such a swing of mood (from turbulence to calmness) calls only for poetry.

Outside, everything is dark. In the distance, small lights from houses shine like tiny dots. The night sky is filled with stars, and I can see some constellations along with the half-crooked moon. They seem to hang in the sky, still and peaceful. This beautiful sight fills me with joy, making me feel as if I have entered another world.

I step onto the balcony. A gentle breeze flows past me, making me feel calm. At this moment, I feel poetic. Words start coming to my mind, and I think of writing them down. But instead, I stand there, looking at the darkness and the endless sky.

Slowly, memories start to fill my mind. They are so clear, as if they are happening again. I enjoy reliving these moments, and without realizing it, a smile appears on my face. A deep sense of happiness fills me, making me feel light, almost as if I am floating.

Time passes. I suddenly remember that I have to write a story. I go inside and look at the clock. I am surprised at how quickly time has passed—minutes have turned into hours. My eyes fall on the blank sheets of paper and the pen, but I do not feel like picking them up. Yet, there is a strange joy inside me, a quiet happiness.

Even without writing, I feel content. I sit for a moment, enjoying this feeling, letting the night and my memories fill me with peace.

This feeling is overwhelming, and it stops me from writing. I wonder, why should I write when I feel so happy? If I start writing now, it might lessen this feeling. I walk to the table, pick up the paper and pen, and put them back in the drawer. I decide to wait for a time when I feel more passion, deeper thoughts—something that often comes when I'm hurt—that will help me write better.

I resign myself to the bed reassuring myself that someday, I'll finish the story.

WHERE IT ALL BEGAN

"Dear Ishaan, we are pleased to inform you that you have been selected for admission to the Bachelor of Technology program in Electrical & Electronics Engineering"

"Your admission has been provisionally approved. We congratulate you on your achievement and welcome you to a new chapter in your academic journey. The orientation and registration process will commence from the 1st of September. You are required to report to the campus by 9:00 a.m. with all necessary documents.

"We look forward to witnessing your growth, curiosity, and passion as you embark on this path"

The letter arrived on a damp July morning, tucked between a stack of newspapers on the veranda. The envelope was thin, the kind that carried both dreams and nightmares. My fingers trembled as I tore it open, the humid air curling the edges of the paper like a slow, unfolding secret.

For a moment, I just stood there, letting the silence wrap around me like a heavy blanket. Electrical Engineering. The words echoed in my mind, sharp and final. The decision was made. The road ahead had revealed itself—and there was no turning back.

The day of admission arrived with the September sky swollen with dark clouds sending down a light drizzle. A soft breeze brushed against my skin, carrying whispers of the journey ahead. The air was filled with a mix of nervous anticipation and quiet optimism.

It had been drizzling since morning, and by the time I reached the outskirts of the college town, the rain had intensified into a steady downpour. My bus dropped me off two kilometers from the campus, leaving me no choice but to drag my Luggage through ankle-deep puddles, my sneakers squelching with every step.

I was already one hour late. Admissions had started at 9 AM, and I reached the college gate at almost 10. I stopped for a moment to catch my breath and looked up at the college building for the first time. It was tall and serious-looking—three floors high, painted a dull grey. The windows were all the same shape and size, lined up like soldiers standing in a row. The boundary walls were high, making the place feel closed off and strict.

It didn't feel like a college. It looked more like a military camp—strong, cold, and unwelcoming. Everything about it showed rules and control. It felt like this place wasn't just built for studying, but to train and shape students with discipline. Maybe that was the goal. Like army training, this college might break us down first, only to rebuild us into something stronger. I took a deep breath and stepped inside.

The guard at the gate gave me a once-over, unimpressed by my soaked clothes and anxious face.

"Admission block?" I asked, panting.

"Straight, then left," he said lazily, waving me in without a second glance.

The campus was vast, dotted with trees that stood still in the rain. Students and parents rushed around, some carrying files, others struggling with umbrellas. I followed the crowd, searching for a signboard.

The problem was, there were no signboards.

I made my way through a courtyard filled with freshers like me—some confident, others as lost as I was. I stopped a senior who was passing by, his ID card swinging around his neck.

"Excuse me, can you tell me where the admission block is?"

He smirked, a flicker of amusement dancing in his eyes. "New admission?" he asked, eyeing the file clutched tightly in my hand.

I gave a nervous nod, my grip tightening. "Yeah, first day."

He chuckled, leaning casually against the pillar. "Well, brace yourself. You're about to step into the best chaos of your life."

He pointed toward a distant building tucked behind a row of trees. "Take that left, then the second right. You'll find a bunch of lost souls standing around, pretending they know what's going on. That's your tribe."

I laughed, the tension in my chest loosening slightly. "Sounds like a party I never signed up for."

He grinned. "None of us did. But somehow, we survive—and sometimes, we even thrive."

I took a deep breath. "Thanks... I think I'm ready."

He gave a mock salute. "Good luck, rookie.

After walking around for ten more minutes in the hot sun, I finally saw a guy standing in the shade near a corridor. He was looking through some papers in a blue folder and seemed stressed—maybe he was dealing with the same admission trouble as me.

"Hey," I said as I walked up to him. "Is this the admission block?"

He looked up, seemed a bit annoyed at first, then nodded quickly. "Yeah, it's right inside. But you're kind of late."

I let out a sigh and wiped the sweat from my face. "Yeah, I know. I've been walking around this campus like it's a maze."

Inside, everything was messy and loud. Parents were arguing with staff, students were standing in long lines, and printers were making noise all around. I looked for the counter that said Electrical Engineering and joined the queue.

I waited in the line for almost two hours. My legs were hurting, and the heat was making it worse. People around me were also tired and restless, but we all had no choice.

"Next!"

Finally, after what felt like forever, I reached the front. The official, a bespectacled man with a tired expression, barely glanced at me before shoving a form in my direction.

"Documents?"

I fumbled with my bag, pulled out a crumpled file, carefully packed with my high school mark sheets, passport-size photos and the printed receipt of the admission fee I had paid online just the night before.

"Here," I said, handing over the stack to the man behind the desk

" He didn't look up. Just flipped through each paper with the efficiency of someone who had done this a thousand times before.

"You're late," he said, still focused on the documents.

"The rain," I replied, trying not to sound defensive.

He sighed, finally meeting my eyes. "Happens every year.

I offered a polite, sheepish smile. He didn't smile back—just motioned me to follow him to a side table cluttered with a printer, a scanner, and a tray full of freshly laminated ID cards.

"Sign here. And here. And again... here," he said, tapping on different sections of the admission form.

I signed like a robot. Name. Father's Name. Course. Branch. Blood Group. The words blurred after a while.

Then came the photocopying. Stamp. Stamp. Another signature. A weirdly angled photo of me was stuck onto a form and sealed with a clear plastic cover.

After fifteen minutes of stamping, signing, and photocopying, I was officially a student of Electrical Engineering.

I took a step back, folder clutched to my chest, a mix of relief and disbelief washing over me. That was it. No drumroll, no motivational speech, no magic moment—just a stack of papers and a man who'd seen thousands of kids like me come and go.

I stepped out of the admin block, the faint smell of damp paper and old furniture still clinging to my senses. The rain had slowed to a drizzle now, but the sky remained heavy, as if holding back a second round just for fun. I pulled my hoodie tighter and looked around.

The campus was alive.

Groups of students—some wide-eyed like me, others seasoned and already bored—were scattered across the open area. Some stood under trees, chatting in animated Hindi-English hybrids. Others marched past me, holding folders similar to mine, searching for lecture halls, hostels, or maybe just a vending machine.

I took a deep breath. Electrical Engineering. That were about to define the next four years of my life. Or ruin them. I didn't know.

But for me, this was the beginning.

Of what? I didn't know yet. But I was in.

FIRST IMPRESSION

Passing out from school is always an emotional moment. Students often express how much they love their school, only to later say the same about college. College is a phase of immense learning—not just academically but also about life itself. It's a time of making new friends, partying all night, and enjoying life to the fullest. These years are the best of our lives, ones that, once gone, will never return.

While memories fade and faces change, life itself moves at a slow pace—if it changes at all. Yet, in recent times, change has come abruptly, unsettling and swift.

Adjusting to this new life wouldn't be easy, but deep inside, I knew that this journey—filled with struggles, friendships, and self-discovery—was just beginning.

I took a left from the admission block and entered a street buzzing with tiny cafes, stationary shops and saloon. Every step felt heavier—not just because of the bag, but because of the weight of this new life. I was in this city, alone, broke, and searching for a survival.

"First time?" a voice said beside me.

I turned. A guy stood there in a worn grey windcheater, his hair sticking out in defiant angles, like he'd either just woken up or hadn't slept in a while—probably the latter.

His eyes had that hazy, sleep-deprived glaze, but his grin was easy, like he belonged here.

"Yeah," I replied, trying to sound more confident than I felt.

He glanced at the folder clutched in my hand, the one with my name scrawled in hurried ink on the top corner.

"Ishaan?" he asked, pointing at it.

I blinked. "Yeah. How did you—"

"Same batch. I saw your name on the folder in your hand," he said. "I'm Nikhil, Mechanical"

I shook it, a little relieved. He didn't seem like the kind of guy who measured worth in entrance exam ranks or CGPA. He looked like he hadn't given either much thought in a long time.

"You're lost?" he asked, tilting his head.

I smiled a little and nodded. "Yeah, kind of. I'm looking for the hostel block."

He laughed. "Typical! First day and already confused. You're right on track"

I smiled awkwardly. "Guess I'm off to a great start."

"No worries," he said, pointing behind him. "Take that path straight till you hit the canteen, then hang a left. You'll see a board that says 'Hostel Block - B'. Just follow the crowd of sleepy faces dragging suitcases."

"Got it. Thanks, man."

Anytime," he grinned. "Welcome to the madness, future engineer."

ṽ

As I approached the hostel, my eyes were drawn to the striking four-story building standing before me. Painted in a warm, yellowish hue, it had an inviting charm that reminded me of a three-star hotel. It was a newly constructed hostel, designed exclusively for first-year students, offering a comforting transition into the new chapter of life.

I had heard various stories about hostel life—some thrilling, others intimidating—but now, standing at the entrance, I felt a blend of excitement and nervousness. The journey to this moment had been filled with anticipation, but now that I was finally here, reality began to sink in.

Reaching the hostel itself had been an adventure. The sprawling campus was a maze of buildings, each one buzzing with students carrying books, chatting in groups, or rushing to their destinations. With my suitcase in one hand and an admission letter in the other, I had to stop a couple of times to ask for directions. A senior pointed me toward a narrow pathway lined with trees, leading to a large, three-story structure—my new home for the next few years.

The atmosphere outside the hostel was lively, filled with students laughing, talking, and even a few playing football in an open area. Taking a deep breath, I stepped inside, my eyes scanning the unfamiliar surroundings. Near the gate, a security guard sat lazily on a chair, his expression indifferent. Determined to get my room assignment, I approached him and asked, "Where is the warden?"

Without shifting much in his seat, he responded in a hoarse, uninterested voice, "Room no. 9."

His tone hinted at irritation, making it clear that he had no interest in engaging in unnecessary conversation. Not wanting to test his patience, I quickly moved towards the warden's office, my footsteps echoing in the corridor.

Upon reaching Room No. 9, I found myself in the presence of an imposing yet dignified figure. Mr. Sharma, the warden, stood tall at six feet, exuding a commanding aura. Dressed in a tracksuit with sports shoes, he carried himself with the confidence of an athlete. His strong build and firm stance left no doubt—he was a man of discipline and authority, likely a seasoned sportsman.

Later, I found out that he was once a player in the national volleyball team. This made me respect him even more. When I introduced myself, he looked at me carefully, but even though he seemed strict, there was kindness in his behavior, which made me feel comfortable instead of scared.

"Your name?" he asked, looking up from the register.

"Ishaan, sir," I replied.

He studied me for a moment before nodding. "Engineering student?"

"Yes, sir. Electrical engineering."

A small smile played on his lips. "Good. A core branch, Stay focused."

"Yes, sir."

He flipped through the pages and finally stopped at one. "You've been assigned a room on the second floor. Your roommate is from the mechanical engineering department."

The information intrigued me. Electrical and mechanical—a classic combination! I could already picture the late-night study sessions, the exchange of notes, and the inevitable technical debates. It seemed like the perfect blend of two foundational branches, a setup that could foster both academic growth and personal camaraderie.

"You'll find your room at the end of the corridor," the warden continued. "Rules are simple—respect your roommate, keep the room clean, and maintain discipline."

"Understood, sir."

He gave a nod of approval. "Good. Now go settle in."

I made my way up the stairs, my heart pounding with anticipation. As I walked through the corridor, I glanced into the open doors of other rooms, catching glimpses of new students settling in, some arranging their beds, others chatting excitedly with their roommates. The walls echoed with a mix of emotions—laughter, nervous whispers, and the occasional deep sigh of those missing home.

Finally, I reached my room, stepping into what would be my home for the foreseeable future. This was it—the beginning of my hostel life, an experience I had eagerly anticipated for years. The thought of living independently, away from the comfort of home, was both thrilling and unnerving.

As I pushed open the door, I was greeted by my new roommate. He seemed like a cool and composed individual, carrying an air of quiet confidence that immediately intrigued me. He spoke little, reserving his words for moments of significance. This was just the kind of roommate I had hoped for—someone who would pose no unnecessary problems. A peaceful coexistence would benefit us both, making our stay easier and more comfortable.

My room was located in the recently constructed wing of the hostel. Though still undergoing some renovations, it had a fresh and modern appeal, adding a sense of novelty to my experience. The faint smell of paint lingered in the air, and the sound of distant hammering reminded me that the building was still a work in progress. Nevertheless, this newness gave me a sense of starting afresh—a clean slate in an unfamiliar place.

As I looked around, I realized that it was time to make the space my own. Though housekeeping had never been my forte, I tapped into whatever organizational skills I possessed. Carefully, I arranged my belongings in the Elmira, ensuring that everything had its designated place. My shoes were lined neatly on a small rack, and my freshly acquired wardrobe found its place on hangers, giving my section of the room a semblance of order. It wasn't much, but it was enough to make me feel at home.

Despite the satisfaction of setting up my space, an unsettling thought crept into my mind. I was alone in a vast campus filled with strangers. How would I navigate this new world? The prospect of making friends was both exciting and daunting. Would I find like-minded people, or would I struggle to fit in? The thought of inadvertently making enemies in such a diverse environment also weighed on me. Hostel life was a melting pot of different cultures, backgrounds, and personalities, and I had to find my place in it.

As these thoughts churned in my mind, I felt a growing sense of restlessness. The room, though now somewhat familiar, still felt foreign. The echoes of laughter and conversation from nearby rooms only amplified my solitude. Yet, I knew that this was only the beginning. Friendships would form, routines would establish themselves, and soon, this place would become a second home.

Exhaustion from the long day began to take its toll. The journey, the moving in, and the emotional whirlwind had drained me completely. My thoughts slowly blurred as fatigue settled in, and before I knew it, I had surrendered to sleep. The bed, though unfamiliar, was surprisingly comfortable, and within moments, I slipped into a deep, dreamless slumber.

Tomorrow would bring new experiences, new challenges, and new opportunities. For now, sleep was my much-needed escape—a brief pause before I embarked on this new chapter of my life.

ũ

RING RING... My phone vibrated loudly, pulling me out of my sleep. Half awake, I rubbed my eyes and checked the screen. It was my alarm. My heart skipped a beat as I remembered—today was my first day of college.

"Welcome to graduation," I muttered to myself, still feeling sleepy. I got out of bed slowly, trying to shake off the drowsiness.

After what felt like hours of thinking about what to wear, I finally decided on formal clothes. But as soon as I stepped outside, I regretted my choice. Most students were wearing casual jeans and T-shirts, while I stood out in my crisp formal attire. I felt awkward, like I didn't belong.

The morning sun was bright, and a soft breeze filled the air as I walked from the hostel to the college campus. I felt like a small child on his first day of school—nervous and unsure. Thankfully, I had met some hostel mates the night before. Knowing they would be there and made me feel a little less alone.

Though a few friends from my hometown were also in the same college, they were in different departments. This made me feel slightly isolated, but I knew I would have to adjust.

The college campus was huge, filled with students chatting and laughing. I saw some of them walking confidently, already comfortable in this new place. Others, like me, looked lost. I took a deep breath and kept moving.

I finally reached the academic hall, where a long list displayed the names of first-year students along with their classroom numbers. My heart pounded as I scanned the list for "Electrical Engineering." After a few seconds, I found my name under "Class F-43."

Taking another deep breath, I walked towards my classroom. Excitement and nervousness swirled inside me. This was the beginning of a new chapter in my life.

I arrived fifteen minutes late, at 9:15 AM. My heart was pounding, but I took a deep breath of relief. It was the first day, so I was sure the teachers wouldn't be too harsh.

As I stepped into the lecture hall, I felt a strange nervousness. The room was big and spacious, but instead of feeling comfortable, I felt small and out of place. I quickly found a seat at the back and dropped my bag on the floor with a soft thud.

The hall was silent. No one turned to look at me. No one said a word. It was as if I had entered a space where I was invisible.

Around me, many students were already talking to each other, laughing, and sharing stories. It was clear that they knew each other well. Watching them made me feel even more alone. I had no one to talk to, and the sense of isolation was heavy.

After some time, the next lecture started. It was a physics class. A professor entered the room, a middle-aged woman with dusky skin. She had a serious look on her face. Sensing that this class might be difficult, I decided to change my seat.

I moved and sat beside another student from my hostel. He was tall, wearing thick glasses that made his eyes look much bigger. His hair was neatly combed and shining with oil. His pants were pulled up so high that they nearly reached his navel.

I hesitated for a moment but then decided to start a conversation.

"Hi, are you from the hostel?" I asked, hoping to make a friend.

"Yes, I am. And you?" he replied, looking at me with curiosity.

"I'm also from the hostel," I said, feeling a little less lonely.

I was desperate to talk to someone, so I quickly asked him more questions.

"What's your name?"

"Where are you from?"

"Why did you choose electrical engineering?"

His name was Kumar Manu. He was from Patna, a city in Bihar known for its culture and history. He seemed friendly, and I felt like I had found someone I could relate to.

Just as we were getting comfortable in our conversation, the professor's sharp voice interrupted us.

"You in the white shirt! Stand up!" she ordered.

My heart started racing. It took me a moment to realize she was talking to me. I stood up slowly, feeling my legs tremble.

"Yes, ma'am," I replied, my voice barely steady.

"Tell me what I just explained," she demanded, her sharp gaze piercing through me like a sword.

Panic hit me like a tidal wave. Explain? What explain? I had absolutely no clue what she was talking about. My mind scrambled for answers, but all I could recall was the muffled sound of her voice in the background while I had been too engrossed in whispering with Kumar Manu about last night's hostel gossips.

My throat went dry as I shifted in my seat. Maybe I could bluff my way through? No, that wouldn't work—not with her. She was the type who could sniff out lies from a mile away.

I hesitated, glancing at my notebook, hoping for a miracle. Blank. Just a few random doodles and scribbled words that made no sense.

I looked up, meeting her expectant eyes. My heart pounded.

"Ma'am, I... I don't know?" I finally admitted, my voice barely above a whisper.

A wave of quiet laughter spread across the room. I could feel the eyes of my classmates on me. Some were amused, while others seemed indifferent.

The professor's face darkened. "You don't even know the question? Stand up for the entire lecture!" she announced firmly.

My heart sank. I had just made a fool of myself on the first day.

With my head low, I remained standing. The minutes stretched endlessly. I could feel the weight of embarrassment pressing on my shoulders.

Some students threw quick glances at me. Others ignored my existence altogether. But inside, I knew I was now the subject of jokes and whispers.

The class continued, but I couldn't focus. All I could think about was how badly my first day had gone.

When the lecture finally ended, I sank into my seat, exhausted.

Kumar Manu gave me a sympathetic look. "Tough start," he said with a small smile.

I nodded, letting out a deep sigh.

ũ

Finally, lunchtime had arrived, I walked towards the hostel mess, my stomach growling with hunger. The morning had been long and tiring, and I could feel my energy draining. As I reached the mess, I saw the usual chaos—students rushing in, some already seated, mess workers shouting orders, and the clattering of utensils filling the air. The sound of sizzling food from the kitchen added to the daily noise.

I sighed and moved forward, trying to navigate through the crowd. Just as I reached the serving counter, a mess worker glared at me.

"Hey boy, make hurry!" he snapped, his voice sharp and impatient.

I felt a flash of irritation. Was it necessary for them to treat us, the future engineers, with such rudeness? I wanted to say something but held back. There was no point in arguing. Instead, I kept my head down and grabbed a plate, piling it with rice, dal, vegetables, and a piece of dessert.

Now came the next challenge—finding a place to sit. The mess was packed, and students were scattered across tables, talking, eating, and laughing. I scanned the room, searching for an empty seat.

Then, a familiar voice called out, cutting through the noise.

"Hey, you! Come here!"

I turned and saw Rohan sitting at a table with Nikhil. I had met them when I had just moved into the hostel.

Rohan gestured towards an empty seat next to them. "Have a seat," he said, pointing to the table where they had already placed their plates.

"Thanks," I said, relieved to have found company.

As I settled in, Rohan leaned slightly forward and asked, "So, how was your day?"

I hesitated for a moment, stirring my daal with my spoon. "It was fine," I replied. "Nothing much happened. And yours?"

"Same here," Rohan said with a shrug. He didn't sound too excited either.

Nikhil, however, was in his usual lively mood. "Why are you both talking like old men?" he said, rolling his eyes. "Come on, guys! College has just started! We should be excited."

I laughed. That was Nikhil—always making sure no conversation turned dull.

As we ate, Rohan introduced me to some of his other friends who joined our table. He had a way of making people feel at ease, effortlessly drawing them into conversations. With his sharp features, confident demeanor, and an undeniable charm, he was a total stud. His slight Punjabi accent added to his appeal, making his words feel both commanding and charismatic. When he spoke, people paid attention, not just because of what he said but because of how he carried himself.

Meanwhile, Nikhil, slim and full of energy, had everyone in stitches with his jokes. He mocked the food, did spot-on impressions of professors, and even mimicked the mess workers, leaving the whole table in fits of laughter. Despite his mischievous nature, he was sharp when it came to studies, balancing his humor with a knack for academics. Even Rohan, usually composed, couldn't resist cracking a smile at Nikhil's antics.

Lunch was turning out to be much better than I had expected. The morning had been stressful, and I had felt a little lost. But now, sitting at this table, surrounded by laughter and friendly faces, I felt more at ease.

As time passed, we continued sharing stories—about school life, funny hostel incidents, and random things that made us laugh. At one point, Nikhil started talking about how he once got caught cheating in an exam but managed to escape punishment with his quick thinking. The way he told the story, complete with dramatic expressions, had everyone in splits.

Eventually, I glanced at the clock and realized that lunch break was almost over. I still had a lot to do, and the day wasn't finished yet.

I put my spoon down and stretched my arms. "I should get going," I said. "Still have things to sort out."

Rohan nodded. "Yeah, we'll catch up later."

"Just don't forget us after making new friends," Nikhil added with a smirk.

I laughed. "Not possible."

As I left the mess, I felt different from how I had felt in the morning. I was still a bit nervous about what lay ahead in college, but at least I knew that I wasn't alone. I had met Rohan and Nikhil, and I had taken my first steps into a world filled with new opportunities and friendships waiting to unfold.

ũ

After lunch, the atmosphere was filled with a mix of excitement and nervousness. We were waiting to be taken to our classrooms, and the anticipation in the air was almost tangible. I walked up the staircase with a sense of reluctance, exaggerating each step as if I were climbing a mountain. The thought of sitting through another lecture felt exhausting already.

As I entered the classroom, my eyes immediately searched for a familiar face. Soon, I spotted Manu and made my way toward him. We quickly fell into a lively conversation, laughing and exchanging stories. Within minutes, I was talking to nearly all the boys in the class, our voices echoing through the room. The energy in the classroom was high, with everyone buzzing about their first day in college.

Just then, the door swung open with a slight creak, and a tall man walked in. He had a strong presence, carrying himself with authority. His long strides and confident posture immediately captured our attention. As he reached the front of the class, he turned to face us and spoke in a deep, steady voice.

"Good afternoon, students," he said, his eyes scanning the room. "I am your mathematics professor from the applied science department."

There was a brief silence in the room. He continued, "Congratulations and welcome to the sports city of India. You are now college students. This is a new chapter in your life, a place where you will gain knowledge, experience, and discipline. College is like a fountain of knowledge, and you must drink deeply from its waters."

He smiled after saying this, as if expecting applause or admiration. However, we only exchanged glances, unsure whether to appreciate his words or suppress our laughter at his dramatic way of speaking.

The professor carried on. "Mathematics is not just a subject; it is a language that explains the universe. It is present in nature, in architecture, in technology, and even in sports. Some of you may have a fear of mathematics, but I assure you, with the right approach, it can become your best friend."

At this point, I could sense the energy in the room shifting. Some students looked genuinely interested, while others were already beginning to lose focus.

"To begin with, let's get to know each other. Please introduce yourselves—your name and the branch you have chosen."

A collective groan rose from the class. Introductions always felt unnecessary and awkward. One by one, students stood up and spoke briefly. Some were confident, while others hesitated and mumbled their words. When it was my turn, I stood up, said my name and branch, and quickly sat back down, relieved to have it over with.

Once the introductions were done, the professor launched into his lecture. At first, he tried to keep us engaged by asking questions and explaining concepts in an animated manner. However, as the minutes passed, the excitement in the room faded. The lecture soon turned into a monotonous explanation of equations and theories. I tried my best to stay attentive, but my eyelids grew heavy. It was as if my brain was refusing to absorb any more information. I looked around and saw my classmates struggling as well. Some were yawning, others resting their chins on their hands, clearly fighting sleep.

My mind drifted, and I found myself staring out of the window. The sunlight outside seemed far more inviting than the dull classroom. Just then, the professor clapped his hands, snapping us back to attention.

"Mathematics requires concentration!" he declared. "If you want to excel in this subject, you must train your mind to focus"

The hours dragged on, and the classroom atmosphere became heavier. Some students began scribbling in their notebooks, not taking notes but doodling instead. I struggled to keep my head up, my mind wandering to thoughts of football, food, and anything but mathematics.

Finally, after what felt like an eternity, the lecture came to an end. The professor wrapped up his lesson, gave us a few instructions for the next class, and dismissed us. A collective sigh of relief filled the room as we packed our bags and hurried out.

As I stepped outside the classroom, I spotted Nikhil and Rohan waiting near the corridor. We exchanged exhausted looks and burst into laughter, knowing we had all struggled to stay awake during the lecture.

A few other hostelers joined us, and we decided to head to a nearby café to escape the monotony of classes. The place was buzzing with students, all trying to recover from their first-day experience. We grabbed a table, ordered some snacks, and soon found ourselves chatting about everything—professors, assignments, and the unpredictable college life ahead.

At first, we were just a group of hostelers hanging out, but as the conversations flowed, something changed. The nervousness and awkwardness of the first day slowly faded. Nikhil, with his laid-back attitude, made us laugh with his sarcastic remarks, while Rohan, always the competitive one, turned even the simplest discussions into debates. I found myself enjoying their company more than I expected.

After spending a good hour at the café, we said goodbye to the day scholars and started walking back to the hostel. The evening air was cooler, and the campus felt more alive, with students enjoying their free time.

"You know," Rohan said, "this college life might not be as bad as I thought."

Nikhil nodded. "Yeah, as long as we survive the lectures."

I chuckled. "And the assignments."

We laughed, realizing that this was just the beginning. The three of us had started as batchmates, but slowly, a bond was forming—one that would carry us through the ups and downs of college life.

THE FRESHMEN TRIALS

The sun was setting over the college campus, painting the sky in shades of orange and pink. A cool breeze flowed through the trees, making the leaves rustle softly. The entire campus seemed to glow under the warm, golden light. It was the kind of evening that made everything look almost like a scene from a movie.

Nikhil, Rohan, and I walked slowly through the grounds, enjoying the peaceful atmosphere. It had only been a few days since we had joined the college, and everything still felt new and exciting. We looked around, taking in every little detail—the tall buildings, the green lawns, and the students scattered all around, some sitting in groups, some walking alone, lost in their own world.

"This place is huge," I muttered, feeling both amazed and slightly overwhelmed.

"Yeah," Rohan replied, chewing his gum as usual. "I wonder how long it will take us to know every corner of this place."

Nikhil, walking slightly ahead, turned back with a smirk. "Well, Rohan, we have four years. I think that's enough time."

We laughed and continued strolling, letting our feet decide where to go next. Without realizing it, we found ourselves near the basketball court. The sound of sneakers squeaking on the ground, the rhythmic bounce of the ball, and the occasional cheer from the spectators filled the air. It was an intense game—two teams competing fiercely, each trying to outscore the other. The players moved with precision, passing, dribbling, and shooting effortlessly.

We leaned against the railing, watching the match with interest. The game was fast-paced, and every move seemed calculated. The players were giving it their all, and the crowd was just as invested. A few other students stood nearby, watching just like us. Their presence was felt even before we turned to look at them.

Something about them was different. The way they stood, their confident expressions, and their casual but firm postures—it didn't take long to realize that they were seniors. A slight tension filled the air as we exchanged glances, silently acknowledging their presence.

One of them, a tall guy with sharp eyes, noticed us and gave a small nod, signaling us to come closer.

For a moment, we hesitated. We had heard stories about seniors interacting with juniors—sometimes it was friendly, but other times, it was more of a test. There was always that uncertainty. Were they going to welcome us warmly, or were they about to make things difficult?

I turned slightly to Nikhil, and that's when I noticed something unusual, something he was rarely seen without. His usual carefree and playful attitude had vanished. Instead, his face looked serious, focused, as if he were about to attend an important job interview or negotiate a huge business deal. It was such a sudden change that I almost laughed, but the situation demanded otherwise.

We took a deep breath and stepped forward, joining a small group of other freshers who had also been gathered near the court. The senior who had signaled us over looked us up and down, taking his time as if he were evaluating us.

After a moment, he spoke with a casual yet authoritative tone. "New students, huh?"

His voice was clear, confident, and to my slight surprise, in English rather than Hindi. I had expected them to speak in Hindi, but maybe this was part of the private college culture. English was often seen as a sign of sophistication and prestige in such places.

I nodded and replied, "Yes."

The senior exchanged looks with his friends, a smirk forming on his lips. Then, with a hint of mischief in his eyes, he said, "Well, we're going to ask you a few questions. Answer them properly, or let's just say, your time here might get... interesting."

There was a moment of silence. The words hung in the air, carrying a weight that wasn't entirely threatening but wasn't entirely friendly either. It was the kind of moment where you weren't sure whether to be nervous or just play along.

Nikhil cleared his throat and finally spoke, "Uh... What kind of questions?" His voice was steady, but I could tell he was choosing his words carefully.

The senior chuckled. "Nothing too difficult. Just a little introduction, some basic college knowledge, and maybe a fun task or two."

Rohan, who had been quiet till now, crossed his arms. "And if we don't answer correctly?"

Another senior, a guy wearing glasses, leaned in slightly and said, "Then things might get more... entertaining. For us, at least."

A nervous chuckle rippled through our group, though most of us seemed equally unsure, some shifting uncomfortably, others maintaining a neutral expression. The message was clear: play along, or face the consequences. So, we accepted the challenge, inwardly bracing ourselves.

"Relax," the first senior said, clapping his hands together. "We're not here to bully you. Just a little fun to welcome you guys."

That made things a little better. There was still an edge of uncertainty, but at least it wasn't outright intimidation.

Another senior stepped forward and pointed at Nikhil. "Let's start with you".

Nikhil took a second before answering, "Nikhil. Mechanical Engineering."

The senior nodded. "Alright, Nikhil from Mechanical. Let's see how well you know your college."

The questions began. Some were simple, like the name of the principal, the founding year of the college, or the location of certain departments. Others were trickier, like naming senior professors or explaining a random rule from the student handbook.

Nikhil answered as best as he could, sometimes getting it right, sometimes hesitating. When he got something wrong, the seniors would laugh, but it wasn't in a mean-spirited way. It felt more like they were testing us rather than looking for ways to trouble us.

When it was my turn, I tried to stay calm. They fired questions at me—simple ones, nothing too intense. My name, where I was from, my schooling, and so on. It felt less like an interrogation and more like a casual chat. The tension I had initially felt started fading away.

Just when I thought we were done, the leader of the group smirked and leaned forward. His eyes held something unreadable, a mix of amusement and challenge.

"Alright," he said, "it's time for the last question. This one is the most important of all."

I stayed quiet, waiting.

"I want to know your thoughts on that girl over there by the canteen."

He gestured dramatically towards a girl standing a short distance away. She wasn't too far, but far enough that she might not have heard the conversation. She was from the girls' hostel, that much was obvious. Her stance, her confidence, and the way she watched our interaction with quiet curiosity told me she wasn't just any random bystander. There was a certain intensity in her eyes, a sharpness that suggested she wasn't easily impressed or intimidated.

It didn't take long for me to realize that she had some kind of connection with the leader of this senior group. Maybe she was someone he liked, or maybe she was someone all of them respected. Either way, it was clear that my answer was about to be judged.

I glanced at her again, taking in her features. She was undeniably attractive. Not in the overly flashy way, but in that effortless, confident manner that made people stop and notice her. Finally, after a moment's thought, I gave my answer.

"Um... Pretty and beautiful lady," I said.

or a second, there was silence. Then, the senior burst out laughing, shaking his head as if I had just missed something obvious.

"Pretty and beautiful?" he mocked; his tone filled with sarcasm. "She's hot, bold, sizzling! And you just call her pretty, like some 'ordinary girl'?"

The others joined in his laughter, though not in a cruel way. It was more like they found my choice of words amusing. I wasn't sure if I should defend my answer or just let it be.

Then, they turned to Rohan, motioning for him to answer the same question.

I turned to look at him. Rohan had been uncharacteristically quiet the whole time. He had even stopped chewing his gum, which was rare for him. He usually had a goofy, light-hearted demeanor, but right now, he was different. His eyes stayed fixed on the girl, and for a moment, he looked almost... fascinated.

Then, without hesitation, he said, "That girl is an item."

The words hung in the air for a moment.

And then—WHAM.

A slap landed hard across Rohan's face.

A senior standing next to me had hit him. His expression was furious, his voice sharp as he snapped, "How dare you?"

The shift in atmosphere was immediate. The casual, playful vibe was gone, replaced by thick tension.

"Do you have any manners?" the senior continued, his anger not fading. "You call someone 'an item' in front of us? Disrespecting a girl like that?"

I was floored; I hadn't expected things to escalate like this over such a simple comment. Rohan's expression was hard, the smoldering rage beneath the surface visible to anyone who cared to look.

"Alright, you're free to go," the main senior said, waving his hand. "But remember, we'll be watching. College is not just about classes and exams. It's about knowing your seniors too."

With that, they walked away, leaving us standing there, still processing everything

Once we were safely out of earshot, Rohan relaxed his angry expression fading as he took a deep breath. Casually, he reached into his pocket, unwrapping another piece of gum, his goofiness back in full force as if nothing had happened at all.

Nikhil exhaled loudly. "Well, that was... something."

Rohan chuckled. "Yeah. Welcome to college life, I guess."

As we walked away from the basketball court, I realized something. This was just the beginning. College wasn't just about books and lectures—it was about experiences, about meeting new people, about facing the unexpected.

And honestly, I couldn't wait to see what came next.

ॐ

Sitting in Rohan's room, the three of us—Rohan, Nikhil, and I—were completely drained. The relentless introduction sessions with our seniors had taken a toll on us. We had spent hours answering their endless questions, introducing ourselves over and over, and completing the random tasks they gave us. By the time they finally let us go, it was already late, and all we wanted was some peace.

Rohan leaned back against the wall, rubbing his forehead. "I swear, if one more senior asks me my name, I'm going to forget it myself."

I sighed, stretching my legs. "This hostel is too noisy. I need some fresh air."

Rohan glanced at the ceiling, feeling the weight of exhaustion. "What if we go to the terrace? It'll be quiet there."

Nikhil's eyes lit up. "That's actually a good idea. No seniors, no noise. Just a little escape."

Rohan nodded. "Let's go before someone else gets the same idea."

Feeling excited about our plan, we quickly left the room and made our way upstairs. But as we climbed the last step, our excitement turned to disappointment.

The door to the terrace was locked.

"Why do these idiots always keep the doors closed?" I shouted in frustration, blaming the hostel security for our disappointment.

"Yeah, man, this suck," Nikhil agreed, looking equally upset. "What do we do now?"

Before I could answer, Rohan gave us a mischievous smile. His eyes twinkled with excitement, which instantly made me suspicious. Whenever Rohan had that look, it meant he was up to something crazy.

"Hey, are you guys thinking what I'm thinking?" Rohan asked, his grin widening.

Nikhil and I exchanged confused looks. Then, at the same time, we both replied, "No!"

We had no clue what Rohan was planning, but we knew one thing for sure—whenever this guy had an idea, it was always something wild. And the craziest part? He had a habit of actually pulling off his plans successfully.

"Okay, forget it," Rohan said with a smirk. "Just tell me one thing—are you two with me?"

I hesitated. "We are with you... but don't do anything stupid," I warned.

"Great," Rohan said confidently. "Now just wait and watch!"

Before we could ask him what he meant, he suddenly turned around and ran down the stairs. He jumped four steps at a time, moving so fast that within seconds, he disappeared from our sight.

Nikhil and I looked at each other, confused.

"What is this idiot up to now?" Nikhil asked.

"I have no idea," I replied, shaking my head.

A few minutes later, we heard footsteps rushing up the stairs. Rohan was back. But this time, he was holding something in his hands.

A fire extinguisher.

"What the hell is that for?" I asked, my eyes widening in shock.

Rohan grinned. "This, my friend, is the key to breaking that lock!" he said casually, as if he had just found a normal solution to our problem.

Nikhil and I were stunned. Was he serious? Did he really plan to use a fire extinguisher to break open the door?

"Screw you, Rohan!" I said, stepping back. "I am not getting involved in this!"

Suddenly, Nikhil turned to me with excitement in his eyes.

"Come on, Ishaan, let's do it," he said eagerly, as if he had just discovered a secret adventure.

I looked at him, confused. "Do what?" I asked.

Before Nikhil could answer, Rohan smirked and pointed a finger at me. "Hey, Nikhil, don't ask him. He is a big loser," he said mockingly.

Wow. What a great way to provoke someone! If you want to make someone do something, just attack their ego, and they will be ready to prove you wrong. I could feel my pride getting challenged, and I was already getting mentally prepared to prove Rohan wrong.

"Come on, Ishaan, let's go! And besides, what is life if it is normal and boring? It must have some adventure; otherwise, all the thrill and enjoyment will be lost," Nikhil said, sounding like a philosopher.

He continued, "You know how much I love movies and all the crazy things that happen in them. This will be fun! And if we pull this off, won't we have a great story to tell our juniors?"

I took a deep breath and thought for a moment. "Okay... but think once again," I said in a low voice, still unsure.

"There is nothing to think again! Let's go!" Rohan said with excitement.

I sighed and finally gave in. "Okay, I will do it. And yes, I am not a loser!" I said, feeling a bit irritated at Rohan's comment. Maybe he was right, but I didn't want to accept it.

While we were talking, Rohan had already grabbed a fire extinguisher and was ready to use it. Without waiting any longer, he started hitting the lock of the terrace door with it. The sound echoed through the corridor. One by one, all three of us took turns smashing the lock. After a few hits, the lock finally broke open.

At that moment, we felt like prisoners who had just escaped from jail. We quickly stepped onto the rooftop, feeling the cool night air against our faces. The view was breathtaking. The city lights were twinkling in the distance, and the stars above were shining softly. It felt like a scene straight out of a movie.

We leaned against the edge of the rooftop, laughing quietly. We talked about all the pranks we had pulled, the sessions with seniors we had struggled through, and the little victories we had achieved just now by breaking the lock. It was a rare moment of peace and excitement.

Suddenly, Rohan pulled out a thin piece of paper, and started rolling something. His fingers moved so fast that in just a few seconds, he had rolled a perfect joint. He took a puff, exhaled slowly, and then turned toward me.

"Hey, do you want a joint?" Rohan asked me casually, as if he were offering a piece of gum.

"No," I replied firmly.

"Oh, come on! Just one puff," he insisted, holding it out toward me. His eyes gleamed with mischief.

I shook my head. "No, I don't smoke."

Rohan smirked and took another deep drag from his joint. "You should try it once. It helps you relax. After daily stress, your body must be sore. This will help you feel lighter."

I shook my head again. "I don't think so. It's not my thing."

He laughed and exhaled another cloud of smoke. "Ishaan, you are too serious. One puff won't make you an addict. Everyone tries it once. Even Nikhil has tried it!"

I raised my eyebrows in surprise. "Nikhil? He smokes?"

"Well, not regularly," Rohan admitted, "but he tried it once. Just for fun."

I sighed. "Look, I respect your choices, but for me, smoking is a waste. It's just like burning money and blowing the smoke into the air."

Rohan chuckled. "You sound like an old man. Loosen up a bit!"

I stayed silent for a moment, watching him as he smoked. He seemed so at ease, like he had no worries in life. But I knew that wasn't true.

"Why do you even smoke so much?" I asked after a while.

Rohan looked at me and shrugged. "It helps me forget things. College stress, family problems, heartbreaks... everything just fades away for a while."

I stared at him. He always seemed so confident and fearless, but maybe there was something deeper hidden inside him.

"I get it," I said softly, "but it's not the right way, Rohan. Running from problems doesn't solve them."

Rohan smiled but didn't say anything. He took another puff and looked at the sky. The smoke slowly rose into the air and disappeared.

Suddenly, a rough voice startled us. Someone had just come to the terrace.

"What the..." I whispered; my throat suddenly dry. "I thought you said no one would come here."

"I don't know, man," Rohan hissed. "Just stay quiet."

But before we could react, a shadow loomed over us, and the dim rooftop light revealed the figure of none other than Mr. Sharma, the hostel warden. His cold, calculating eyes scanned the scene before him—the broken lock dangling from my fingers, the dented fire extinguisher near Nikhil, and the cigarette smoldering between Rohan's fingers. We were caught red-handed, and from the look on his face, he was not about to let this slide. We looked like we were competing to break the most rules.

My heart pounded in my chest. My body felt weak, and I prayed for the ground to open up and swallow me. How were we going to get out of this nightmare?

"What on earth do you think you're doing up here?" Mr. Sharma's voice was calm, but there was a dangerous edge to it.

Rohan stammered, "S-sir, we just... w-we were just..."

Nikhil lowered his head and mumbled, "We're sorry, sir."

I knew this was bad. This wasn't just breaking a minor rule—this was a series of violations stacked on top of each other. And Mr. Sharma wasn't the type to let things slide. I took a deep breath, trying to find the right words.

"Sir, we... we know this was wrong. But please, we're new to this college. We just wanted one night up here, to—"

Before I could finish, a sharp slap landed on my cheek. The sting burned across my face, and my vision blurred for a moment. The thrill of rebellion disappeared instantly. I was no longer some daring rule-breaker; I was just a student who had made a terrible mistake. The silence that followed was suffocating.

I cursed under my breath. What a day this had been. First, there were endless introduction rounds with the seniors, during which Rohan had been slapped. And now, just when the three of us had decided to escape the stress for a while, I was the one getting slapped.

Without another word, Mr. Sharma turned on his heel and gestured for us to follow. We obeyed, trudging behind him down the stairs, each step heavier than the last. The echoes of our footsteps bounced off the hostel walls as we descended to his office on the ground floor.

ũ

Once inside, the room seemed even smaller than usual. The walls, lined with books and hostel records, felt like they were closing in on us. We stood stiffly as Mr. Sharma settled into his chair, his gaze piercing through us.

"I should report this to the Management," he said finally, his voice low and deliberate. "You three would be out of this college in no time. But I won't."

I looked up, hope flickering in my chest. Maybe, just maybe, we would get out of this.

Then, his next words shattered that hope. "Give me your parents contact numbers".

My stomach dropped. My mother disappointment was something I never wanted to experience.

Rohan clenched his fists, his jaw tightening, while Nikhil took a sharp breath. Then, to our utter shock, he fell to his knees.

"Sir... please... don't call my home," he sobbed, his voice breaking.

Crying was a desperate move, but sometimes, in difficult situations, it worked. And Nikhil was using it perfectly. His shoulders shook as he continued pleading, his words barely coherent. Mr. Sharma exhaled deeply, rubbing his temples.

"Okay, stop crying," he said after a long pause. "I won't call your parents. But there are conditions."

We straightened up immediately, eager to listen.

"You want my forgiveness? Then you'll have to earn it," he continued. "Each of you will write a detailed apology letter. I want to know exactly why rules matter, why your actions were unacceptable, and what you learned from this."

Rohan exhaled in relief. "That's it, sir?"

Mr. Sharma's eyes hardened. "That's it? Do you think this is a joke, Rohan?"

"N-no, sir," Rohan muttered, looking down.

Mr. Sharma leaned forward; his fingers interlocked on the table. "You boys think you're invincible, don't you? You think rules are made for others, not for you?" He shook his head. "This hostel is meant to be your home. A place where you learn discipline, respect, and responsibility. You're not children anymore. You're supposed to be future engineers, future professionals. And yet, you're here, breaking locks, destroying property, and smoking on the rooftop like delinquents."

His words stung. The weight of our actions truly settled in at that moment.

He turned his gaze to Nikhil. "You—what if something had happened up there? What if one of you had fallen? Would your parents ever forgive me?"

Nikhil sniffled, shaking his head silently.

"And you," he said, looking at me. "You were supposed to be the sensible one, weren't you?"

I swallowed hard. I had no excuse.

Mr. Sharma sighed and leaned back in his chair. "Look, boys. I was a student once too. I get it. You wanted to do something adventurous, something thrilling. But rules exist for a reason. Not to suffocate you, but to protect you. To prepare you for the real world, where consequences are much worse than a slap or an apology letter."

We remained silent, absorbing his words.

"Now," he said, softening slightly, "I want those letters on my desk by morning. If I find even a hint of insincerity in them".

We nodded quickly, eager to escape further punishment.

A faint smile tugged at the corner of his lips. "Go back to your rooms. And don't let me catch you on that terrace again."

We wasted no time in leaving. The moment we stepped outside his office, we let out deep sighs of relief. We had escaped the worst. Barely. The night had not gone as planned, but we had learned an important lesson.

As I lay in bed that night, my cheek still sore, I thought about what had happened. This night would stay with me forever. Not because of the excitement of breaking the rules, but because of the lesson we had learned.

Rules exist for a reason. Respect and discipline matter. And sometimes, even strict people like Mr. Sharma can show kindness in their own way.

Finally, I was thanking to Nikhil and to God as well for saving me from this drastic situation and who knows I will be writing many apologies like this in future.

ũ

As the days of our first semester continued, the strict rules imposed by our seniors gradually began to ease. The long nights spent answering their ridiculous questions, running errands, and participating in their so-called "social awareness" activities had become part of our routine. While some freshers resented it, others, like me, began to see it as a strange bonding experience. In a way, these trials forced us to interact, to rely on each other, and to forge friendships we wouldn't have otherwise made.

Our nights were controlled by seniors who gave us strange and sometimes ridiculous tasks. Every evening after classes, we had to follow their orders. Some of us wrote assignments, others completed lab records, and sometimes, they even made us answer questions from a porn magazine, calling it "social awareness." It was both funny and frustrating.

One night, things got even crazier when two seniors started fighting over who would get to "claim" a particular junior. It was a bizarre moment that showed just how absurd the whole situation was. I followed their commands without arguing, just hoping this madness would end soon.

There were strict rules for freshers like us. We had to wear a special dress code, and talking to girls from our batch was nearly impossible. Even making eye contact with them felt like breaking a rule. Our batch had hundreds of students across different streams, but the seniors controlled everything.

However, once the much-awaited Fresher's Party finally arrived, it marked the beginning of a new chapter. The unofficial restrictions on us were lifted, and for the first time, we felt the real freedom of college life. No longer were we confined by the fear of seniors dictating our every move. We could now choose our own paths, our own adventures. It was at this moment that I started to truly absorb the essence of college—this place wasn't just about academics or hierarchy; it was about experiences.

THE SPACE BETWEEN

I had spent quite some time in what people called the "Sports City of India," but soon, my life started feeling boring. Every day was the same—going from the hostel to college and back again. My days were filled with classes, assignments, and textbooks, making life feel dull and tiring. A part of me wanted something different, something exciting, but I just couldn't bring myself to do anything about it. Everything around me felt lifeless, and I felt the same way.

Exams were always near, assignments kept piling up, and even my favorite habit—taking peaceful naps—had disappeared. Life had turned into a never-ending cycle of studying, yet people kept saying that college was the place where you "find yourself." Some even believed it would turn me into a "real man," but I couldn't understand how. It was strange how some managed to find purpose in this daily grind, while I remained as lost as ever, still searching for a meaning I couldn't seem to find.

"Today is a gift; that's why it's called the present."

So, I did follow too. This part was what I hated but the other part I like the most was the next phase of my life.

Days passed fast and the semesters even faster.

I was hostler over here and always "happy to help" others. I thought my friends shouldn't feel helpless and not at all lonely at any time. There is of course a tremendous happiness in making others happy, despite our own situations. We make friends because shared grief is half the sorrow, but happiness when shared, is doubled and that is the big reason to make friends. We have many things which we can only share with our friends. If you want to feel rich and happy, just count all of the things you have that money can't buy. Happiness also comprises a most beautiful feeling called 'love'.

When I was with my best friends chatting about everything from classes to dreams, but mostly, about love. It was as if each one of us had our own hidden story, waiting to be written. We spoke about people we admired, half-wondering where these moments would lead. Love and friendship were two different things, yet both left you wondering about what lay just around the corner.

"If you had just one wish," someone asked, "what would you choose for, Wealth, fame, love or friendship?

I didn't even have to think about it. I'd choose love, every single time, no matter what had happened in my past. Friendship had been a constant, a loyal companion through the years. But love—that was still an unknown.

Truthfully, I was still searching for it.

Being single, they say, is supposed to be liberating. No heartbreak, no expectations, no pain. But doesn't that also mean anyone to lean on, no one to tell you how good you look, or someone to hold your hand and promise to be there through everything? Imagine someone waiting to pull you into a hug and say, "I missed you—take care." Someone brushing a kiss on your lips, saying, "I love you." Is that really so bad? So, what if you haven't found love—what harm could there be in letting someone love you?

It's worth thinking about, at least once, the people who genuinely care.

And yet, as the days dragged on, nothing seemed to change. It was the same campus, the same classrooms, the same life. I remained the back-bencher, my grades hovering in mediocrity, and though I'd sit in quiet corners, secretly observing her—yes, her—I could never muster the courage to speak. Maybe it wasn't "girls" in general who held my interest. No, it was just one. And for now, I was content simply to watch her, waiting, perhaps, for the courage to do more.

ũ

Ahana! Her name was enough to make my heart race from the moment I first saw her. It was love at first sight, plain and simple. She was shy, almost reserved, with an understated grace, always lost in her own world. And those eyes—a mysterious depth that only drew me in further. Unlike her quirky friend who would constantly glance my way, Ahana barely even noticed me

I remember the day I saw her. I, Rohan and Nikhil were sitting on a corner of a Cafeteria, which was the place where we use to sit every time when we are free during college time, it was the day when I would have butterflies in my stomach when she passes by me. It was the day when I see her smile and feel that the world is so beautiful. It was the day when my heart skips a beat if she accidentally looks at me. It was the day when I was going to fall for her all over again.

I wanted to tell her how I felt, but I couldn't gather the courage on my own. I needed my friends to back me up—my brothers in arms, each unique in their own way.

The one on the left was Nikhil. He broke in his high school with his girlfriend Nikita. She left him for some other guy which left him heartbroken. He started drinking and develops some weird attitude. He turned even more slim. But the flip side of it, He was very good in academics. Last two semesters, he was the top scorer. Another exceptional skill he has, he predicts things before it happens. Whether it may be cricket match or college gossips, it always happens as he told.

On my right was Rohan, my new roommate and the undisputed charmer of the college. Rohan was born for three things—*girls*, *girls*, and *girls*. A classic Romeo, he went on dates almost every weekend, swapping girlfriends faster than I could keep track. His rule was simple: no girlfriend lasted more than two weeks. It seemed absurd, but Rohan never seemed to tire of the game.

And then there was me—neither as smart as Nikhil nor as good-looking as Rohan. Just an average guy, caught somewhere in the middle, desperately in need of any help I could find

"Hey, look at that girl," I nudged them, pulling their attention toward Ahana.

"Wow, she's hot," Rohan said, barely glancing before going back to his food.

"Hey, do you guys believe in love at first sight?" I asked, already bracing myself for their reactions.

Nikhil stared at me like I'd lost it. "Wait a minute. You're saying you've fallen for that girl?"

"Yes, I'm in love with her, but I don't know a thing about her," I confessed.

"Her name's Ahana, first-year batch," Rohan said immediately. Not surprising—he had a talent for knowing everything about every girl in college.

"Come on, Ishaan. Just go and talk to her before it's too late," Rohan encouraged, always the love expert.

"Maybe... just not right now," I muttered.

"Does it soon, dude? Or someone else will," Rohan warned.

"Common leave it, let's go," I said and we all leave for class.

ॐ

As days passed, my mind was full of thoughts about her. Questions, doubts, and hopeful imaginings swirled in my head as I wondered what her reaction might be if I finally proposed. Gathering every ounce of courage, I resolved to open my heart to her, to say everything I'd kept hidden for so long. With these thoughts racing through my mind, I made my way to the cafeteria where she usually had lunch, hoping to catch a glimpse of her familiar face.

My eyes scanned the crowded hall like a child looking for their mother in a sea of strangers. I looked left and right, growing more anxious by the second, but she was nowhere to be found. Worried, I asked a friend if they'd seen her, only to find out that she hadn't come that day. My heart sank, and frustration surged within me. Today was supposed to be the day, and it felt like the universe itself was conspiring against me.

Unable to sit with my friends at the cafeteria, I drifted aimlessly back to the college building, lost in thought. The classes went by in a blur; I didn't hear a single word of the lecture, my mind trapped in a hazy fog of questions and "what ifs." Why wasn't she there? Had something happened? Or was this a sign that I should let go of this unspoken love? These thoughts haunted me, refusing to grant me a moment of peace.

When lunch came around, I joined my friends at the mess, but I could barely taste the food on my plate. Time slipped through my fingers like sand, no matter how hard I tried to grasp it. I wished for the impossible—to stop the hands of the clock from moving forward, to freeze the calendar so the date wouldn't change, to keep the sun in the sky so evening would never come. But the days marched on relentlessly, and so did my silent yearning.

The day of our semester completion loomed closer, and my heart grew heavier. Every night in my hostel room, I would resolve that the next morning would be the day I finally spoke to her. But morning would come, and I'd find myself hesitating all over again, the courage I'd mustered slipping away like a fading echo.

I had spent more than half of the year carrying this love for her, wordlessly, hoping somehow that she would notice. At the start of the new academic year, I made it my resolution: I would tell her how I felt. I promised myself that I would not wait any longer for the "perfect" moment, because if I did, I might never find it. I had to get through this, to bare my heart and finally hear her answer, whatever it might be.

As days dwindled, I felt the weight of time pressing down on me. The fear of losing her forever if I remained silent outweighed the fear of rejection. I knew that soon enough, we'd go our separate ways, and I'd be left with nothing but regrets if I didn't try. So, I prepared myself, hoping for the right moment when I could finally express everything that had been building up within me.

ũ

The cafeteria was buzzing with the usual lunch-hour hum, but I barely noticed it. Rohan and I sat at our usual spot, our coffee cups steaming between us. I kept my gaze fixed on the entrance, watching with a sense of nervous anticipation.

"Look, look, Rohan. There she is" I muttered, nudging him eagerly.

Rohan glanced over at the girl I'd been quietly admiring for months. She was there with her friend, laughing over something, the sound lost in the general din of the room but visible in her easy, radiant smile.

"Of course, she's here, dude. This is the cafeteria," Rohan said, rolling his eyes.

"What does it mean?" I asked, a touch of desperation slipping into my voice.

"What does what mean?" he replied, taking a sip of his coffee, fully aware of my obsession but pretending as if this was the first time, he'd ever heard about it.

"Her presence here, man! what else?" I said, hoping for some validation.

Rohan shrugged nonchalantly. "It means she and her friend are here to have coffee."

"Man, you're such a wet blanket," I said, sighing as I watched her laugh at something her friend said.

Rohan shook his head, chuckling at my nervousness. "Hey, why don't you just go over and say 'hello'?" he suggested, his tone both encouraging and teasing.

"Now?" My heart pounded at the thought, but a part of me wanted to wait for some miraculous "perfect moment."

"No, after she marries someone else," he said, smirking.

I glared at him, feeling my cheeks heat up. "There's no risk? I mean...what will she think?"

"You'll never know unless you try," he replied, patting my shoulder. "What's the worst that can happen?"

I took a deep breath, steeling myself. "Should I go now?"

Rohan chuckled, leaning back in his chair. "I bet a hundred bucks you don't have the guts."

He knew me too well. But I was determined. "Wait and watch, man," I said my voice firmer than I felt. I stood up, my legs feeling like jelly as I headed toward her.

The cafeteria felt miles long, and as I walked, my mind began to race. She was right there, just across few tables, yet it felt as if we were separated by worlds. She was the most beautiful girl I'd ever seen; even my friends agreed. In fact, I'd overheard people around the campus, even people from other departments, commenting on her beauty. She had this aura around her—a mix of elegance and quiet confidence—that drew people in without her even trying.

For more than half a year, I'd admired her from a distance. I'd convinced myself that words weren't necessary, that I could somehow communicate with her through stolen glances and quiet smiles. "Why bother with words when you can talk with your eyes?" I thought, a tiny spark of confidence creeping into my heart. But the voice in my head nagged, "You don't know anything about her except her name." I swallowed, feeling a pang of doubt. But another voice, louder this time, urged me, "Go ahead, she's alone. At least say 'hello.'"

I forced myself to take another step forward, my heart pounding louder with each stride. But suddenly, the ground seemed to shift beneath me, like someone had slicked the floor with butter, something distinctly unpleasant.

What the—" I muttered, bending down to see the mess. It was a half-eaten pizza, carelessly thrown on the floor.

"Great! Just great!" I groaned. "Who even does this?"

I scraped the mess off my shoe, feeling both disgusted and annoyed. This was not how I imagined my big moment.

After what felt like ages, I managed to clean it up, my face hot with embarrassment. As I straightened up, I cast a nervous glance in her direction, half-convinced she'd vanished while I'd been fussing over my shoe. But she was still there, thankfully, waiting for her friend who seemed preoccupied with her phone.

This was my chance. I took a deep breath, gathering every ounce of determination I could muster. I started walking toward her, feeling like I was striding down a beach on New Year's Eve. In my head, there were fireworks exploding, the thrill of the moment wrapping around me. I could practically hear the cheers of an imaginary crowd urging me forward.

I was nearly there, my heart racing as I closed the final gap between us. She looked up and saw me approaching, her expression calm but curious. I offered a tentative smile, my voice catching as I said, "Hi."

But she didn't smile back. She simply looked at me, her expression unreadable, as if she were trying to decide who I was and why I was talking to her. I forced myself to hold her gaze, despite the uncomfortable silence stretching between us. Maybe she was just shy, I reasoned, or maybe she thought I was about to confess some grand, romantic feeling out of nowhere.

She turned to walk away, and in a small panic, I called out, "Wait! I just wanted to say 'hi.'"

She stopped, turning to face me again, this time with the faintest hint of a smile. It was small, almost imperceptible, but it was enough to make my heart soar. She understood—I could feel it. She knew I'd been looking at her, knew I wanted to be close to her, even if just for a moment.

But before I could take another step, I felt something slam into my face, a sharp, sudden pain blooming around my left eye. Dazed, I stumbled back, hearing a voice growling in my ear, "Stay away from her."

Blinking, I tried to regain my balance, my brain struggling to make sense of the situation. I glanced around, half-expecting to see an angry boyfriend or some furious protector materialize out of nowhere. But there was no one else; the cafe was just as it had been before, the hum of voices and clinking cups continuing as if nothing had happened.

Still, I pressed forward, determined not to let this phantom pain hold me back. But by the time I looked up again, she had vanished into the crowd, leaving me alone on the cafeteria floor, my heart heavier than before.

I walked back to Rohan, feeling as if I'd just returned from some epic battle only to realize I'd been defeated before it even began. He raised an eyebrow, trying not to smile.

"See? It wasn't so bad, was it?" he said, though his eyes were full of sympathy.

I shook my head, managing a weak smile. Maybe I'd never have another chance with her, but at least I'd taken a step, even if it ended with me standing alone.

And somehow, that felt like the beginning of something—of what, I couldn't quite say. But maybe, just maybe, I'd find out one day.

ũ

The cafeteria incident haunted me for days. I replayed every moment in my head, imagining different outcomes, wishing I had said something cleverer, more charming, and more memorable. Instead, all I had managed was an awkward "hi" and a face full of phantom pain. It wasn't the romantic beginning I'd envisioned—far from it. But somehow, I couldn't shake the feeling that this wasn't the end of my story with her.

Ahana, even her name felt magical, rolling off the tongue like a melody. I spent hours wondering about her, speculating on the kind of person she might be. Was she into books or music? Did she prefer coffee over tea? Was she the kind of person who cried at movies or the kind who laughed at the cheesy parts? I didn't know, and it felt impossible to find out.

But something shifted one afternoon, a week after the ill-fated cafeteria encounter. I caught sight of her sitting alone at a small table near the window in the cafeteria. She was scrolling through her phone, a cup of coffee steaming gently in front of her. Sunlight streamed through the large windows, casting a soft glow around her, making her seem almost ethereal. It felt like a sign, or perhaps just a fleeting moment of courage, but I decided to take my chance.

Balancing my tray of coffee, I walked over to her table. Each step felt heavier than the last, my heart pounding in my chest like a drumbeat. When I reached her, she glanced up, her expression neutral but not unkind.

I debated for a moment, my heart racing. Should I try again? Could I risk another embarrassing encounter? The memory of my failed attempt still stung, but a small, stubborn part of me refused to give up.

"Hey," I began my voice steady but my palms slightly clammy. "Do you mind if I sit here? It's pretty crowded today."

She turned, her eyes meeting mine. For a moment, I thought she might ignore me, but then she smiled faintly, a polite but distant expression.

"Sure," she said simply, her voice as soft and melodic as I remembered.

"Thanks." I slid into the chair, trying to appear composed as I set my tray down. For a moment, we sat in silence, the distant hum of conversations and clinking dishes filling the space.

"Ahana, right" I asked, even though I already knew.

Her eyebrows lifted slightly, and she nodded. "Yes. And you are?"

"I'm Ishaan," I said, trying to keep my tone casual. "Our classes are in the same building. I think I've seen you around."

She nodded again; her expression unreadable. "Nice to meet you, Ishaan"

I took a deep breath, steadying my nerves. "I'm from the Electrical Engineering branch. What about you?"

She tilted her head slightly, her expression softening. "Ah, I'm from Electronics and Communication."

"Ah, so we're kind of neighbors then, department-wise," I said with a small grin, hoping to lighten the mood.

She chuckled softly, and the sound, though brief, gave me a sliver of confidence. "I guess you could say that."

"Likewise," There was a pause, and I scrambled for something to say. "So, uh, do you always take your coffee black?" I asked, gesturing to her cup.

She glanced at her coffee and then back at me, a hint of amusement flickering in her eyes. "Not always. But it's been a long day."

"Tell me about it," I said, chuckling nervously. "I've had so much coffee today, I'm pretty sure I'm part espresso now."

She smiled again, this time a little more genuine, and I felt a tiny surge of triumph.

The conversation didn't last long. She excused herself after a few minutes, saying she had to get back to her class. But those few minutes felt like a breakthrough. For the first time, I had spoken to her without tripping over my words or embarrassing myself. It wasn't much, but it was a start.

ũ

Over the next few weeks, I made it a point to say hello whenever I saw her. Sometimes it was in the hallway, sometimes in the cafeteria, and occasionally in the Campus. Our interactions were brief but pleasant, and I began to learn little things about her. She liked her coffee black only when she was tired. She had a quiet, understated sense of humor that came out in the form of dry, witty remarks.

One day, the library was unusually quiet that afternoon, even for a place meant for studying. The soft rustle of pages and the occasional muffled cough were the only sounds that broke the stillness. I was buried in my notes, attempting to decipher a particularly confusing diagram, when I heard the gentle scrape of a chair being pulled out across from me.

I looked up, and there she was—Ahana. She had her backpack slung over one shoulder, her other hand clutching a notebook and a cup of coffee. Her hair was slightly tousled, as though she'd rushed here from somewhere, and her glasses rested on the bridge of her nose in a way that made her look effortlessly intelligent.

"Mind if I sit here?" she asked her voice soft but clear.

I blinked, surprised. This wasn't the usual setup where I sought her out; she had chosen to sit with me. I nodded quickly, trying to appear nonchalant. "Of course, make yourself comfortable."

She settled into the chair, placing her things neatly on the table. "You're always here, aren't you?" she said with a small smile, taking a sip of her coffee.

I chuckled. "Guilty as charged. This is my battle station. Between deadlines and exams, this place feels like peace"

"Could be worse," she said, glancing around. "At least the library has a decent vibe. Better than the cafeteria during lunch rush."

"True. Though I'd argue the cafeteria's chaos has its own charm," I countered. "You get to witness some top-tier drama over spilled coffee or missing chairs."

She nodded her smile lingering as she opened her notebook. For a few moments, we both worked in companionable silence. I tried to focus on my notes, but my attention kept drifting back to her. The way her brow furrowed in concentration, the absent-minded way she twirled her pen between her fingers—it was fascinating.

"What are you working on?" I asked, finally breaking the silence.

"An assignment for my electronics class," she replied without looking up. "Analyzing the efficiency of different circuit designs"

I grinned. "Sounds deep, any discoveries so far"

She glanced up, her eyes meeting mine. "That I'd rather be doing anything else, what about you, what's that mess you're staring at?"

"Oh, this?" I gestured to my notes. "Just trying to untangle the mysteries of Mechanics equations, it's like a bad relationship. Complicated and constantly making me question my life choices."

She laughed again, shaking her head. "Well, at least you've got a sense of humor about it. That's half the battle, right?"

"True," I said. "But enough about my struggles, but enough about my misery, any tips for surviving these boring assignments?"

She tilted her head thoughtfully, considering for a moment. "Well, breaking it down into smaller chunks helps. That way, it doesn't feel so overwhelming. And I try to remind myself that it'll all make sense one day."

"Yeah, I keep telling myself that too," I said, rolling my eyes. "But it never seems to make sense when I need it to. Anyway, speaking of breaking things down—what about you? What's the end goal for all of this? Engineering, right"

Her eyes lit up as she smiled. "Yeah, definitely, I've always wanted to be an engineer. There's something about problem-solving and designing things that really excites me. I love the idea of creating something that can have a real impact on people's lives. Maybe designing more efficient energy systems or improving technology for everyday use."

I nodded, impressed. "That sounds amazing. Engineering definitely seems like it has a lot of potential to shape the future. It's a solid career path, for sure."

She tilted her head, curious. "What about you? What's your career goal?"

I leaned forward, setting down my pencil. "I've never really been drawn to engineering. My dream is to join the defense forces, want to be army officer"

Her eyebrows raised in surprise. "Really.... That's a big decision."

"Yeah, it is," I said with a smile. "But it's something I've always known I wanted. My father was in the army, and he always talked about the sense of pride and fulfillment that came with serving the country. I want to follow in his footsteps and contribute to something bigger than myself. Being an officer isn't just about leadership; it's about serving the nation, protecting it, and making a difference in people's lives."

She was silent for a moment, clearly processing what I had said. "That's incredible. I can see why you'd feel so strongly about it. It's not just a career choice; it's a calling."

I nodded, appreciating her understanding. "Exactly, it's about doing something that matters. I want to help make the world a safer place and give back to the nation that's given so much to me."

She smiled warmly. "I respect that a lot. It's a noble goal, and I'm sure you'll be great at it."

"Thanks," I said, feeling a sense of pride in her words. "It's going to take a lot of hard work, but I'm up for the challenge."

She chuckled. "Well, at least we both have big goals, even if they're in totally different fields. We're both on our own paths to making an impact"

"Exactly," I agreed, feeling a renewed sense of determination. "Here's to figuring it all out, one step at a time."

The conversation continued, shifting between moments of seriousness and lighthearted banter. We laughed about some of the absurdities of campus life, our shared frustrations with professors who seemed to enjoy giving the most difficult assignments, and even debated over which coffee in the cafeteria had the best brew. I realized how easy it was to talk to her—her openness and humor made me feel comfortable in a way I hadn't expected.

As we exchanged stories about our classes, I couldn't help but notice how similar our experiences were. We were both in our first year of engineering, navigating the same challenging subjects, trying to stay afloat amidst the pressure of exams and assignments. In some ways, it felt like we were in this together, even if our goals were different.

Eventually, I glanced at the time and noticed she was packing up her things. It had been over an hour already, and I didn't want the conversation to end just yet.

"So, uh...," I began hesitantly, not sure how to phrase it. "Would you mind if we exchanged numbers? I mean, since we're both in the same boat with these assignments, maybe we could help each other out."

She paused for a moment, a flicker of hesitation crossing her face. I could tell she was weighing the request, her fingers hovering over her bag. For a brief second, it felt like the air between us thickened, but then she gave me a small smile.

"Alright," she said, pulling out her phone. "I guess it wouldn't hurt."

She handed me her number, and I couldn't help but feel a sense of relief mixed with excitement. I quickly saved it, trying to hide the smile creeping onto my face.

"Thanks," I said, feeling a bit more confident now. "I'll definitely reach out if I need help with anything."

"Same goes for you," she replied, standing up and slinging her bag over her shoulder. "Good luck with everything."

"Good luck to you too," I said as she turned to leave.

As she walked away, I sat there for a moment, staring at the phone number on my screen. The library, which had once felt like an uninspiring pit of exams and deadlines, now seemed just a little brighter. Maybe it was the prospect of working together on assignments—or maybe it was something more.

That day in the library changed everything. After that, we started talking more. Our conversations became longer and more comfortable. I found myself looking forward to every moment I got to see her.

We talked about all kinds of things—work, movies, music, and even our childhood memories. I learned that she loved indie films and had a soft spot for animals. She found out that I was terrible at cooking but could make amazing instant noodles.

As weeks passed, our bond grew stronger. We didn't just talk in class anymore. We started meeting outside, grabbing coffee or having lunch at the cafeteria. She introduced me to her favourite books, and I showed her the best spots on campus.

We spent hours discussing lectures, assignments, and dreams for the future. The campus buzzed around us, but we were lost in our own little world.

Somewhere along the way, I realized that she had become an important part of my life. It wasn't just about casual conversations anymore. I cared about her. And maybe, just maybe, she felt the same way too.

MORE THEN WORDS

The first year of engineering had finally come to an end, and a new term was just beginning. It felt like a fresh start, but the memories of the past year lingered.

It had been a while since I spent time with Ahana—since we shared that quiet connection of friendship. She was just a friend, but there was something about being around her that made others notice. I couldn't figure out why, but whenever we were together, it felt like the world somehow noticed us.

Every time we met, I almost wanted to tell her how I really felt—how much I cared and how much I wanted to be with her. But I always hesitated to say those words out loud.

Sitting alone in my classroom, my thoughts drifted, and I couldn't stop thinking about Ahana. It had been a few days since we last talked, and I missed our chats. I knew it was time to tell her how I felt—not just as a friend, but something more.

Lunch break seemed like the right time. It was the only calm part of the day when the classrooms were quieter and not as busy. I decided this was the moment—the right time to finally talk to her and share how I truly felt.

As I walked through the corridor, a few glances and whispers followed me. Near her class, her friends passed by with teasing looks. "There he goes," they said loud enough for me to hear. I couldn't tell if they were joking or accusing. Why was it so strange for a guy and girl to be friends?

"Arrey, there he goes," one of the girls said loud enough for me to hear. The rest of them laughed, adding their comments. I couldn't figure out if they were joking or if they genuinely disapproved. "Look, it's him again," another one added, as if I was someone, they had been keeping tabs on.

I rolled my eyes, pretending not to care. But inside, a mix of nervousness and irritation churned in my stomach. I kept walking, trying to ignore their stares and whispers.

Finally, I reached her classroom. There she was, standing by the door. She hadn't noticed me yet, so I took a moment to observe her. Her hair was loose, with a few strands falling across her face, catching the light perfectly. She looked beautiful, not because she was trying to, but because she just was. Her soft smile made her seem like she was lost in some happy thought. Her eyes sparkled with a quiet kind of joy that made her stand out even more.

I called her name, and she turned to look at me. Then, she walked towards me.

Leaning against the wall, I tried to look relaxed and casual, even though my heart was racing. She had a way of making everything around her feel brighter. But it wasn't just her appearance that drew me in. It was who she was—her confidence, her laughter, and the graceful way she carried herself.

"What's up?" I finally asked, trying to sound calm, though my heart was racing. I wondered if she could tell.

She just smiled, her eyes sparkling with mischief, saying nothing. It was like she knew how flustered I felt.

I sighed, feeling a mix of nervousness and curiosity. Her silence always spoke louder than words.

Just then, a few of her friends walked by, giggling and teasing her, one nudged her, making her blush as she told them to stop. They ignored her, clearly enjoying the moment.

After what felt like forever, she turned back to me and said, "Nothing much. What about you?"

Nothing…Just boring classes…

So…. What else?

Just as I was trying to think of a clever response, she turned to talk to her friends, her scarf slipping from her shoulder as she adjusted it, laughing. Her earrings caught the light, swaying gently as she moved. I couldn't help but stare, completely captivated. It was as if everything around me faded into the background, leaving only her. The world went silent, and all I could see was her face, her laugh, the light in her eyes.

I must have looked silly, grinning like an idiot, but I couldn't help it. She looked at me and caught my gaze. Her smile hinted at a little embarrassment, but she didn't look away.

"Oh god," I thought to myself. "I'm in love."

The realization hit me like a wave, overwhelming and sudden. It was as if I'd been standing on the edge of something for so long, and now, finally, I'd fallen. I was in love, and I could feel it in every part of me. How had this happened? I'd known her for a while, but today, in this moment, something was different. Maybe it was the way her hair danced in the wind or the way her laugh filled the space around us, but I knew, without a doubt, that I was in love.

"You didn't go to the hostel mess for lunch?" Ahana asked, her voice soft but curious.

I shook my head. "No, not feeling hungry," I said simply.

She didn't reply immediately. Instead, she let the silence settle between us, but it wasn't awkward. It was... comfortable. The kind of silence that didn't need to be filled.

Then, out of nowhere, she spoke. "You know," she said, her voice thoughtful, "you're not what I expected."

I glanced at her, intrigued. "What do you mean?" I asked, tilting my head slightly. I tried to read her expression, but she just smiled, her gaze drifting towards the city lights in the distance. The evening glow painted her face in warm, golden hues, making her look almost unreal.

"When we first met," she continued, her voice almost lost in the night air, "I thought you were just another guy trying to impress me. Saying the right things, acting cool, like so many others."

I frowned slightly. "And now?"

She turned to look at me, her eyes searching mine. "Now, I see you're different," she said softly. "You're real. Genuine. And I like that."

Her words hit me in a way I hadn't anticipated. It wasn't just a compliment—it was an acknowledgment of something deeper. I felt my chest warm at the thought, a smile creeping up my face. "Well, I'm glad I could prove you wrong," I said, my voice soft and almost shy.

There was a moment of quiet between us, the kind that felt comfortable, not awkward. We simply stand there, sharing the tranquility of the moment. I wanted to say more, to share just how much her words meant to me, but something about the stillness made me hesitant.

After a few moments, she turned towards me, her expression shifting slightly. The spark in her eyes dimmed a little, and I could tell something was on her mind. "Ok then, I had to go for lunch now," she said, her voice bringing me back to reality.

"Oh, right, of course. I didn't even realize how late it's getting," I replied, standing up with her. A part of me wanted to extend the moment, but I knew this wasn't the time.

"Maybe we can talk later" she suggested with a smile.

"I'd like that," I said, hoping the connection would continue long after she walked away.

I felt a strange mix of emotions—happiness, sadness, excitement, and a bit of fear. I wanted to tell her right then and there how I felt, but I couldn't find the words. Instead, I forced a smile and waved as she walked back into her class, her friends in tow. I stood there, watching her go, feeling as though I'd just discovered something monumental, something that would change everything.

As I walked back to class, my mind was a whirlwind of thoughts and feelings. I couldn't wait to tell her, to let her know just how much she meant to me. But again, for now, I would hold onto this feeling, this beautiful, aching happiness, hoping that one day, she might feel the same way too.

ũ

The night was quiet, with only the hum of the ceiling fan filling the room. I paced back and forth, my mind racing with thoughts of Ahana. She was my friend—or rather, we were in that strange in-between space where "just friends" didn't quite fit, yet we hadn't defined it as anything else either. I had always thought of her as more than a friend, but now, finally, I felt it was time to be honest with her, time to tell her everything that was swirling inside my heart.

An idea struck me—simple yet perfect. Why not message her? I knew it was the easiest way to put everything out there without stumbling over my words. And at this late hour, sending a message would let me take my time, finding the right words to express how much she truly meant to me.

It felt safer to write it down than say it out loud and risk seeing any disappointment on her face. With a text, she could read my thoughts in private, in her own time.

So, with my phone in hand, I sat down and began to type. It was strange—I'd never been good with words, and writing anything heartfelt had always been a struggle. Yet, as I thought of Ahana, the words seemed to flow from my heart with ease.

It was as if she unlocked something inside me, something I didn't even know existed. I started typing, and slowly, my feelings and emotions began to take shape in the form of words on the screen.

I think it is the right time to tell her. I don't want to live with a title of just friends. She might have surprised but definitely will accept as we know each other. I want to do it all by myself.

"Dear Ahana

I don't know how to say this, but I have to tell you what's in my heart. We've been friends for a while now, and I truly enjoy every moment we spend together. You make even the simplest things feel special—whether it's studying, laughing at silly jokes, or just talking about life.

Every time I see you, my day gets better. Your smile, your kindness, and the way you care for people make you one of the most wonderful people I know. I never expected to feel this way, but the more I get to know you, the more special you become to me.

I don't want to lose our friendship, but I can't hide my feelings anymore. I like you—more than just a friend. I don't know if you feel the same, and that's okay. I just wanted to be honest with you because you mean a lot to me.

No matter what, I will always respect our friendship. But if there's even a small chance you might feel the same, I'd love to know.

Take your time, and no matter what, I'll always be here.

Love always"

As I reread the message, panic started to rise within me. Was I truly ready for this? I knew the weight of sending such a message—it wasn't just something casual. It had the potential to change everything between us, and that thought made me nervous.

I couldn't stop thinking about our recent hangouts. I replayed the laughter, the glances we shared, those little moments that felt special at the time. But now, looking back, they seemed more significant, almost as if there was an unspoken connection between us.

Yet, with each memory, a feeling of uncertainty grew. There was a sense that something deeper was there, something that made my heart race, but also made me nervous. I wondered if she felt the same way or if I was reading too much into it.

What if she didn't want to take that next step? What if she saw me only as a friend, and nothing more? The fear of ruining our friendship with a declaration like this kept me from hitting send, even though a part of me was desperate to express how I truly felt.

My thumb hovered over the "Send" button, my heart racing faster than ever. Each beat echoed in my ears, drowning out the laughter and chatter around me. Time seemed to stretch endlessly as I debated the risk. Sending that message could either bring us closer or push us apart forever. The fear of losing her friendship loomed larger than my desire to confess my feelings. What if I lost her altogether? The thought was paralyzing.

Finally, I exhaled deeply, feeling the weight of the decision pressing down on me. In that moment, clarity washed over me, and I knew I couldn't do it. Not yet. Not like this. The thought of confessing my feelings felt too daunting, too final. With a heavy heart, I deleted the message, watching the words vanish from the screen like a secret lost to the ether.

The relief that followed was almost palpable, yet it was quickly overshadowed by a wave of disappointment. I felt a part of me slip away with those unsent words, a secret that might never be revealed. It was as if I had locked away a piece of my heart, the part that dared to hope.

As i closed my eyes, the room still bustling with life, i made a silent promise to myself again: I would find the courage to tell her. But for now, i would cherish the moments we had, keeping my love safely tucked away, hidden beneath layers of friendship and unspoken feelings.

I lay on my bed, staring at the ceiling. Outside, life went on as usual, unaware of the quiet love story waiting for its time to bloom.

NO MORE FEAR

The college campus was alive with energy. Students filled the corridors and lawns, creating a buzz of excitement and nervousness. It was the first week of the new academic session, and everything felt fresh and full of possibilities.

Every face seemed new, each corner bristling with the promise of a story waiting to unfold. This wasn't just a place of learning; it was a crucible where dreams were forged, friendships were tested, and characters were built. For the first-year students, the campus was an intimidating maze; for the seniors, it was a familiar stage where they knew their parts by heart.

First-year students wandered around, wide-eyed and unsure, trying to make sense of the large and lively campus. For seniors, it was like returning to a familiar stage. They knew their roles and moved through the crowd with confidence, sharing smiles and laughter.

Among all the students, two names stood out: Rohan and Nikhil. They didn't try to grab attention, but something about them made people notice. Rohan had a natural charm and confidence that made people want to be around him.

Nikhil with a full of energy that balanced Rohan's lively personality. Together, they were like two sides of the same coin—a perfect team that everyone admired.

One such afternoon, the sun cast long shadows across the mess hall, but I wasn't in the mood to join them. My stomach felt heavy, and I wasn't particularly hungry. When Rohan and Nikhil dropped by my room to drag me along, I waved them off with a half-hearted excuse.

"Not today, guys. You go ahead. I'll catch up later," I said, leaning back against my chair.

"You sure" Rohan asked, raising an eyebrow. "You might miss out on something epic, like that time the cook almost burned the rotis, and the entire mess turned into a smokehouse."

I laughed, shaking my head. "I'll take my chances. Bring me back some gossip, though."

But Nikhil wasn't convinced. "Come on, Ishaan. You've been sitting in this room all day. Fresh air, food, and our glorious company—what more could you want?"

"I'm just not hungry," I muttered.

Rohan smirked. "Then come for the chaos. Someone's bound to start a debate over whether the dal is too watery again."

I sighed. They weren't going to let me off easy. "Fine, fine. Let's go."

Grinning, they pulled me up, and together we headed to the mess, where the usual noisy, chaotic atmosphere awaited.

The mess hall was full of life. Students walked in with trays, looking for a place to sit. The sound of plates and spoons filled the air. People talked in low voices, and sometimes, a burst of laughter came from different corners. The smell of hot curry and fresh rotis made the place feel warm and familiar. This was hostel life—busy and noisy, but also comforting.

Rohan, Nikhil, and I moved through the crowd, exchanging casual nods with familiar faces before settling into our usual spot by the window.

Sunlight poured in, casting a golden hue over our table, making the scratched-up wooden surface gleam. The warmth of the light made the moment feel almost peaceful, a small respite from the exhausting routine of college life.

Between mouthfuls of food, we chatted about the day's events—professors who seemed to take pleasure in torturing students with surprise quizzes, and, of course, the ever-present struggle of balancing assignments with sleep, Rohan had his own theories about the best completion of the assignments, while Nikhil playfully argued against him. I mostly listened, enjoying the familiarity of our banter, the way it felt like an anchor in the unpredictable sea of college life.

But just as the laughter reached its peak, the atmosphere shifted.

The mess hall doors slammed open with a resounding bang, making heads snap up. In walked Dhama, the infamous hostel bully, his broad frame cutting an imposing figure against the backdrop of his rowdy gang. The lively chatter stuttered into hushed whispers as his cold gaze swept across the hall, and for a moment, it felt like the very air had thickened with tension.

Dhama was the kind of person who thrived on chaos and intimidation, and he had a long history of clashing with other students. He was the best basketball player in college, a fantastic dancer, and had even won the **Mr. Fresher** award. But despite his talents, he loved power and control—he had a knack for sniffing out vulnerabilities and exploiting them mercilessly. First-year students, still finding their footing, were his favorite targets.

Back on our table, unaware of the unfolding drama, I had settled into the quiet, blissfully ignorant of the storm brewing in the mess hall

Dhama's eyes scanned the room like a predator seeking prey. Today, his target was a first-year student struggling to carry a tray of food.

"Hey, come here," he called two juniors roaming around the mess area. One was a short and chubby fellow with unruly curly hair, while the other was tall, skinny, and awkwardly lanky. Both of them had an air of nervousness that betrayed their inexperience. It was clear this was their first encounter with seniors, and they were unsure of what lay ahead.

"Yes, Bhaiya," one of them said hesitantly, his voice quivering as he tried to mask his apprehension.

Dhama and his gang surrounded the boys, jeering and laughing as they deliberately blocked his path. The boy's face turned red with embarrassment, and the commotion drew the attention of everyone in the mess.

"Screw that! Bloody hell, we're not your Bhaiya. Call us 'sir,' you idiot!" His voice, slurred and uneven, echoed across the hall. The juniors flinched at his tone, their wide-eyed expressions a mix of fear and confusion. To anyone else, Dhama's demeanor might have seemed laughable, but to these juniors, he was a towering figure of authority.

"You bloody juniors, dozing off, eh? Rascals! Who's going to speak first?" Rishi, a person from Dhama gang broke the silence. His voice carried the authority that years of being a senior naturally bestowed. It was a tone that demanded immediate compliance.

"Sir... sir..." One of them managed to stammer in a deep, husky voice, his attempt at formality betrayed by the tremor in his tone.

Dhama, now visibly irritated, roared, "You idiots!" His anger seemed disproportionate, fueled more by the response than the situation. "We're going to be here together for years—studying, having fun, everything. Since we got here first, you will respect us. We'll help you out when needed, but you better remember who's in charge."

"Yes," Rishi continued his voice unsteady as his body swayed drunkenly. "In this college, we rule the roost. You have to do what we say. Now, give your proper introduction."

The shorter junior seemed on the verge of tears, his eyes welling up as he tried to muster the courage to speak. The taller one, though equally scared, clenched his fists as if trying to steady himself. Finally, the shorter one lifted his head slowly, agonizingly slow, to meet their gaze

"Sir... I am..." he began, his voice cracking under the weight of his fear. Then, unexpectedly, he broke down. Tears streamed down his face as he sniffled audibly, unable to hold back his emotions any longer.

"For God's sake," Dhama snapped, throwing his hands in the air in exaggerated frustration. "It's basic common sense—we're not asking you to solve rocket science!" His voice was louder now.

The junior continued to look at him, his tear-streaked face frozen in a mask of helplessness. He seemed unable to form the words, his fear paralyzing him.

"I don't have the habit of repeating myself," Dhama said, raising his voice slightly to assert his authority. "What is your name?"

Still, no answer, He simply shrugged his shoulders in a gesture of helplessness, as if to say, *I don't know what you want from me.*

The taller junior, realizing the situation was escalating beyond control, finally stepped forward. "Sir, my name is Raghav," he said, his voice shaky but resolute enough to pierce the heavy tension. "I'm from Kanpur and have joined the Mechanical Engineering department."

"Good," Rishi said, nodding in approval. "That wasn't so hard, was it?"

But Dhama wasn't satisfied. "And what about you?" he demanded, pointing at the shorter one who was still sniffling. "Speak up, or do you need your friend to hold your hand?"

The shorter junior wiped his face with his sleeve, trying to compose himself. "Sir... my name is Aditya," he finally managed, his voice barely above a whisper. "I'm from Lucknow, and I've joined the Computer Science department."

"There you go," Rishi said, softening his tone slightly. "Now was that so difficult? See, when you're respectful and cooperative, we don't have any problems."

But Dhama wasn't done. "Respectful? That was pathetic!" he scoffed. "Look at you two—shaking like leaves. Is this how you're going to survive in college? You need to toughen up if you want to make it here."

Dhama staggered closer, leaning in so that his face was mere inches from Raghav's. "Listen, junior," he said his voice low and menacing. "This is your first and last warning. Next time we call you, you run. Got it?"

The boys nodded again, their heads bobbing like puppets on strings. Without another word, they turned and bolted, their footsteps echoing down the hallway as the door slammed shut behind them.

ũ

Rohan, Nikhil, and I watched the scene unfold, our plates of food forgotten in front of us. The tension in the hostel mess was palpable, like a rubber band stretched to its limit. Dhama's antics were nothing new, and we all knew better than to intervene when he was in this state—drunk on power and cheap ego.

But as I stared at the empty doorway where the juniors had fled, I couldn't shake the pang of guilt gnawing at my chest. Hazing was a tradition, yes, but was this really the best way to build camaraderie? Was fear the glue that held us together?

The mess buzzed with murmured conversations as people cautiously returned to their meals, trying to pretend nothing had happened. But not Rohan. His shoulders were tense, his jaw clenched as the irritation boiling inside him reached its peak. Suddenly, he shoved his chair back with a screech, the sound cutting through the din like a knife.

"What are you doing?" Nikhil hissed, grabbing his arm. "Let it go, man. It's not worth it."

But Rohan shook him off, his eyes locked on Dhama. "Hey, Dhama!" he called, his voice sharp and unwavering.

The mess fell silent once more, every pair of eyes swiveling to Rohan. Even Dhama paused in mid-sip, the mug in his hand frozen as he turned toward the source of the challenge.

Rohan stepped forward, his chin held high, his voice clear and defiant. "How about you pick on someone your own size for a change?"

A ripple of whispers spread through the crowd. No one ever talked back to Dhama—not unless they wanted to end up on the receiving end of his wrath.

Dhama lowered his mug with deliberate slowness, the smirk on his face growing wider. His voice, when it came, was laced with mockery. "Well, well. Look who's got a spine today. Hey, Rohan, why don't you keep it down? Not everyone wants to hear your nonsense."

The room held its breath, the air charged with anticipation. Nikhil shot me a nervous glance, silently pleading for someone to step in and diffuse the situation before it spiraled out of control. But I stayed rooted to my seat, unable to look away as Rohan squared his shoulders and stood his ground.

Rohan didn't flinch. "This isn't nonsense, Dhama. It's about respect—something you clearly don't understand." His words rang out, firm and unyielding, daring Dhama to make his move.

For a moment, Dhama just looked at him, his smile fading a little. The dining hall was so quiet that even the soft sound of the ceiling fan seemed loud. Then, with a small laugh, Dhama pushed his chair back and stood up, towering over Rohan like a dark storm cloud about to rain.

The stage was set, the battle lines drawn. And as the tension reached a fever pitch, I realized that this wasn't just about juniors or tradition anymore. This was about standing up to a bully, about breaking the cycle of fear that had held us all in its grip for far too long.

Rohan looked up, his sharp eyes meeting Dhama's. "You've got nothing better to do than harass people? Grow up, Dhama." he replied coolly, though his tone carried an edge. I smirked beside him, but Nikhil shifted uncomfortably.

Dhama came forward, his hulking frame casting a shadow over his table. "You've got a big mouth for someone who doesn't know when to stop talking," he sneered.

The mess fell silent as everyone's attention turned to the brewing confrontation. Tension crackled in the air like a live wire. Rohan stood, refusing to back down. "And you've got a lot to say for someone who can't take a joke."

It escalated quickly. Dhama's friends exchanged uneasy glances. hey knew Rohan was not someone to mess with. But Dhama's ego was too large to back down. Dhama's group moved to surround Rohan's table, but Nikhil and i rose to stand beside their friend. "Alright then," he sneered. "Let's settle this"

Dhama threw the first punch, a wild swing aimed at Rohan. But Rohan was quick—he ducked and hit back with a strong jab to Dhama's side. I could see Dhama's friends getting ready to attack, so I stepped in. One of them tried to grab me, but I blocked him, while another came at me with a raised hand, and I quickly stopped him too.

The fight broke out in the canteen, filling the air with shouts and the sound of fists landing. Chairs toppled over, and tables slid across the floor as chaos spread. Nikhil, always the peacemaker, tried to stop the fight, but someone shoved him aside. His voice got lost in the noise.

Despite being outnumbered, Rohan and I held our ground. my agility and Rohan's calculated strikes proved too much for Dhama and his two friends. One by one, they faltered, retreating as the realization set in that they had underestimated their opponents.

But Dhama wasn't ready to give up yet. Angry and hurt, he made one last attempt, lunging straight at me. Rohan and I fought back together, refusing to let him win. Rohan's punches were sharp and full of determination, while I fought just as hard, not for myself, but for my friend. Together, we managed to overwhelm Dhama, forcing him to retreat with a bleeding lip and a bruised ego.

"Enough," Nikhil said, firm voice but not unkind. "This isn't about proving who's stronger. It's about respect. You don't earn it by bullying others."

Dhama glared at me, his eyes still burning with anger, but the fight had drained from his body. He knew he had lost. Clenching his jaw, he wiped the blood from the corner of his mouth and pointed a finger at us—me and Rohan.

"I promise, this isn't over. I'll make sure you get the worst of it," he spat, his voice laced with fury.

With that, he turned sharply and stormed out of the hostel mess, his friends trailing behind him, their faces a mix of frustration and humiliation. The mess, once filled with chaos, now echoed with silence as everyone watched Dhama disappear through the door.

As the crowd dispersed, we collapsed onto a chair, our bodies aching and our hands marked with fresh bruises. Our shirts were torn, a testament to the intense fight we had just endured.

As the crowd slowly dispersed, a first-year student, whom we had defended, approached Rohan hesitantly, his eyes filled with gratitude and nervousness.

"Thank you, Sir" he said, his voice filled with gratitude. "I didn't know what to do."

Rohan smiled, patting him on the shoulder. "Stick up for yourself next time. But don't worry; we've got your back."

Nikhil nodded. "And remember, bullies like Dhama only have power if you let them. Stand tall."

After the intense brawl in the hostel mess, we finally rushed back to my room. Our adrenaline was still pumping, our knuckles bruised, but there was a strange satisfaction in knowing we had stood our ground.

As soon as we entered, Rohan slammed the door shut and collapsed onto the bed, breathing heavily, while I grabbed a bottle of water, taking quick gulps to cool down. The room was dimly lit, the ceiling fan creaking as it spun lazily above us.

"That was insane," I muttered, rubbing my jaw where I had taken a hit.

Rohan chuckled, wiping a bit of blood off his lip. "Insane? That was legendary, did you see his face when I landed that punch? We finally shut those guys up."

Nikhil sat down on the chair, exhaling deeply. "Yeah, but they won't stay quiet for long. Dhama's not the type to take a beating and move on."

"Yes, he's not going to let this go," I warned a note of apprehension in my voice. Rohan brushed it off. "Let him try. We'll handle whatever comes."

A tense silence settled between us. We knew this wasn't over. But for now, we had won. For now, the hostel belonged to us.

A NIGHT IN THE SHADOWS

The fight between us and Dhama had been over a week ago, but I knew he was still waiting for the right moment to take revenge. Things had been quiet, but an uneasy feeling lingered in the air.

One night, around 9 PM, we were lounging in Rohan's room, lazily chatting and passing time after a long day of classes. The ceiling fan creaked softly as it spun, and the faint hum of distant conversations from other rooms filled the air.

"I'm starving," Nikhil suddenly groaned, stretching his arms behind his head. "Let's go have some Maggi at the small stall outside the college campus."

Rohan, lying on his bed scrolling through his phone, shook his head without even looking up. "I just ate at the mess. You guys go."

I hesitated. "I don't know, man. It's late. And the cafeteria already closed."

"Oh, come on," Nikhil pressed, sitting up. "You know nothing hits better than midnight Maggi. Just imagine that spicy, steaming bowl right now."

I glanced at Rohan, who shrugged indifferently. "Your call."

After a few more minutes of persuasion and my own stomach starting to agree with Nikhil, I caved. "Alright, fine. Let's go."

Leaving Rohan behind, the two of us slipped out of the hostel into the cool night air. As we walked the kilometre-long stretch to the stall, we laughed and joked, the stress of the day fading away.

We reached the small roadside stall, and the smell of hot, spicy Maggi made us feel happy and hungry. Our late-night trip suddenly felt worth it.

Steam rose from the big pan where the old shopkeeper, who always seemed to be awake, cooked the noodles. He stirred them with skill and looked at us with a smile.

"Hungry at this hour?" he asked, laughing.

"Something like that," Nikhil said with a grin.

A few moments later, he gave us our plates. The noodles were shiny with masala and cooked just right. As we took our first bites, the buttery, spicy Flavors filled our mouths. Each bite felt amazing, warming us up in the cool night air.

We laughed and talked while enjoying our food. Before leaving, we grabbed some chips and a cold drink to complete our midnight meal.

As we walked back, our conversation was relaxed and carefree. Nikhil laughed about how badly he had played in the last cricket match, saying he had dropped an easy catch and even missed a simple run-out. I couldn't help but tease him about his never-ending crush on a girl from the literature department. He blushed and tried to change the topic, but I kept pushing, making him groan in frustration.

The night air was cool, and the street was quiet except for our footsteps and laughter. But as we turned a corner, everything changed. A group of people stepped out from the shadows and came in front of us.

Their expressions were serious, and their body language was stiff and threatening. My heart started beating faster. Nikhil also noticed the change, and I could feel his tension beside me. The relaxed mood from earlier disappeared in an instant. Something didn't feel right.

As soon as I saw them, I knew. These weren't just random guys—they were Dhama's men. The same Dhama we had thrashed last week in the hostel mess. He wasn't the type to let things go, and now he had sent his friends from the city to settle the score.

One of them stepped forward, his eyes burning with hostility. "Thought you could just walk away after what happened?" he sneered, his voice sharp with anger.

I exchanged glances with my friends. There was no mistaking it—this was payback. We weren't dealing with hostel politics anymore; these guys meant business. The air felt heavier, the space around us shrinking.

There was no running now. No backing down. It was our turn to face them. My fists clenched instinctively. We had to be ready, because this fight was coming whether we wanted it or not.

I raised my hands in a placating gesture. "We're just here to buy some snacks. Let's not make this a bigger deal than it already is," I said, trying to keep my tone calm.

But the group had other plans. One of them produced a hockey stick, another a baseball bat, and within moments, the situation spiraled out of control. The first blow landed on Nikhil's shoulder, sending him sprawling to the ground. I tried to shield Nikhil, but a sharp swing of the bat caught me on the side of my head. Pain exploded in my skull, and i stumbled, blood trickling down my temple.

The attack was relentless. We both tried to defend ourselves, but we were outnumbered and unarmed. The beating lasted only a few minutes, but it felt like an eternity. Every blow that landed, each kick, each strike, felt like it was taking away a piece of my soul. When the group finally retreated, we were left battered and bruised, lying bloodied on the cold pavement.

Our breaths were ragged and shallow, and the world around us spun out of control. I could feel the warmth of blood pooling beneath me, mixing with the grime of the street. The night, once peaceful, had turned into a violent blur. Nikhil, who had always been calm, seemed as though he had already given up, his body limp beside me.

I mustered every ounce of strength I could find, my hand trembling as I reached for phone in my jeans pocket. The screen flickered under my fingers, and I almost dropped it, too weak to hold it steady. But I forced myself to focus. I knew I had to call for help, or we would both bleed out right here on this street. I couldn't bear the thought of it, of leaving our families to find us like this.

My breath came in shallow gasps as I fumbled with my phone, my trembling fingers tapping the screen to dial Rohan's number. The ringing tone echoed in my ears, distant and muffled, as panic surged through me. Nikhil lay motionless on the side of the street, blood seeping from a deep wound on his head. My body trembled violently, still reeling from the brutal attack.

Pain throbbed in my skull, my vision swimming in and out of focus, but I refused to give in to the darkness creeping at the edges of my mind. I had to stay conscious. I had to do something. Rohan needed to pick up. Every passing second felt like an eternity as I waited, helpless and desperate. The cold night air bit at my skin, but all I could feel was fear—fear that I might lose my friend before help arrived.

It took what felt like an eternity for Rohan to pick up.

"Hello?" His voice sounded distant, muffled, as if he had just woken up. But the moment he heard the tremor in my voice, the panic in the air, he became alert.

"Rohan..." I whispered, barely able to make the words come out. "Get the college ambulance."

I could hear Rohan's breath catch on the other end of the line, a mixture of disbelief and fear rising in his voice. "What's happened? Where are you?"

"Near the college main gate... close to the highway.... Nikhil...and I... Dhama." I paused to catch my breath, the pain overwhelming me as I spoke. "We're hurt... badly. Please, Rohan... hurry."

I could hear him scrambling in the background, the sound of him moving quickly. I heard the rattle of keys, and the sharp sound of the door opening. "I'm on my way; I'll call the ambulance right now. Stay with me, okay? Stay with me!"

His words were frantic, but they felt like a lifeline. I wanted to respond, to reassure him, but I didn't have the strength. My eyelids fluttered as I tried to keep myself awake. Every movement, every tiny shift of my body sent waves of pain through me. I couldn't imagine what Nikhil was feeling beside me. His breathing was erratic, and I could tell he was slipping in and out of consciousness. His hand was limp in mine, his skin cold and clammy. I pressed his hand tighter, trying to offer some kind of comfort, though I knew he probably couldn't even feel it.

"Rohan... please..." I rasped my voice barely audible. I wanted to say more, to tell him everything would be fine, but the words were lost to the dizziness taking over my body.

"I'm coming, don't hang up," Rohan's voice was closer now, his urgency palpable. I could hear him shouting something to someone in the background, but my hearing seemed to distort, the world around me narrowing into a blur of sound and color.

The seconds stretched on forever. The harsh, metallic scent of blood filled the air as I lay there, trying to breathe, trying to stay alive. Time felt irrelevant. The world outside my pain didn't matter. The only thing that mattered was getting help, getting us out of here. The sirens in the distance were like a distant promise, an anchor that I clung to in the storm.

"Rohan... don't hang up," I whispered again, barely conscious of the words leaving my lips.

"I'm not going anywhere, stay with me, please," Rohan replied, his voice steady now, but tinged with concern. "The ambulance is on its way. You're going to be okay."

A few minutes passed, but it felt like an eternity before I heard the unmistakable sound of sirens growing closer. The wail of the ambulance sliced through the night air, a sound that, in that moment, I couldn't have been more grateful for. I tried to lift my head, to see the flashing lights, but I couldn't. My body was too weak, my limbs like lead.

I heard Rohan's voice again, louder this time, more frantic. "They're here! Hang on, okay? Help is here!"

I could hear the screech of tires as the ambulance pulled up to the curb, the doors slamming open, the sound of feet running towards us. A pair of strong hands grabbed under my arms, lifting me with surprising ease. A sharp pain shot through my side as I was moved, and I gasped, the pain making everything go dark for a moment. But the voices around me cut through the haze. I could hear the paramedic working quickly, his instructions sharp and clear.

"Vitals are weak. We need to move, now!" he called out, checking Nikhil's pulse before quickly injecting a cold needle into both his arm and mine. Warmth spread through my body, easing the pain just enough for me to relax for a split second. But even that fleeting comfort couldn't hide the weight of what had happened. Nikhil… he was still lying there, motionless. He hadn't made a sound since the attack, and I could hear the paramedic shouting his name, desperately trying to rouse him "Get him on the stretcher; we need to stabilize both of them!" The urgency in their voices sent a spike of fear through me, but I had no strength left to feel anything beyond the numbness that had settled over my body

The ambulance doors shut quickly, and I was lifted inside. The engine started, and we sped away. The sirens were loud, cutting through the night. The tires screeched on the road as we rushed to the hospital, but I couldn't focus on anything. My eyes felt heavy, and my mind kept drifting in and out. The only thing keeping me awake was Rohan's voice, still echoing in my ears, like a lifeline.

"We're almost there, Stay with me. You're going to be okay. Both of you will be fine. We won't leave him. We'll make sure those responsible pay, Dhama and the ones who all involved in this will face a fate worse than this.

I wanted to believe him. I really did. But every time I blinked, the world became darker, the edges of my consciousness fading. I thought about my family, my friends, about all the things I still had left to do. And I realized with a sickening clarity that I didn't know if I would ever see them again.

The hospital loomed ahead, its sterile lights flashing like a beacon in the distance. I felt the ambulance slow, the screech of brakes signaling our arrival. I was swiftly unloaded from the back, my body jerking as they moved me, the pain now a constant companion. My vision blurred again, and I heard distant voices, the sound of doctors and nurses working quickly, calling out orders

I was wheeled through a series of doors, the bright white lights above me flickering as I was rushed down a corridor. I could see Nikhil in the bed beside me, the paramedics still working on him, trying to stabilize him. His face was pale, his chest rising and falling weakly. I tried to reach out to him, but my arms were too heavy, too uncooperative.

And then, as if a switch had been flipped, I was pushed through the ICU doors. The cold, sterile environment of the ICU greeted me, and I felt my body relax as the bed was tilted back, the pressure on my wounds lessening, if only slightly.

The last thing I remember before the darkness fully took over was Rohan's face, blurry and distorted through the glass of the ICU room, his eyes filled with fear, but also determination. He mouthed something to us, something I couldn't hear, but I could see it in his eyes.

"Stay strong," he seemed to say. "You're going to make it." Nikhil lay in the adjacent bed.

Whole night the dull ache in my head reminded me of the assault. And then, the world went dark.

I slowly regained consciousness, the sterile smell of the ICU filling my nose. My body felt heavy, like it was trapped under a thick, suffocating blanket, and I could hear the faint beeping of machines surrounding me. The soft murmur of voices in the background made me aware that I wasn't alone.

I blinked a few times, trying to clear the fog from my mind. It was then that I noticed Nikhil, lying in the bed beside mine, his face pale and his head wrapped in bandages. He looked weak, but there was a familiar smile on his lips.

"Nikhil" I rasped, my voice sounding foreign to my own ears.

His eyes fluttered open, a small grin spreading across his face as he glanced toward me. "You're awake," he said, his voice a little hoarse but filled with relief.

"Barely," I replied, trying to push myself up but quickly giving up as the pain in my head surged. "What's the damage?"

Nikhil let out a low groan, adjusting himself in the bed. "Concussion and a bunch of stitches and you"

"Same," I muttered, trying to shift into a more comfortable position. "But I've got this killer headache..."

He chuckled softly, but then winced at the movement. "Yeah, we both have enough battle scars to make a gladiator jealous." He paused for a second, his eyes narrowing playfully. "But do you think these nurses know how cool we are?"

I couldn't help but laugh, though it sent a sharp pain shooting through my skull. "They probably think we're action heroes. Fighting for honor or something"

Nikhil raised an eyebrow, his grin widening. "Or clowns who messed with the wrong people."

We both burst into laughter, careful not to agitate our wounds too much. The sound of our laughter echoed in the otherwise quiet ICU room, a stark contrast to the cold, clinical environment. Slowly, the atmosphere in the room began to shift as our hostel friends and juniors started to trickle in. One junior, holding a bouquet of mismatched flowers, was the first to make his way over to us.

"Bhaiya, how are you feeling?" he asked, his voice a mix of concern and curiosity.

I smirked at the bouquet, which looked like something a kindergartner might have put together, before replying, "Like Dhama's cricket bat—overused and broken."

Nikhil, ever the comedian, added with a dramatic sigh, "Don't worry, though. We're planning our revenge. This time, with more damage"

The entire room burst into laughter, the tension lifting from the sterile air. Even the nurses, who had been strictly monitoring our conditions, couldn't hold back their smiles. It was a rare moment in an ICU, where instead of pain and fear, there was life—laughter filling the space.

As more people came in, the room felt less like a hospital ward and more like a lively gathering spot. The nurses went from being all business to joining in on the banter, one even commenting, "You guys sure know how to stay in ICU, you feel very excited to be here and treating it to be party hall"

Nikhil, ever the entertainer, had already begun naming his stitches after the people of Dhama's gang, by pointing to a long stitch across his arm.

I shook my head, a smile tugging at my lips despite the pain. "You're ridiculous."

"Don't underestimate the power of a superhero wound," he winked, clearly enjoying his role as the ICU's official comic relief.

But as the laughter settled down and the crowd thinned, the door to our ICU room opened again, this time with a familiar face entering. Rohan, our best friend, strode in with a determined look on his face, his eyes scanning the room until they landed on us.

"Ah, the mighty warriors are awake," he said with a grin, but there was a hint of seriousness in his tone. "How are my two injured heroes?"

I grinned at him. "Surviving, just barely"

Nikhil nodded, his smile fading slightly. "Yeah, we're lucky to be alive."

Rohan's eyes darkened as he looked between us, his jaw tightening. "Dhama's going to pay for this," he said, his voice low but filled with promise. "I don't care how we do it, but we're getting him back for this."

I gave him a pained smile. "As long as it's not with cricket bats or anything that'll put us back in here"

Rohan laughed but quickly sobered. "No more fighting with cricket bats. We'll plan something smarter...and more painful he added, giving Nikhil a playful nudge.

"You know what? I'm all for that," Nikhil said with a mischievous gleam in his eye. "We'll get him back, and this time, no one gets hurt."

We all shared a look, our bond stronger than ever in that moment. It didn't matter how bad things had gotten—we were a team, and together, we'd make sure Dhama didn't get the last laugh.

"Deal," I said, feeling the weight of my injuries but also a sense of determination growing within me. "We'll take them down, one person at a time."

Rohan chuckled, shaking his head. "You two are insane."

"Maybe," Nikhil agreed, his smile never faltering. "But we're going to make sure Dhama remembers that he messed with the wrong guys."

ũ

After two days confined to stiff hospital beds, softened only slightly by painkillers and the endless volley of jokes between us, Nikhil and I were finally discharged. The long walk back to the hostel was more of a limp, our bodies still sore but our spirits unbroken.

News of our return had spread like wildfire, and as we approached the gates, a buzzing crowd of hostel mates gathered to welcome their "wounded warriors." But beyond the smiles and greetings, hushed whispers filled the air—everyone was murmuring, gossiping in hushed tones. We were the talk of the town, our injuries turning into exaggerated legends before we even stepped inside.

Dhama and his boys were conspicuously absent, their usual swagger replaced by the shadows of warnings issued by both the warden and the college authorities. They had been explicitly told to steer clear of us, and for once, they complied.

As we shuffled into the hostel, the atmosphere shifted. A cheer erupted, Rohan along with few hostlers rushed forward to greet us, while the seniors stood back, their amused glances laced with a quiet respect. Nikhil, despite the stitches on his forehead, managed to raise his hand in mock triumph.

Rohan strode forward and clapped on my back—lightly, knowing the pain. "Next time, call me before you go hero mode."

Nikhil raised his arms, despite his bandaged wrist. "Back from the dead, boys!" he shouted.

The group burst into laughter. I exhaled, feeling a strange warmth despite the pain.

"Come on, let's go inside" Rohan said, throwing an arm around Nikhil and me. Together, we walked inside, bruised but undefeated as Today, pain didn't matter—brotherhood did.

As we made our way down the corridor, familiar faces peeked from their rooms, smirking and whispering. Someone patted Nikhil on the back, while another whistled. "Heard you two took on an entire gang," one junior piped up.

"Yeah, and lived to tell the tale," Nikhil shot back, wincing slightly but grinning through it.

Rohan shook his head. "Idiots. Both of you."

Despite his words, I could hear the pride in his voice. We reached our room, and as I slumped onto my bed, I felt the exhaustion creep in. But even through the throbbing pain, one thought remained—some fights weren't about winning. They were about standing together.

That night, the hostel turned into a celebration. Snacks and soft drinks flowed, and I and Nikhil were the stars of the evening. We recounted our version of the battle, embellishing details to make it sound like an epic Bollywood fight scene.

"There were at least ten of them," I exaggerated, holding court in the common room.

"Fifteen," Nikhil interrupted, adjusting his bandage like a war hero. "And they had chains. But we stood our ground."

"Before getting knocked out," a junior piped up cheekily, drawing a round of laughter.

The incident had a lasting impact on the hostel dynamics. Word of the assault spread quickly through the college, and the administration took swift action. Dhama and his gang were summoned and they faced a grilling from the disciplinary committee. Witnesses were called, statements were taken, and the evidence of our injuries—painful as they were—spoke volumes.

The verdict came swiftly. Dhama and two of his closest accomplices were suspended from the hostel for an entire semester. While they were still allowed to attend classes, they had to find accommodation off-campus. For a group that had ruled the hostel corridors with intimidation, the punishment was nothing short of a public dethroning.

The hostel buzzed with gossip in the days that followed. Relief was the dominant emotion, though it was tinged with caution. Dhama's departure left a power vacuum, and while no one missed his oppressive presence, there was an unspoken fear of what might come next. For now, though, peace reigned, and the corridors felt lighter without the looming shadow of his gang.

For Dhama, the suspension was a crushing blow. Forced out of the hostel, he faced the dual burden of practical inconvenience and a bruised ego. His friends, once loyal to a fault, began to distance themselves, unwilling to share in his downfall. The hostel, once his kingdom, now seemed like a distant, hostile memory.

A week after our return, Nikhil, Rohan, and I were lounging in my room. Nikhil sat cross-legged on the bed, holding a small mirror to inspect his stitches. "You think these will leave scars?" he asked, tilting his head for a better angle.

I looked up from the book I was pretending to read. "If they do, we'll just call them battle marks. Adds to our charm"

Rohan snorted. "You mean your charm. Pretty sure those stitches won't help Nikhil's face."

Before Nikhil could retort, a knock at the door interrupted us. Rohan opened it to find a mutual friend standing there, looking unusually serious

"Hey, guys. Dhama wants to talk. He's waiting for you at the café near the library. Says he wants to clear the air"

Rohan raised an eyebrow. "Clear the air? After what he did"

The friend nodded. "He knows he messed up. Meet him at the café near the library"

I exchanged a glance with Nikhil, who shrugged. "Fine," I said. "Let's see what he has to say."

Later, we three arrived at the café to find Dhama already seated a coffee cup in his hands. He looked different—quieter, subdued. As we approached, he stood up awkwardly.

"Hey," he said his voice devoid of its usual bravado.

We sat across from him, our expressions guarded.

Dhama took a deep breath. "I'll be honest. I made a big mistake. What I did was wrong, and I've had a lot of time to think about it. I'm really sorry to all of you."

His voice sounded sincere, which surprised us. He didn't seem like the arrogant bully we knew. Instead, he looked truly sorry.

Rohan, who never trusts easily, leaned forward. "Why now? What made you change?"

Dhama sighed, his eyes dropping to the coffee cup in front of him. "Because I've hit rock bottom, man, the suspension, the isolation... It's been tough. I've had all this time to think about what I've done, and it hit me just how much damage I caused. It's not just about the fights or the stupid stuff I said. It's about the people I hurt—especially you guys." His voice broke a little, but he quickly composed himself.

I narrowed my eyes. "You didn't think about it then? When you were hitting Nikhil? When you got us all tangled in that mess?"

Dhama flinched slightly but nodded. "I was blind, honestly. Just... wrapped up in this stupid pride, this need to prove something, to everyone and to myself, but after everything that happened, I realized how far I'd fallen. I used to think I was untouchable, but the suspension—it shattered that. I lost everything. And it made me see how wrong I was, how wrong I'd been to you guys."

He took a deep breath, his hands trembling slightly as he set the coffee cup down. "I'm not asking for you to forgive me right away. I know I don't deserve it. But I need you to know how deeply sorry I am for everything I did. For the way I treated you both... and the way I acted. For making Nikhil feel like he was less than me, for pushing you both into that fight, I wish I could take it all back. I wish I could've been better."

Nikhil looked at him, his expression unreadable. "You hit me, Dhama. You were ready to take it all the way. How do you expect me to just... forget that?"

Dhama's eyes softened, and his voice dropped. "I don't expect you to forget. I know that's impossible. But I want you to know that the person who did that is not who I want to be anymore. I don't want to be that guy who throws punches or belittles people. I don't want to be the person who hurts his friends because of his own insecurities. I've thought about it a lot, and I regret it all. I regret hurting you, Nikhil. I regret putting you both in that situation. I'm sorry."

There was a long silence as we processed his words. It felt strange hearing him speak like this, with such raw honesty, when just a week ago, he was the one who had planned to take revenge from us.

I glanced at Rohan, who still looked wary but less angry. "You hurt us, Dhama. A lot, you think words are going to fix that?"

Dhama nodded slowly, his eyes never leaving mine. "I don't expect words to fix anything. I just needed to say them. To own up to what I did. I know I have a long way to go to make things right, but I want to try."

Rohan crossed his arms. "What does that even mean? What are you going to do differently?"

Dhama met his gaze steadily. "I don't have all the answers yet. But I'm going to start by making sure I never let something like that happen again. I'm going to work on myself, on being a better person, on being someone you guys don't have to look at and think 'this guy is just a jerk.'"

There was another pause, this one longer, as we all sat with the weight of his words. Finally, Nikhil spoke up, his voice quieter than usual "I don't know if I can just forgive you right away. It's going to take time, Dhama. But I'll give you a chance. I'll see if you're really serious about changing. But if you slip up even once, don't think we'll just let it slide. You've got one shot at this."

Dhama nodded his expression a mix of relief and guilt. "That's fair. I don't expect anything less. Thanks for hearing me out."

As we left the café, the weight of the past week began to lift. The scars we carried, both visible and invisible, were a testament to the battles we'd fought. But they also served as a reminder: sometimes, even the worst of us can find a path to redemption. The choice to walk it, however, is theirs alone.

As Nikhil, Rohan and I settled back into our routine, we couldn't help but reflect on the events that had unfolded. The fight, the pain, the camaraderie of our friends—it all felt like a strange, chaotic chapter in our lives. But it also brought us closer, cementing bonds of friendship that would last a lifetime.

A DANCE OF DOUBTS

Over the next few months, Dhama's transformation was evident. He kept a low profile, avoided conflicts, and seemed genuinely remorseful. His efforts didn't go unnoticed, and slowly, the hostel's attitude toward him began to shift. It wasn't forgiveness—not yet—but it was a start.

One afternoon, as Rohan was poring over paperwork for the upcoming college fest, Dhama approached him in the library. The quiet hum of whispered conversations and the rustling of papers filled the air, but Dhama's hesitant footsteps seemed to echo in Rohan's ears.

"Hey," Dhama said his voice soft but steady. He stood near the table, holding onto his backpack strap.

Rohan glanced up, his pen pausing mid-scribble. He raised an eyebrow, not entirely sure where this was going. "Hey," he replied cautiously.

"I heard you're on the fest organizing team" Dhama continued, his tone betraying a mixture of nervousness and determination. "Need an extra hand?"

Before Rohan could respond, Nikhil seated a few chairs away, snorted. He leaned back in his chair, crossing his arms "Trying to score some good karma, huh?"

Dhama chuckled; the sound self-deprecating. "Something likes that," he admitted, his eyes briefly meeting Nikhil's before shifting back to Rohan. "But seriously. Let me help. I've got time, and I want to make myself useful."

Rohan set his pen down and leaned back in his chair, studying Dhama. The guy looked different—not just in how he carried himself, but in the way his words felt genuine. It wasn't the cocky, defensive Dhama he was used to seeing.

"You want to help," Rohan said his voice slow, testing.

"Yeah" Dhama nodded, a little too quickly. "I know I've... I've screwed up a lot. But I'm trying to turn things around. And I thought, maybe, this could be a way to start."

Nikhil scoffed, closing his notebook with a loud thud. "You've got to be kidding me, Rohan. Letting *him* help with the fest? What if he screws it up on purpose? Or worse, tries to sabotage the whole thing? We've all seen what he's capable of."

Nikhil rolled his eyes and glanced at Dhama "And why should we trust you? What's stopping you from ditching halfway through or messing things up?"

Dhama took a deep breath, his jaw tightening for a moment. He turned to Nikhil, his gaze steady. "Nothing," he admitted. "You don't have to trust me.

But I'm not asking for a free pass here. Give me something to do, anything. If I screw it up, you'll know I haven't changed. But if I don't..." He trailed off, shrugging slightly. "It's your call."

Rohan tapped his fingers on the table, his mind racing. He exchanged a glance with Nikhil, whose skeptical expression hadn't softened. Turning back to Dhama, Rohan asked, "What kind of work are you talking about? This isn't just putting up posters or moving chairs. We've got deadlines, logistics, budgets—real responsibilities. Can you handle that?"

"Or it's a trap," Nikhil countered. "You're being too trusting, Rohan. What's the first rule of damage control? Minimize risk. And he's the biggest risk you could take."

Rohan shook his head. "Maybe, or maybe this is the risk that pays off. Dhama, if I let you help, you follow my lead, no questions asked. You mess up even once, and you're out. Fair?"

"Try me," Dhama said his voice firm.

Rohan hesitated for a moment longer, and then sighed, a small smile tugging at the corner of his lips. "Alright," he said, grabbing a stack of papers from the table. "Here, we need someone to coordinate the sponsorship team. It's not glamorous, and it's a lot of cold-calling, but it's important. Think you can manage?"

Dhama took the papers, his expression serious. "I'll do my best," he promised.

Nikhil sighed and raised his hands in frustration. "Fine, but if anything goes wrong, don't say I didn't warn you."

As Dhama pulled up a chair and started going through the documents, Rohan watched him out of the corner of his eye. It was a small gesture, letting Dhama in, but it marked the beginning of something new. His willingness to contribute—to be part of the hostel community in a positive way—spoke volumes.

Rohan glanced at the documents spread before Dhama and nodded approvingly. It was strange seeing him this serious, but maybe things were changing for the better. Nikhil, however, seemed restless. His earlier exasperation had faded into something more guarded.

"So," Nikhil started his voice low as they stepped outside for a break. "You really think Dhama's turning over a new leaf?"

Rohan a frown creasing on his forehead turned to Nikhil. He had been thinking about the same thing, but hearing it aloud felt different.

"What do you mean?" he asked, looking at Nikhil curiously.

Nikhil smirked; his eyes gleaming with amusement. "You know exactly what I mean. Dhama, the troublemaker, the one who never missed a chance to stir up some chaos,

He's been acting all... responsible lately. I'm not sure I can buy it."

Rohan chuckled, shaking his head. "Come on, he's been trying. You've seen it yourself. He's been actually putting effort into the fest planning and helping with the arrangements. I know it's hard to believe, but maybe he's changed."

Nikhil raised an eyebrow, still unconvinced. "Yeah, well, I'm waiting to see how long that lasts. But you'll love this," he said, his tone dripping with mischief. "He's enrolled in dance with Ahana for the college fest."

Rohan's eyes widened in surprise, He had not expected that, Dhama and Ahana—two completely different people. Ahana, always graceful and poised, and Dhama, got known for his uncoordinated and awkward movements "What?" Rohan laughed, trying to process the news. "Wait, he's seriously going to dance with Ahana? That's—interesting."

Nikhil's face broke into a mischievous grin. "I know, right? He's been practicing with her for the past week.

Rohan still couldn't wrap his head around it. He glanced over at Nikhil, who was watching him intently. "Well, I guess that's a good thing. He's contributing to the fest in some way, even if it's... unconventional."

"Yeah, but there's a catch," Nikhil added, leaning forward, lowering his voice. "Someone else isn't exactly thrilled about it."

Rohan paused, his thoughts immediately jumping to me. The only person he knew who could possibly react negatively to Dhama dancing with Ahana was me, who had always been more protective of her.

"Ishaan" Rohan guessed, raising an eyebrow.

"Exactly," Nikhil said with a sly grin. "Ishaan's not going to be thrilled about Dhama and Ahana spending so much time together. I think he's worried Dhama might, I don't know, get too close to her or something."

Rohan exhaled deeply. "I get Ishaan's protective side. He's always been close to Ahana, and the idea of anyone getting too close to her—especially someone like Dhama—doesn't sit well with him. But honestly, I don't think Ahana would ever fall for Dhama. She's way too sharp for that."

Nikhil laughed, shaking his head. "You're right. Ahana is way out of Dhama's league, but you know how possessive Ishaan can be. He might just blow this out of proportion."

Rohan thought for a moment, rubbing his chin. "Hmm, I don't know. We should probably tell Ishaan about it before it blows up in our faces. He'll find out eventually."

Nikhil winced. "Yeah, but I'd rather not be the one to break it to him. He'll probably throttle me just for mentioning it. You're his friend too, Rohan. Why don't you tell him?"

Rohan chuckled, his tone teasing. "Me? Not a chance, man. I'm not stepping into that minefield. Ishaan's no picnic to deal with when he's mad. You're braver than me, so this one's all yours."

Nikhil shook his head, grinning. "Fine, I'll do it. But when Ishaan blows up, you better be ready to back me up."

"I'll back you up, sure," Rohan said, laughing. "Just don't expect me to say anything. You're the one who decided to stir the pot."

Just then, Rohan glanced down at the pile of papers he had been sorting through earlier—event schedules, participant lists, and task assignments for the fest. The reality of the work ahead settled back into his mind. "Look, I better get back to this," he said, gathering the papers and preparing to dive back into the planning. "We're running out of time, and there's still so much to do before the fest kicks off."

Nikhil nodded, stood up, and stretched. "Yeah, I should go too. But I'll see you later. You'll probably be here for a long time."

Rohan laughed. "Yeah, I will. No one else will do the work. Take care, man."

Nikhil gave a lazy wave as he started walking toward the exit. "Alright, I'm off. Don't work too hard. And remember, if Ishaan blows up, you owe me one."

Rohan waved him off as Nikhil disappeared into the distance. Rohan turned his attention back to the fest papers, diving into the work with renewed determination. As much as he wanted to be done with it all, he knew the fest wouldn't organize itself. There were deadlines to meet, tasks to assign, and last-minute changes to handle.

He looked up at the ceiling again for a moment. A deep breath filled his lungs, and with a sense of resolve, he began tackling the next task on the list. There would be time for everything else later, but for now, the fest was his responsibility, and he was determined to make it a success.

ॐ

The moonlight filtered through the dusty windowpanes of our hostel room, casting faint shadows on the walls. The room was a cluttered mess—textbooks half-open on the study table, a stack of empty instant noodle cups in one corner, and a faint smell of cigarette smoke lingering from Rohan's habit. He had just stepped out for his usual late-night smoke, leaving Nikhil and me in relative silence.

Nikhil lay sprawled on his bed, one earphone hanging out from his ear while the other played faint music. I sat on my bed with my legs crossed, playing with a pen. The quiet sound of the ceiling fan filled the void.

"Man, Rohan smokes like a chimney," Nikhil commented, removing the earphone and glancing toward the door.

I chuckled, but my thoughts were elsewhere. Nikhil must've noticed because he tilted his head and gave me a curious look.

"You've been zoning out a lot lately," he said. "What's up? Something on your mind"

"Nothing major," I said, trying to brush it off.

Nikhil raised an eyebrow. "Nothing major, come on, I've known you long enough to tell when you're holding something back. Spill it."

I hesitated for a moment, and then sighed. "Ahana and I talked for hours on the phone last night."

"Oh?" Nikhil said, his tone teasing. "Do tell. What did she have to say this time?"

I rolled my eyes but couldn't help the smile tugging at my lips. "She's signed up for some dance event in the college festival. You should've heard her talk about it— like a little kid who just discovered candy. She's so excited."

Nikhil smirked. "I thought you talked to her every night."

"We used to," I admitted, my smile fading. "Not anymore."

"What's changed?" he asked, his voice laced with genuine curiosity.

I shook my head. "Drop it. It's not important."

Nikhil didn't press further, but the energy in the room shifted. The comfortable silence that had settled earlier now felt awkward and heavy. After a moment, Nikhil broke it.

"Do you know about Dhama?" he asked casually, though there was an edge to his tone.

I frowned. "What about him? He's helping out Rohan with the fest proceedings and participating in some activities. Why?"

"Nothing specific," Nikhil said a trace of something unreadable in his tone. "It's just... he's been flying high these days."

"Why? What happened?" I asked, narrowing my eyes.

"You know Dhama and Ahana are performing a dance together in the college festival, right?" he said, glancing at me cautiously.

The words hit me like a punch in the gut. My hands curled into fists at my sides. "What?" I snapped, stopping in my tracks. "Dhama, With Ahana"

"Yeah," Nikhil said, trying to sound casual but clearly bracing for my reaction. "He's been spending a lot of time with her lately. I think he's trying to get close to her."

"That bastard," I muttered under my breath, anger bubbling up inside me. Dhama had been my rival for as long as I could remember—arrogant, conniving, and always looking for ways to one-up me. The thought of him getting close to Ahana, the girl I cared about more than anything, made my blood boil.

"You're wearing out the floor, Relax, man. It's probably just a dance thing. You know how these college events are." Nikhil said from his spot on the bed, his head propped up on a pillow. He was scrolling through his phone, but his tone hinted at the concern he didn't voice often

"No," I said firmly, my jaw tightening. "I need to see this for myself."

""Wait, are you serious?" Nikhil asked. But the small smile on his face showed he wasn't really surprised.

"I'm not letting that guy weasel his way into her life, the way he talks, the way he acts—it's all calculated. I'm not going to let him manipulate her." I said, leaning against the window frame.

Nikhil frowned, rubbing his temples. "Fine, let's say you're right. What are you planning to do about it? March in there and start a fight again?"

"No," I said, though the temptation flickered in the back of my mind. "I just... I need to see for myself. To confirm if he's crossing lines."

He shook his head, leaning back against the wall. "This is starting to sound like one of those bad rom-com plots where the jealous guy screws everything up. Why don't you just talk to her?"

"I will. After I know the truth," I replied, my jaw tightening again. "She deserves to know who she's dealing with."

"Alright," Nikhil said, throwing up his hands in surrender. "So, what's the plan? Are you just going to crash their rehearsal and glare at him until he confesses his evil intentions?"

I smirked despite myself. "No. We'll watch from a distance. If he's being inappropriate or pushing too hard to come close to her, I'll step in. Otherwise, we'll leave without making a scene."

"Easier said than done," Nikhil muttered but didn't argue further. He picked up a notebook from the table and flipped it open.

"Alright, detective, what is the plan?"

I glanced at him. "Okay, what time is the rehearsal?" I asked.

"Probably in the afternoon," he replied. "They usually use the main auditorium for these things."

He wrote something down and then gave me a serious look. "Fine, we'll go. But remember, we're only watching. No drama."

I nodded, even though I felt restless inside "Only watching."

The night dragged on as I replayed the day's events in my mind, trying to pinpoint what exactly had triggered this unease. Nikhil eventually fell asleep, his snores punctuating the stillness, but I stayed up, staring at the ceiling and planning every possible scenario for the next day.

ũ

The next afternoon, the campus buzzed with its usual rhythm. Students milled about in groups, some rushing to their next class, others lounging under the shade of the sprawling neem tree near the canteen. Nikhil and I had decided to skip lunch, our focus solely on the rehearsal.

As we left the hostel and made our way toward the academic buildings, Nikhil tried to lighten the mood. "You know, if we get caught, they might think we're the creepy ones."

I shot him a look. "We're not doing anything wrong. Just observing"

"Sure, because stalking always comes across as innocent," he quipped, though his tone lacked any real bite. "Seriously, though, try not to look like you're about to charge into battle."

I didn't reply, my eyes scanning the path ahead. The road widened into two lanes as we passed the gate of the academic main building. Its ship-like design always fascinated me—a bold architectural choice that stood out against the otherwise conventional campus structures.

The road began a gentle descent, leading us toward the academic hall. The farther we walked, the quieter the campus became, as though the chatter and noise of the upper areas were being swallowed by the surrounding trees. By the time we reached the main auditorium, the faint sound of music floated through the air, its rhythm enticing and filled with energy.

My heart raced with anxiety and anger as I neared the glass doors. Beyond them, the backstage appeared—a space covered by a red canvas roof, supported by metal rods. Sunlight poured in, casting a warm, glowing light inside. The air buzzed with quiet chaos, where people worked quickly and creatively. It was a place where ideas came to life under pressure.

Through the open canvas, I caught sight of Ahana and Dhama rehearsing their dance alongside a few other dancers. Their movements were fluid and synchronized, their feet tapping rhythmically against the wooden stage. The music played from a small speaker, filling the air with an upbeat tempo that resonated with their enthusiasm. Ahana's posture was poised, her hands cutting through the air with precision, her face carrying an intensity that only enhanced her grace. Dhama, ever the showman, added a dramatic flair to his every step, his laughter echoing occasionally as he interacted with the others.

Rohan, dressed in his festival management team attire, stood a few feet away, assisting the host with his microphone. He was still wearing the remnants of his earlier costume from the rehearsals, a mix of sweat and effort etched into its fabric. As I entered with Nikhil, we quietly took seats behind, careful not to disturb the ongoing preparations. The wooden floor creaked faintly underfoot; adding to the symphony of sounds—music, footsteps, and muffled conversations.

The stage shook slightly as the dancers moved. Ahana's focus was amazing, and every move she made had meaning. But inside, I felt nervous and uneasy. Nikhil leaned in and spoke, pulling me out of my thoughts.

I felt a sharp pang in my chest. It wasn't jealousy—it was anger. Anger at Dhama's audacity, his ease, the way he seemed to insert himself into her space as though he belonged there.

Nikhil nudged me. "Relax. He's not doing anything wrong."

"Yet," I muttered, my eyes never leaving the stage.

We stayed there for several minutes, watching as the rehearsal continued. Dhama was undeniably charismatic, his movements confident and his voice commanding as he directed the group. But something about him still felt... off. Like he was playing a role rather than being genuine.

"She looks happy," Nikhil said softly, breaking the silence.

I didn't reply, my mind racing. Was I overreacting? Reading too much into his actions? Or was there something real beneath my unease?

"Come on," I said, tugging Nikhil's arm. "We've seen enough. Let's go"

"You don't want to watch it?" he asked, his voice a mixture of curiosity and concern.

"No," I replied, my tone sharper than intended. "I've had enough."

The rehearsal ended with a loud cheer, showing the hard work and talent of the performers. The dancers took their final positions, holding them momentarily before stepping offstage. Applause erupted from those gathered, and a sense of accomplishment lingered in the air. Ahana and Dhama emerged from the left exit, their faces flushed with exertion and triumph. They walked together, their conversation animated as they relived the moments on stage, punctuating their words with laughter.

Ahana noticed me and walked toward us; her face covered in sweat. The sun was blazing, making the heat unbearable. I sat there calmly, my sunglasses hiding my eyes. My posture showed confidence—I had my right leg resting over my left knee, and my arms were relaxed.

I wore a blue shirt with white frills on the sleeves. The fabric stuck to my skin because of the heat. The sun shone brightly, making everything around me feel even hotter. The red canvas beside me seemed to burn under the scorching light. The air was thick, heavy, and suffocating.

Ahana's eyes widened in surprise as she spotted me. "What a surprise! You're here?" she said, her voice carrying both delight and curiosity.

I smiled but didn't answer right away. She took a step closer, her expression shifting to something more serious. "So... how was it?" she asked, her voice light but probing. Her eyes searched mine, looking for validation.

I removed my sunglasses deliberately, folding them with care before hanging them on my collar. "Good job," I said, extending my hand. She hesitated for a brief moment before shaking it, her grip firm yet tentative.

"Was I anywhere near the others?" she asked, her voice tinged with self-doubt.

"Don't say that," I replied, my tone softening. "You were better. You'll always be better."

Nikhil, standing nearby, chimed in enthusiastically, "Your performance was splendid!"

Ahana's face lit up at the compliment, though her smile carried a hint of humility. "Thank you," she said, turning to Nikhil and shaking his hand. The simple gesture seemed to carry more weight than it should, and I felt an inexplicable pang of irritation.

Her friends soon joined in, forming a cheerful group around the dancers. Everyone talked at once, sharing their thoughts about the performance—some praised it, while others gave helpful suggestions. I slowly stepped back, feeling unnoticed in the lively conversation.

My gaze lingered on Ahana. Her smile, though steady, seemed rehearsed, a mask for the exhaustion and emotions brewing underneath. The sun's rays painted her in shades of red, intensifying the vibrancy of her presence.

"Excuse me," I said quickly and stepped away from the group. I put my sunglasses back on and moved through the crowd, making my way to the far end of the backstage area. The red canvas fabric shifted gently in the breeze, almost as if it were alive. I found a small open space near the wall and bent down slightly to step outside.

The sun greeted me with its unrelenting heat, a stark contrast to the charged atmosphere inside. I took a deep breath, the air outside fresher but heavier with unsaid thoughts. The noise from backstage faded into a distant hum as I leaned against the wall, my mind replaying the scene I had just left.

Ahana's voice, her movements, and her smile stayed in my mind and wouldn't fade away. The way she reacted to Nikhil's compliment and how her eyes still sparkled even though she was tired kept bothering me. I clenched my fists as the feelings I had tried to ignore started rising like a wave I couldn't stop.

I glanced back at the canvas wall, its vibrant red stark against the blue sky. Behind it, Ahana and the others continued their celebration, their laughter occasionally piercing the quiet I had sought. For a moment, I considered walking back in, confronting the turmoil head-on. But instead, I stood still, letting the sun beat down on me, its warmth grounding me amidst the chaos of my thoughts.

The sun hit me full force, a sharp contrast to the dim, chaotic backstage. It was blinding but liberating. I walked a few paces, letting the heat envelop me, the silence of the open space settling my nerves. A gust of warm wind rustled the sparse trees nearby, a stark reminder of the unrelenting summer.

I heard footsteps behind me, light but deliberate. "Can't you wait there?" Nikhil's voice was calm, but there was a curious edge to it. He'd followed me out.

I turned slightly and held out a water bottle, offering it to him. My words were clipped as I responded, "It was a rotten fest."

He took the bottle but didn't drink. Instead, he looked at me, his brow furrowing slightly. "I think it was good," he said after a pause.

"You're free to think that," I replied, my tone neutral but dismissive.

"What is with you?" he asked, his voice carrying a mix of irritation and concern.

"There is nothing with me," I said, turning my gaze to the horizon. The sun was starting its slow descent, painting the sky in hues of orange and red.

"Why did you come out of the auditorium?" he pressed.

waved my hand toward the open area around us. "This place is nice."

He wasn't buying it. "You left in the middle of the conversation."

I shrugged. "I had already watched them practice." I answered quickly and shortly, hoping to end the conversation, but Nikhil didn't give up.

"You know everyone's talking about them," he said, his tone shifting to something more playful. He laughed lightly and slapped my leg, as if to jolt me out of my mood.

"Bastard planned it right," I muttered, the words slipping out before I could stop them. They carried a bitterness I hadn't intended to voice.

Nikhil raised an eyebrow, intrigued. "Hey, you are thinking too much now"

I ignored his question and stood up, taking the bottle from him and placing it on the counter of the makeshift cafeteria nearby. The place was deserted except for a few staff members tidying up. The aroma of stale coffee and fried snacks lingered in the air.

"Okay, spill," Nikhil said, pulling up a chair and sitting across from me. "What's really going on?"

I leaned back against the counter, crossing my arms. "It's nothing. Just tired of pretending."

He tilted his head, studying me. "You've been acting strange all day. It's not just about the Ahana, is it?"

I sighed, the weight of the day pressing down on me. "It's not the Ahana. It's everything around her. The fake smiles, the overdone admiration, the way everyone fawns over her."

Nikhil's expression changed. His eyes softened, and a small smile appeared on his face. "Ahana, huh?"

I didn't reply right away. My silence was enough to give him an answer. He leaned forward, resting his elbows on his knees, watching me carefully.

"Look, man," he said after a moment, "she's really good at what she does. People notice talent. That's just how it is. It's not her fault that everyone keeps talking about her."

"I know that," I murmured, my voice quieter now. "But sometimes, it feels like she's living in a completely different world. A world I can't step into."

Nikhil let my words settle in the air. He didn't rush to respond. Then, he asked, "So, what's stopping you from trying?"

His question caught me off guard. I turned to him, frowning slightly. "You make it sound so easy."

"It's not easy," he admitted with a small shrug. "But it's better than standing here, doing nothing, and feeling bad about it. If you have something to say, say it. What's the worst that could happen?"

I let out a short, humourless laugh. "The worst? She could laugh at me. Or even worse, feel sorry for me."

Nikhil shook his head. "You're overthinking it. She's not that kind of person."

I narrowed my eyes at him. "You seem to know her pretty well," I said, my voice sharper than I meant.

He caught it but didn't rise to the bait. "We've talked a few times. She's nice. Genuine, you should give her a chance."

I looked away, the knot in my chest tightening. The day had dipped lower, the sky now a deep, fiery orange. The staff at the canteen began to pack up, their movements brisk and efficient.

Nikhil stood, stretching lazily. "Anyway, I'm heading back. Think about what I said." He clapped me on the shoulder before walking away, leaving me alone with my thoughts.

I stayed there for a while, the quiet hum of the evening settling around me. The voices from backstage were faint now, a distant echo of the world I'd momentarily escaped. I closed my eyes, letting the breeze brush against my face. Maybe Nikhil was right. Maybe it was time to stop hiding and start living. But for now, I just needed a moment to breathe.

FALLEN FOR THE FALLEN

Days pass, a thousand words written and unspoken to Ahana remained undelivered, hanging in the air like unfinished symphonies. In the depths of my mind, there are familiar faces—Rohan and Nikhil, my best friends, my confidants, the unsung heroes in my tangled love story. They have always been there for me, offering support and laughter during my most vulnerable moments.

It was the third year of college, a time when everything felt like it was speeding toward an uncertain future, yet some emotions remained timeless. Today, I felt the need to confide in them, to unravel the complexity of my feelings for Ahana, the girl who turned my world upside down.

I was sitting on my bed, thinking about our conversations and the time we spent together. Suddenly, my phone rang, snapping me out of my thoughts. I looked at the screen and saw her name—Ahana. It felt like I had come back to life, like a fish put back into water after struggling to breathe. I paused for a moment but then answered the call, trying to sound calm and casual.

"Hey, Ishaan! Where have you been this week?" Her voice was light, yet there was an underlying tone of concern that tugged at my heart.

"I was just... busy," I replied, trying to sound casual. There was a brief silence on the other end, a moment filled with unspoken questions that I felt deeply.

"Busy? Doing what?" she probed, her curiosity evident.

"Just some stuff," I said, my voice trailing off. The air was thick with anticipation, and I could feel my heart racing.

"I actually wanted to ask you something," she finally said, breaking the silence. My heart leaped; finally, a chance for clarity, a chance to understand her feelings.

But then, as if someone had pressed pause on our conversation, she hesitated, and all I could hear was the faint sound of her breathing. The suspense was unbearable.

"Uh, you know what? I forgot what I was going to ask," she said, abruptly ending the moment.

A wave of disappointment washed over me. "Oh," I muttered, feeling the weight of unspoken words crushing my chest. I disconnected the call, frustration bubbling inside me. I flipped onto my bed, staring at the ceiling, my mind racing with thoughts of what could have been.

I pulled out my phone to text Ahana, desperately wanting to know what she had intended to ask. My fingers hovered over the screen, but the words eluded me. Just then, Rohan burst into my room, full of energy, and jumped onto my bed like a child.

"What's up?" he asked, kicking my leg playfully.

"Nothing," I replied, too engrossed in my thoughts to engage. I continued texting, hoping to spark some clarity between us.

Nikhil, ever the impatient one, kicked me again. "Seriously, what's going on?"

I was frustrated, and in an attempt to regain control of the situation, I tried to snatch my phone back from him. He had always been a bit of a pest, but today it felt unbearable. "Give it back, Nikhil!" I shouted, my patience wearing thin.

He simply laughed and tossed my phone onto my back. "Fine, let's go to the mess. You're no fun!"

I sighed, knowing that food was the only thing that could get Nikhil to cooperate. "Okay, but I need your help first. Sit down," I insisted.

Nikhil was already thinking about food and couldn't tolerate delays. "Can we do this after dinner? The food won't be there if we're late," he said, his eyes darting towards the door.

"Listen, this is important," I said, trying to bring the conversation back on track. "This isn't casual gossip; it's about love. I'm seriously in love with Ahana."

"What? Come on, man! Not this again. Why don't you just open your heart to her? How long are you going to stay just friends?" Nikhil's reaction was exactly what I had anticipated. He had always been the sensible one, the voice of reason.

Just then, Rohan walked in, sensing the tension. "What's the problem?" he asked, looking between us.

"You are the problem; you've turned him into a hopeless romantic!" Nikhil shot back, not missing a beat.

Rohan raised his hands in surrender, "What did I do? I just got here!"

I quickly intervened, sensing that if they started bickering, it would spiral into an endless exchange of insults. "Guys, focus! The real issue here is that I'm in true love with Ahana."

Rohan's confusion turned to curiosity. "Since when did this love become *true* love?"

I sighed, realizing he had probably seen it all along. "Yeah... maybe it was always there," I confessed. Saying it out loud felt strangely liberating, as if I had lifted a weight off my chest.

"You didn't even tell me, that you are so serious about her" Rohan sounded offended but intrigued at the same time.

"I didn't want you to announce it on a loudspeaker!" I shot back. Rohan had a terrible habit of spilling secrets, especially to his girlfriend, who then shared them with her friends, turning my private matters into gossip.

"So, have you told her about your felling or still in the list of best friends?" he asked, changing the topic again.

"No," I admitted, my heart racing at the thought.

"Then what are you waiting for?" Rohan pressed a spark of excitement in his eyes.

I hesitated, busying myself with my phone as another message from Ahana popped up. "I don't know," I mumbled, unsure of how to respond.

"It's been years since you both have been close. When are you going to open your heart to her? After graduation? Or when she's already with someone else?" Rohan asked, his eyes fixed on me.

I hesitated, unsure of what to say.

"If you really want her in your life, I can help you," he added, his voice filled with certainty.

My heart pounded. "Okay, tell me!" My curiosity got the better of me, and a surge of adrenaline rushed through me.

Rohan smirked. "Here's the plan: Call her somewhere private and just propose. Sweet and simple."

"Are you serious? That's your master plan?" I scoffed, unable to believe how ridiculous it sounded.

"If you want her, follow it! Otherwise, just stay friends," he said, getting up to leave the room.

"Okay, I'll do it," I said, determination surging through me.

Rohan's eyes lit up. "That's great news, dude! Nikhil, not everyone is a saint like you!" he teased.

Nikhil frowned, "Ishaan, what's gotten into you? Why are you suddenly so eager?"

"I love her! I need to tell her before its too late," I replied, my voice steady. "If I don't act now, I'll lose my chance forever."

Rohan approached me and hugged me tightly. "That's my boy! You need to be strong in your decision. I'll help you figure it out."

"Love is messy," Nikhil warned. "And you have your exam the day after tomorrow. Are you sure you want to get into this right now?"

I groaned, running a hand through my hair. "I know, I know. But if I don't tell her how I feel, I'll regret it forever."

"Tomorrow is Sunday," Rohan announced, his eyes sparkling with mischief. "Call her and ask her out!"

I stared at him, incredulous. "Are you serious? I can't just drop everything and meet her tomorrow. I need to study for my exam."

"Oh, come on," Rohan said, waving a hand dismissively. "You've been studying all semester. One afternoon won't make a difference. Besides, Café Chronicles is the perfect place for couples on weekends. If she agrees to meet you there, it's a good sign."

Nikhil frowned. "I don't think this is a good idea, Ishaan. Rohan's plans always sound fun, but they're reckless. What if it goes wrong?"

"Exactly, what if she says no?" I added, feeling a wave of panic. "I'll have ruined everything."

"Or you'll finally know how she feels," Rohan countered. "Look, life is about taking risks. If you don't act now, you'll always wonder 'what if?'"

I hesitated, torn between my fear of rejection and my desire to confess. "But the exam…"

"We'll help you study after," Rohan promised. "Right, Nikhil?"

Nikhil interjected, "I don't think you should do this, Ishaan. It's too risky."

"Relax, Nikhil; it's a good start. I'm calling her," I said, trying to reassure both of them.

ũ

"Hello, Ahana?" my heart pounding in my chest.

"Hey, Ishaan! Thank God you called. I'm so bored right now," she responded, her voice immediately brightening my day.

"Bored, huh?" I teased. "Well, I might have the perfect cure for that. Are you free tomorrow? Maybe we can go get some lunch?" My voice was steady, despite the adrenaline coursing through me.

There was a pause on the other end, and then she sighed. "Tomorrow?" she asked in her hesitant tone. "I don't think I can, Ishaan."

"Why not?" I pressed, trying to keep the disappointment out of my voice.

"I have my exam the day after tomorrow," she explained. "I really need to study. I've barely gone over half the syllabus, and I'm so stressed about it."

"Ahana, you're always over prepared. You'll do fine," I reassured her. "You deserve a little break. Just an hour or two, and then you can dive back into studying."

She let out a small laugh. "I wish it were that easy. You know me—I can't concentrate once I step out. I'll end up feeling guilty about not studying the whole time."

"Okay, fair," I conceded, though I couldn't help feeling a pang of disappointment. I hesitated for a moment before adding, "But don't you think you'll do better if you relax for a bit? You're not a robot, Ahana."

She chuckled softly. "I know I'm not a robot, but this exam is really important. I can't afford to mess it up."

"Isn't it important to stay sane, too?" I countered. "Look, I get it. You're worried, and I respect that. But I'm just saying, a quick lunch break won't ruin your preparation."

There was silence for a moment, and I could almost hear her deliberating. "I don't know, Ishaan," she said finally. "Maybe after the exam?"

I sighed but decided to push just a little further. "How about coffee instead of lunch? Just a short outing, I promise. I know you love coffee, and it'll be less of a commitment than sitting down for lunch and talking for hours."

She laughed again, this time more openly. "You really don't give up, do you?"

"Not when it comes to you," I admitted honestly.

"Okay, coffee sounds tempting," she said after a pause. "But where?"

"How about Café Chronicles, it's a beautiful place, and the coffee there is amazing," I suggested, my excitement creeping into my tone.

She hesitated again. "I'm not sure about Café Chronicles. It's a bit far, and I'll need to get home early to study in the evening."

"That sounds fair," I replied quickly, eager to secure the opportunity before it slipped away. I didn't want to risk overthinking or giving them a chance to change their mind. Leaning in slightly, I added, "How about City Café? It's just around the corner, so it'll be more convenient, and they have an amazing selection of coffee flavors.

"City Café, huh?" she repeated thoughtfully. "That actually sounds perfect. I'll just have to make sure I'm back by 4 p.m."

"Deal" I said, a grin spreading across my face.

"Okay then," she said, her tone lightening. "It feels like my dad's coming home soon. I'll call you tomorrow to confirm. Goodnight, Ishaan!"

"Sweet dreams," I replied, hanging up with a sense of accomplishment.

For the first time in weeks, I felt hopeful. Even though Ahana was stressed about her exam, I was glad I could convince her to take a small break. Tomorrow couldn't come fast enough.

Nikhil and Rohan were waiting eagerly for my update. "She agreed! We're going to the City Café," I announced, a smile spreading across my face.

Nikhil's demeanor changed. He started asking unnecessary questions, like an examiner ready to grade my performance. "When exactly are you taking her?"

"At noon tomorrow," I said, a bit confused by his sudden seriousness.

"I know that! But what time?" he pressed.

"Around 2 or 3 in afternoon, but why are you asking?" I questioned, puzzled.

"I'll tell you tomorrow," he replied with a mysterious smile before heading out for dinner.

Nikhil went for his dinner. Rohan prepared me all night for tomorrow's mission. He suggests me to wear his blue shirt where he considers it as his lucky one. He gave me lots of tips and I can't keep all that in mind. So, I took notes of it in a small bit paper. These are Rohan's theory of the proposal.

"In order to propose a girl, you need to talk more about Love. There are lots of ways to start this topic. He gave me some examples like Dress code, Flirting, Other couples etc. Once you get it in to the topic, wait for the perfect time to propose."

ũ

I was waiting for Ahana at the Café entrance, hands tucked into the pockets of denim jeans, fingers curling around a small, folded note that held Sid's theory. I knew the words by heart, but something about having it on paper, as if it were a magic spell, gave me comfort. I have rehearsed them all night—Sid's foolproof "theory," the same one that had supposedly won over his own girlfriend in the past.

The bustling Café around me hummed with activity. The sound of distant laughter, the clinking of coffee cups, and the soft echo of announcements over the loudspeakers created a patchwork of ambient noise, a fitting background for the butterflies in my stomach.

Every few seconds, i gaze darted to the entrance gallery, my heart hitching each time i saw a flash of pink, only to deflate when it wasn't her. Ahana, as usual, was late, and i didn't mind. i chuckled to myself, shaking my head. "Ahana and punctuality... sworn enemies," i whispered, smiling.

Finally, she appeared, and i felt my heart skip a beat. Her soft baby-pink top, three-fourth jeans that hugged her form perfectly, and the light bounce in her steps made her look like she was walking on air. Her hair was tied in a loose ponytail, and as she walked toward me, I noticed the faint blush on her cheeks. Was it the Café lights, or was it something more?

"Why the hell do I fall for her every single time?" i thought to myself, feeling that familiar ache in my chest. With each encounter, it felt like a new beginning, like a wave of affection i couldn't resist. i knew i was in deep—maybe too deep—but i was willing to take the plunge. Today was my day to know. Was there any possibility she'd be my "sweet dreams"? Was there any chance she'd be my answer?

"Hey! Waiting for long?"

"Nope, just got here," I lied. I always tried to play it cool, even though she must have known by now that I'd been waiting.

She giggled, probably seeing through me, but didn't call me out on it. "Shall we?" I gestured towards the restaurant, and she nodded.

We entered the Café as many other couples enjoying lunch there. Lights and the theme were all set for weekends. I realize this is the perfect place for this.

"Take your seat, madam," I said, trying to keep my voice steady as I pulled out her chair.

"Appreciate it! So, what's the reason behind this unexpected invite at such an expensive café?" she asked, leaning back with a teasing smile and a spark of curiosity in her eyes.

My heart did a little flip. I'd anticipated this question, and i could feel my palms start to sweat. This was it. This was the moment I'd been waiting for. I took a deep breath, feeling the paper with Sid's theory burn in my pocket like a live ember.

I chuckled. "Well, maybe I just wanted to treat you to something nice. Or maybe..." I paused, raising an eyebrow dramatically. "Maybe there's a deeper reason."

Ahana narrowed her eyes, tilting her head slightly. "Hmm... a deeper reason, huh? Now you've got me curious. Spill it, Ishaan."

I smirked. "Alright, alright. Truth is, we've been so caught up with college, exams, and everything else that I figured we deserved a break. Thought we could just sit back, enjoy some good coffee, and talk without the usual chaos."

She tapped her fingers on the table, pretending to think. "Hmm... sounds reasonable. But you could've chosen a regular café. Why this fancy one?"

I shrugged. "Well, you always talk about how much you love the Coffee here but never get around to trying them. So, I thought—why not?"

She shook her head, chuckling. "True". A small, satisfied smile crossed her lips before she glanced up at me. Her expression softened, but there was something else in her eyes—hesitation, maybe even curiosity.

"You know, Ishaan, there's something I've been meaning to ask you..."

"Off course" My heart skipped a beat.

"Go ahead, shoot," i said, doing my best to keep my voice steady.

She looked at me seriously, almost as if she were weighing her words. "Look around, only young couples are there. Do you think love fades after marriage? Do couples simply stop loving each other as time passes?"

Her question caught me off guard, but only for a moment. I had thought about this before, wondered about how love could survive the tests of time and life. After all, I'd seen both sides—the friends who were still madly in love years later, and those who had grown distant, caught up in the routine of everyday life.

I leaned forward, thoughtful, as i tried to answer. "I think it's not that they stop loving each other. It's just that life gets busy. They get comfortable, you know? The kind of love changes... but it's still there."

"Hmm" She seemed unconvinced. "But isn't love supposed to keep you excited? Keep you on your toes?"

I thought for a moment, and then reached for an analogy. "It's like... when you first buy a new watch. At first, you're obsessed with it. You can't wait to wear it; you show it off to everyone. It's shiny and new, and you're careful not to scratch it. But as time goes on, you get used to it. It becomes a part of your routine. Doesn't mean you don't appreciate it, though. It's still ticking, right?"

Ahana looked down at her own wrist, her fingers brushing over the watch she wore. She smiled softly. "So... you're saying love doesn't fade. It just changes?"

"Yeah," I said quietly, hoping his words might be enough to nudge her closer, to make her think about love, about them, in a different light. "It just changes."

She looked back up at me, her eyes searching his face. I wondered what she saw, wondered if she felt even a fraction of what he felt for her. The moment hung in the air between us, delicate and unspoken, and i held my breath, hoping it would lead us somewhere new.

"So, you are saying. They need a new person like a new watch to celebrate love." Girls always merge themselves in the talk and will imagine the worst ever possibilities. She asked me with a smile.

"No. I will take my word back. It was a stupid example." I don't want to get into this topic anymore. So, I put a full stop to it.

She drifted me afar from the topic "Love". So, I try to go with 2nd rule but just as I opened my mouth to answer, a waiter appeared beside our table. "Your order, sir," he announced, effectively breaking the spell.

I turned, trying not to show my irritation, and took in the waiter's dark, slightly rotund appearance. He had an oddly devilish look to him, and in that moment, I couldn't help but inwardly grumble at his timing.

"Perfect timing" I said sarcastically, before turning to the waiter. "For me, one coffee, please."

I loved coffee; it was the perfect companion for long conversations. Plus, it was affordable, and I didn't want to blow my budget on something extravagant.

"And for you, Ahana?" I asked her, softening my tone.

She glanced through the menu briefly before deciding, "I'll have a cold coffee and maybe some noodles—oh, wait! Let's start with ice cream first. What about you, Ishaan? You want it?"

I shook my head. "No, I have a bit of a cold. Better to skip it."

I reached into my pocket, fumbling with my phone, wondering how I could steer this conversation towards a confession. How was I supposed to flirt with her when everything suddenly felt so real? She'd gone back to studying the menu, but I couldn't take my eyes off her.

The air inside the Café felt charged, like every little sound and movement was amplified. My hands felt clammy as i reached for the glass of water in front of me, but i set it down without drinking. My mind was racing, flipping through scenarios of how she might react when I told her how I felt. I'd imagined this moment so many times—her smiling, her eyes lighting up, maybe even a quick laugh that would melt into that quiet look I loved, the one that made me feel like the world faded away and it was just us.

This was it. If i didn't tell her now, i wasn't sure i ever would.

"So," i said, trying to keep my voice steady. My heart thumped loudly in my chest, and i wondered if she could hear it. "There's actually something I wanted to talk to you about."

Ahana looked at me, curiosity sparking in her bright brown eyes. She leaned forward, resting her chin on her hand. "Go on. You seem nervous," she said, half-smiling.

I chuckled, trying to shake off my nerves, but her eyes held me in place. "Well, I guess I am. It's not every day I put myself out there like this."

She gave me a look, a mix of teasing and genuine interest. "Wow, this must be serious then. Ishaan, I'm all ears."

"You look beautiful today," I ventured. "Pink really suits you."

She glanced up, her expression a mixture of surprise and amusement. She seemed pleased, but then quickly turned it into a joke, trying to brush it off.

"Really?" She scooped up a spoonful of ice cream, then held the bowl out to me with a playful smile. "Are you sure you don't want a taste of something sweet?

I shook my head, amused by her deflection. "No thanks," I replied, laughing.

Just then, I noticed a couple at a nearby table, their conversation growing tense. The guy leaned forward, frustration in his eyes, while the girl looked away, biting her lip. "Look over there," I whispered to Ahana, subtly tilting my head. "That couple looks like they're about to break up."

She turned to glance at them, her expression unreadable. Then, she sipped her Coffee and murmured, "I bet she's the one ending it."

I frowned. "What makes you say that?"

Ahana tapped her fingers lightly against her glass. "See how he's trying to explain something? And she won't meet his eyes? She's already made up her mind."

A moment later, the girl shook her head and stood up, her face a mix of sadness and resolve. The guy slumped back, defeated. I exhaled, caught off guard by how accurate Ahana's prediction was.

"How did you know?" I asked, genuinely curious.

She shrugged, still watching them. "Love doesn't fall apart in a single moment," she said thoughtfully. "It cracks slowly, over time, until one person finally gathers the courage to walk away."

.

Her words lingered between us, a quiet weight settling in my chest. "So, how do you stop love from breaking?" I asked softly.

She looked at me then, her gaze deep. "You don't let it fade. You hold on before it's too late."

And somehow, her answer felt far heavier than the question itself.

I absorbed her words, a subtle ache forming in my chest. She had such a clear thought, her expectations so vividly defined. Yet, something about her perspective unsettled me. With a gentle voice, I asked, "If love is meant to be cherished, then why is it always the man who must take the first step, who must propose?"

She looked at me, a little surprised. "Because a girl can't"

"Why not?"

She shrugged, giving me a small, almost sad smile. "I don't know."

I felt a stirring inside me, a need to dig deeper, to understand more. "Ahana, can I say something?" I asked, hardly daring to hope as I held my breath.

She hesitated, and then nodded slowly. "Yes."

I took a deep breath, searching for the right words. I thought of Rohan's theory again, the one about taking the leap, about being open and honest because life was too short for half-truths. But suddenly, all the clever phrases and careful rehearsals I'd practiced felt flimsy and useless. All I could do was be myself, let her see the part of me that had been waiting for her.

Ahana... we've known each other a long time. You've been there through everything for me, and you mean a lot to Me." i paused, watching her expression closely. She was listening, still and attentive, but i couldn't read her eyes. "I just... I guess what I'm trying to say is that, over time, it's become more than that for me. I think about you all the time, and I... I love you, Ahana."

I said it softly, so quietly I wondered if the words had even reached her. But I'd said it. I'd crossed that invisible line. I could feel my heart pounding, and i held my breath, waiting.

Ahana's face changed, her eyes widening slightly. She looked down for a moment, and i saw her swallow, almost as if she were struggling to find the right words.

"Seriously...Ishaan..." she began, her voice soft. She didn't meet my eyes right away, and i felt a flicker of dread rise up, unwelcome and cold. She looked up, and i saw a tenderness in her gaze, but there was something else there too—an apology, a sadness.

"Ishaan, you're one of the most important people in my life," she said quietly, her voice barely above a whisper.

"And I don't know what I'd do without you. You're... amazing, really. But..."

The word hung in the air like a stone dropping into water, sending ripples through my mind.

She took a deep breath. "I don't know how to say this without hurting you, and I never wanted to. But... there's someone else. Someone I like" Her cheeks flushed, and she looked away for a second, before finally meeting my gaze

My heart pounded, and I felt butterflies rise in my stomach. "What's his name?"

There was a long pause before she answered. "Leave it, I can't tell you, "She whispered.

"Come on, Ahana," I urged. You can trust me."

She looked at me intently, and then sighed, as if resigning to some inner battle. "Promise you won't tell anyone?"

"Promise," I said, leaning in, hanging on her every word.

She took a breath. "It's...Rohan. Your friend"

For a moment, the world went silent. I stared at her, the words echoing in his mind but not fully sinking in. Rohan? She like my best friend? My mind reeled, scrambling to make sense of what she was saying, to process it. Rohan, the friend I've trusted, and the one I've looked to for advice on how to win Ahana's heart.

To love without expecting anything in return—it's a brave thing, they say. And I was feeling the full weight of it now. I was bracing myself for the pain, the emptiness of knowing my feelings could never be returned. But I was willing to bear it if it meant she was happy.

"Who, Rohan?" I managed to choke out.

She nodded, looking away shyly. "Yes, Rohan"

"I didn't know how to say it," she murmured, her voice just above a whisper. "It all unfolded so effortlessly—I never even noticed when my feelings for him began to grow."

I nodded, swallowing hard. I knew she wasn't trying to be cruel, but it hurt all the same. i forced myself to breathe, to let the pain settle, trying to keep my voice steady. "I get it, Ahana. I just... I didn't see it coming. I thought..." i trailed off, the words fading as i realized how futile they were. What was the point in telling her how much I have hoped, how much I've dreamed? It was all meaningless now.

A thick silence stretched between us, full of unspoken words and lingering sadness. The sounds of laughter and clinking glasses around us felt distant, muted, as if we were in a different world. I forced myself to meet her gaze, the weight of her words sinking in fully.

"Well," i said softly, a faint smile tugging at the corner of my mouth. "I guess I should thank Rohan then. His theory really worked... just not in the way I thought it would."

Ahana looked stricken, her lips parting as if to say something, but she closed them again. She looked down, her fingers fidgeting with the edge of her napkin.

"Ishaan, I'm so sorry. I wish things could be different."

I shook my head, offering her a weak but genuine smile. "Its okay, Ahana. You can't control who you fall for. Believe me, I know." i let out a dry chuckle, hoping it might lighten the heaviness in my chest, but it only felt emptier.

I looked around the surroundings, taking in the soft glow of the lights, the sound of couples laughing, of conversations blending together. Somewhere, I've read that you don't choose the moments that change your life. They happen when you least expect them, turning everything, you know upside down in an instant.

I took a deep breath, standing up from my seat. "I think... I need a little air," i murmured, trying to keep my voice from wavering.

"I think we should leave now," I said, swallowing my anguish.

She looked at me, her face falling. "What's wrong? You've always been a best friend of me, Ishaan. I was hoping you'd help me with Rohan."

That broke me even more, but I kept my face still, hiding the turmoil inside. "You should leave now, you are getting late" I repeated, barely able to contain my pain

Ahana looked up at me, her face full of concern, guilt, regret, but i couldn't bear to see it, not right now. I nodded to her, a quick farewell, before turning and walking away, the weight of the confession pressing on me with every step.

Her eyes filled with confusion and hurt as she stood and walked away, leaving me alone to pick up the pieces of my broken heart.

After settling the bill, I stepped out of the café, the crisp evening air brushing against my face, I let out a long, shuddering breath. I leaned against the wall, the noise of the Café filling my senses, grounding me, even as my heart felt like it was breaking.

ṽ

I am the one who introduced Ahana with Rohan. Rohan never showed any intentions in her. Why everyone falls for him. He won't even have a girlfriend more than a Month.

The day Ahana met Rohan was a day I remember with a bitter taste in my mouth. I had arranged for them to meet, thinking it was harmless. Rohan had this magnetism about him that I thought Ahana might appreciate, but I never imagined it would lead to this.

My phone rang, it was Rohan. Probably wondering how the whole thing went down, I thought. But I couldn't bring myself to answer. It wasn't anger—at least not directed at him. I just didn't have the words for the strange ache in my chest.

Instead, I dialed Nikhil.

"Where are you?" I asked.

"Oak Bar," he said, his voice carrying that casual slur I recognized all too well.

Nikhil was the one I talked to when things went wrong. He had his flaws—he drank too much—but I could always count on him in his own way.

"You're drinking at noon? Man, you're crazy," I said.

"No, no," he said seriously. "It's for you."

"For me?" I frowned. "What are you talking about?"

"Dude, you told me yesterday that you might need this. I just got ahead of the game."

Something in his tone made me pause. He wasn't joking. He knew.

"She rejected you, didn't she?"

The words stung, but I exhaled sharply. "Yeah."

"Dude, it's simple. She's not going to agree. Girls like Ahana—they don't go for guys like us. It's always someone like Rohan."

The truth of his words hit me harder than I wanted to admit.

"Nikhil," I said after a long pause, "you're a genius man, how come you know this, She likes Rohan," I admitted, forcing the words out.

There was silence on the line. Then, his voice came, laced with surprise. "Wait... what? You've got to be kidding me."

I sighed. "I wish I was."

Nikhil smirked, his voice laced with confidence and mischief. "That's just how life works, man. No point dwelling on it. Come with me—I've got the perfect solution for your heartbreak." He always made his arguments sound reasonable, even when they weren't.

I hesitated. I had a Power Systems exam the next day. The thought of drinking and showing up unprepared was an idea I'd never entertained before. My academic life was one of the few things I could control. But Nikhil had this uncanny ability to make his arguments sound reasonable, even when they were far from it.

"I can't drink," I said. "I have an exam tomorrow."

"Oh, come on," he scoffed. "One drink isn't going to ruin your exam. Besides, you're smart enough to wing it."

"That's not the point," I argued. "I need to focus."

"Focus on what? How to get true love?" he shot back. "You've already lost focus. You're stuck in this loop, man. Trust me; one drink will clear your head."

I sighed, conflicted. "Why do you always make bad ideas sound like good ones?"

"Because I'm not wrong," he said with a grin I could hear through the phone. "Now, come over. We'll talk it out, and I promise you'll feel better."

I sighed, hanging up before tossing my phone onto the passenger seat. Pulling on the car ignition, I listened as the engine rumbled to life. Maybe it wasn't the healthiest coping mechanism, but at least I wouldn't have to stew in my thoughts alone.

BOTTOM OF THE GLASS

The bar wasn't crowded. A few lone souls were scattered across the tables, each lost in their own private battles. The air inside was thick with cigarette smoke and the tang of roasted paneer and spicy fries coming from the kitchen. Dim orange lights flickered intermittently, barely lighting up the room. A soft murmur of quiet conversations filled the space, like the gentle hum of bees. It was a place for tired souls, a small escape for those looking for a break from the struggles of life. Here, people could sit, think, and forget their worries for a while.

Nikhil sat slouched at the corner table, looking unhappy while the room buzzed with chatter. His shirt was wrinkled, his shoulders drooped, and smoke from his cigarette partly hid his face. He slowly swirled the last bit of whiskey in his glass, staring at it as if it could answer all of life's tough questions. The table in front of him was worn out, covered in scratches, burn marks, and water rings, each telling a story of past nights.

"Ah, there you are," he said, offering a small, knowing smile. His voice was warm, but there was a heaviness behind it.

Without saying a word, I walked over and took the seat across from him.

Before I could even settle in, Nikhil signalled the bartender for another bottle. He knew. I didn't have to say anything—he could see it on my face.

I sighed and poured myself a drink from the Half-empty bottle already on the table. The sound of glass touching glass seemed unusually loud, cutting through the quiet buzz of conversation around us.

"To the ones who got away," Nikhil said, raising his glass.

"To the ones we never even had," I muttered, clinking mine against his.

He chuckled, a humourless sound. "Funny, isn't it? We spend years building dreams around people who barely notice."

"Or worse," I added, taking a sip, "they notice just enough to give us hope, but never enough to stay."

Nikhil exhaled smoke, shaking his head. "Here's to the fools we are."

"And the lessons we never learn," I said, lifting my glass again.

We drank in silence for a while. The burn of the alcohol was sharp, a cleansing fire that dulled the edges of my thoughts. Around us, the bar's patrons continued their quiet rituals—a man in a rumpled suit nursing a beer, a young woman scrolling through her phone with a cocktail untouched beside her, an older couple whispering over a shared plate of fries. Each of them seemed to carry an invisible weight, their stories etched in the lines of their faces.

"Do you ever feel like you're stuck in the middle of the road?" I asked suddenly. The words spilled out before I could stop them, borne of a restlessness I couldn't quite name.

Nikhil looked up from his glass, his dark eyes locking onto mine. He didn't answer right away. Instead, he swirled his drink, took a slow sip, and let the silence stretch between us.

"All the time, man," he said finally, his voice quieter than usual. "Life is like that for people like us."

I frowned. "People like us?"

He exhaled sharply, leaning back in his chair. "Yeah. The ones who never quite make it. We're the 34s out of 100—always just one short of passing, always a step behind where we need to be. It's like no matter how much we try; we're always stuck in the 'almost' phase. Almost winning, almost succeeding, almost happy."

I tapped my fingers against the table, thinking. His words struck a nerve. "So what do we do?" I asked after a moment.

Nikhil smirked, but it didn't reach his eyes. "That's the real question, isn't it?" He leaned forward, resting his elbows on the table. "Some people break the cycle. They push harder, find a way to turn that 34 into a 40, then a 50, then a 90. Others…" He trailed off, staring at his drink.

"They get used to it," I finished for him.

He nodded. "And that's the scariest part. You stop trying after a while. You tell yourself it's fine, that maybe being stuck in the middle is just how life is supposed to be. And before you know it, you've settled."

His words struck a chord, echoing something I had felt but never articulated. My life had been a series of almost, a collection of near-misses that formed a patchwork of frustration. I almost took a leap toward my dreams, but hesitation held me back. I cared for someone deeply, but remained just a friend in their story.

"Why do we do this to ourselves?" I asked. "Why do we keep chasing after things we'll never have?"

Nikhil shrugged, a bitter smile playing on his lips. "It's human nature, I guess. We see someone else's story—some song, some movie—and we think it's ours. But it's not. It never was."

I stared into my glass, the amber liquid reflecting fragments of my face. The conversation had veered into dangerous territory—the kind of introspection that only late-evening drinks and melancholy company could summon.

"What are you thinking about?" Nikhil asked, his voice pulling me back to the present.

I hesitated, but there was no point in lying. "Ahana," I admitted, exhaling her name like it was something I had been holding onto for too long. It lingered in the space between us, heavy with memories, regret, and things left unsaid.

He nodded knowingly. "You're not mad at her, are you?"

"No," I said quickly, shaking my head. "How could I be? She doesn't owe me anything." I paused, searching for the right words. "I guess I'm just mad at myself for hoping—for believing, even for a second, that things could have been different."

Nikhil sighed, staring into his own glass. "Hope's a dangerous thing, my friend," he said, lifting his drink. "It's like a tightrope. One misstep and you're plummeting into despair."

I let out a dry chuckle. "So, what, then? Never hope?"

He smirked, but there was something sad in his eyes. "No. Just don't let it blind you. Don't let it trick you into seeing something that isn't there."

I ran a hand through my hair, frustration clawing at my chest. "It's not that easy."

"No, it's not," he agreed, downing the rest of his drink. "But neither is falling from that tightrope. The higher your hope, the harder the fall."

I stared at him for a long moment before looking away. He was right. But that didn't make it hurt any less.

ũ

The evening wore on, and the bar began to fill with more people. The murmur of voices grew louder, blending with bursts of laughter and the occasional burst of music from the old jukebox in the corner. Nikhil and I stayed in our corner, insulated from the growing crowd by the invisible wall of our shared thoughts.

The bottle in front of us was almost empty. We poured the last few drops into our glasses and lifted them. The golden liquid shimmered under the dim light of the bar. We clinked our glasses together—perhaps in a silent toast to our sorrows—and then gulped down the final peg. The bitter warmth of alcohol burned its way down my throat, making me feel heavy yet strangely light at the same time.

Outside, the night deepened. The clock on the wall showed that it was already ten. The bar's door swung open every now and then as people entered or left, letting in the cool night air. I noticed that it had started to drizzle. The faint smell of wet earth mixed with the strong scent of alcohol and cigarette smoke inside the bar.

Nikhil looked at me and sighed. "Ishaan, we should leave now," he said, his voice slightly slurred. "We've had enough. Let's go back to the hostel before we do something stupid."

I leaned back against my chair, staring at the half-empty glass in front of me. The golden liquid swirled lazily under the dim bar lights. The warmth of the alcohol in my veins dulled the ache in my chest, the one I had been carrying for weeks.

"I don't want to go yet," I said, my voice quieter than I intended. "One more."

Nikhil groaned. "No, Ishaan."

I waved my hand lazily at the waiter. My fingers felt heavy, clumsy. The world around me had taken on a hazy, dreamlike quality. The music, the chatter, the clinking of glasses—it all felt distant, like a muffled memory.

Nikhil grabbed my arm. His grip was firm. "No more," he insisted. His brows were drawn together in frustration. "We are already too drunk. Let's go."

I hesitated.

Outside, the rain tapped softly against the windows. The city lights blurred through the wet glass, casting distorted reflections. The hostel, our messy rooms, and tomorrow's exam—they all felt like a distant reality, something I wasn't ready to face.

Nikhil's grip tightened. "Ishaan," he said, his voice more forceful this time. "Come on."

I sighed, rubbing my temples. "Fine," I mumbled.

We got up, swaying slightly. The bar felt warmer than I realized as we stepped toward the exit. The Oak Bar's fluorescent sign flickered above us, buzzing faintly.

As soon as we stepped outside, the cold night air hit me like a wave. It was raining, a slow drizzle that clung to my skin. The faint smell of rain mingled with the metallic scent of the cooling city. I shivered.

"Where's your car Ishaan?" Rohan mumbled, scanning the dimly lit parking lot.

"Over there," I said, pointing with a wavering hand, my footing was unsteady as my speech. My one leg dragged slightly as if it had suddenly grown heavier. Nikhil smirked at the sight, though his own steps weren't much steadier.

"You good to drive" Nikhil asked, his words slightly slurred.

I nodded, though I wasn't entirely sure. We made our way to the parking lot; our steps unsteady but guided by an unspoken understanding. The rain soaked through my Shirt, its cold fingers clawing at my skin, but I welcomed the sensation. It felt real, unlike the dull feeling left by the drinks at the bar.

The old Maruti model sat under a flickering light, its windshield glistening with condensation. I fumbled in my pocket for the keys, my mind foggy. As we reached the car, i placed the keys in the ignition, turned the engine off to roll the windows up.

Nikhil, who was with me on the other seat, stepped out to smoke a cigarette. Seeing him step out, I also decided to get out for a moment. But before leaving, I turned the engine off and rolled up the windows.

Once outside, I absentmindedly shut the driver's door. Without thinking much, I locked the car. The moment I heard the soft *click* of the lock, my heart dropped. My mind suddenly became clear—I had just locked the keys inside the car.

A creeping sense of dread tightened around my chest.

"Nikhil," i croaked my voice barely above a whisper. "The keys are inside the car."

Nikhil turned, swaying slightly, his expression blank. "What?"

I repeated myself, my words trembling this time. Nikhil stared at me, then at the car, and then back at me. "You locked the keys inside?" he asked slowly, as if trying to process the information through the haze of alcohol.

I nodded; sweat forming on my forehead despite the cool night. The realization was setting in like an encroaching storm. The bar was heading to close, the streets were almost deserted, and the car wasn't exactly parked discreetly. Worse still, the handbrake was on, leaving the car jutting slightly into the narrow lane of parking.

Nikhil leaned against the car, running a hand through his messy hair. "Well, that's just fantastic. What now?"

For what felt like an eternity, the two of us stood in awkward silence, our foggy minds grappling for solutions.

"We could break a window," I suggested half-heartedly, but the thought of the repair costs made me cringe.

Nikhil scoffed, shaking his head. "That's the dumbest thing I've ever heard. Do you know how much that would cost to fix?" He pulled out another cigarette, lit it, and took a deep puff. The smoke curled into the air as he exhaled slowly.

I crossed my arms. "Well, do *you* have a better idea?"

He shrugged. "Maybe we should ask someone for help. There has to be a way to get the car open without smashing it."

I sighed. "Yeah, but it's late. Who's even going to help us at this hour?"

Nikhil glanced around. The street was quiet, only a few dim streetlights flickering. "Let's at least try. Maybe there's a Mechanic nearby, who knows a trick to open locked cars."

I nodded. "Alright, fine. But if this doesn't work, we're breaking that window."

Nikhil laughed. "Let's hope it doesn't come to that."

And with that, we set off to find help.

ũ

The two of us walked up and down the street, searching for help. After nearly twenty minutes with no luck, we finally spotted a small Mechanic shop that was still open. A thin man wearing a torn shirt sat there, looking relaxed.

I stepped forward, feeling desperate. "Bhaiyya, need your help," I said. "Our car is parked at Oak Bar, and the key is locked inside."

The mechanic looked at me with a crooked smile. He took a long drag from his half-burnt cigarette before speaking. "I can open your car," he said confidently, as if it was an easy task.

"Really?" I asked, feeling relieved. "That would be great! Please help us."

He leaned back in his chair and shook his head. His weary eyes flickered toward the dimly lit street outside. "Not now. It's late, and I am closing," he said casually, exhaling a thin stream of smoke from the half-burnt cigarette clinging to his lips. His tone was final, indifferent to our desperation.

"Please, Bhaiyya! It's very late, and we are stuck, you can take extra charges" I pleaded, my voice laced with urgency. The thought of being stranded here for the night sent a shiver down my spine.

He sighed, stretching his arms with deliberate slowness, as if weighing his decision. Then, without much enthusiasm, he grabbed a screwdriver and a plastic ruler from his cluttered workbench. The tools looked worn from years of use; the ruler slightly bent at the edges. Finally, he stood up, adjusting his oil-stained shirt.

"Come, show me the car," he muttered.

Feeling relieved, we quickly guided him to our vehicle. Our footsteps made soft sounds as they hit the empty road, which was quiet all around us. He moved around the vehicle confidently, running his rough fingers along the doors and windows. His eyes gleamed as he took in the situation, Then, all of a sudden, he smiled widely.

"This is easy," he said with quiet confidence. "Give me a minute."

He rolled the ruler between his fingers, as if getting ready for a delicate task. Then, moving slowly and carefully, he slid it between the window and the door, trying to unlock it. His Screwdriver, which he had been holding between his lips, moved slightly as he focused on the task. The night was quiet, except for the soft sound of metal rubbing against plastic.

"You do this often?" I asked, watching him work.

The mechanic chuckled. "Let's just say, I know my way around locked cars." He moved the ruler up and down, searching for the lock mechanism.

The car rocked slightly as he applied pressure. "Almost there," he muttered. A faint scratching sound came as the ruler rubbed against the glass.

Then, with a sudden click, the lock popped open.

"There you go!" he said proudly.

We sighed in relief. "Thank you so much!" Nikhil said, smiling.

The mechanic smiled and gave a friendly wink as he handed the keys back. "Next time, don't forget your keys," he said in a playful tone.

"Thank you! How much?" I asked, already reaching for my wallet, relieved that the ordeal was over.

He glanced up, wiping his hands on his worn-out Pants. "That'll be five hundred rupees," he said, holding up five fingers.

"Five hundred?" I froze, my fingers barely grazing the edge of my wallet. "That's way too much!"

He shrugged, unfazed by my reaction. "Night charges," he said, his voice carrying the indifference of someone who had this argument far too often. "And let's not forget, I saved you time, didn't I?"

I sighed, knowing there was no point in arguing. It was past midnight, and I was exhausted. He had me cornered—literally and financially. With a reluctant nod, I pulled out the notes and handed them over. He took them with practiced ease, slipping them into his pocket like he had done a hundred times before.

As he turned to leave, he paused. "Oh, and one more thing," he added, almost as an afterthought. "The original key won't work anymore in the lock. You'll have to replace the locks."

"Perfect," I muttered under my breath, watching as he disappeared into the night, leaving me with a lighter wallet and yet another problem to solve.

ṽ

We climbed into my car, the interior cold and smelling faintly of stale car freshener and forgotten fast food wrappers. The engine sputtered to life, and I turned on the heater, the warm air filling the space with a low hum. Nikhil leaned back in his seat; his eyes half-closed.

The drive back to the hostel was very quiet, except for the sound of rain hitting the car roof and the tires splashing through water on the road. The city lights shone in the distance, looking like a promise of something ahead. But right now, it was just me, deep in my thoughts, listening to the rain. Beside me, Nikhil was asleep, mumbling something I couldn't understand.

As we walked back to the hostel, I broke the silence and said, "Nikhil, you were talking about 34 out of 100." He was half-asleep, walking slowly and unsteadily, but I couldn't stop myself. That number stayed in my mind, bothering me like a puzzle I couldn't solve.

He blinked lazily, barely processing my words. "Huh?"

"Football, studies, love—it's all the same," I said, letting out a tired laugh. "I'm always just one mark short of passing. No matter how hard I try, that one mark always seems out of reach."

For a moment, Nikhil said nothing. His usual sharp wit seemed dulled by the weight of exhaustion, but then, out of nowhere, he muttered something that hit me harder than I ever expected.

"Maybe that's the problem," he said his voice slow and deliberate. "You're so focused on that one mark you don't have that you forget about the other 34 you already do."

I looked at him, searching his face for any hint of sarcasm, but there was none.

"What are you saying?" I asked.

He yawned, stretching his arms. "I'm saying, you spend too much time chasing what's missing instead of valuing what you have. Maybe that one mark isn't the real problem. Maybe it's your way of looking at things."

I stopped in my tracks, his words sinking in. It felt like a punch to the gut, but not in a bad way. More like the kind of blow that wakes you up, the kind that forces you to look at things differently.

As we walked on, his words refused to leave my mind. The night air was cool, a faint breeze brushing against my face, but I felt strange warmth inside, a stirring realization. Maybe Nikhil was right. Maybe I'd been looking at life all wrong.

I'd spent so much time obsessing over the things I didn't have—chasing after that elusive one mark—that I'd overlooked the 34 marks I already possessed. Those 34 weren't perfect, but they were mine. They were proof that I'd tried, that I'd fought, that I'd lived.

Ahana might not be mine, but that didn't take away the moments we shared. The laughter that came so easily when we were together, the conversations that stayed with me long after they ended, and the memories that would always hold a special place in my heart—all of it mattered. Even if she didn't love me the way I loved her, she gave me something priceless: a glimpse of what it truly feels like to care for someone.

And Rohan—perfect, charming, effortlessly magnetic Rohan—might be the guy everyone admired, the guy Ahana had chosen, but that didn't make him better than me. We were different, and that was okay. I didn't need to be him; I just needed to be me

Then there was Nikhil. Flawed, sarcastic, with an uncanny ability to cut through the noise and see things for what they truly were. He wasn't just my best friend; he was my anchor, the person who reminded me that life was more than just a series of grades, goals, and missed opportunities.

Life, I realized, might never be perfect. But perfection wasn't the point. The point was to keep going, to keep trying, to find joy in the journey even when the destination seemed impossibly far away.

As the night drew to a close, I felt something shift inside me. I didn't have all the answers—not by a long shot—but for the first time in a long time, I didn't feel like I needed them. What I had was something better: the courage to keep moving forward, one step at a time.

Even if I was 34 out of 100, I wasn't finished yet. Life wasn't a pass-or-fail test; it was a story, and I was still writing mine. Who knew? Maybe the best chapters were still ahead.

For now, I was just grateful to be heading hostel, my best friend snoring beside me, and the promise of a new day waiting on the other side of a few hours' sleep.

As we got close to the hostel gates, I couldn't help but laugh quietly. The craziness of the night was finally sinking in. I realized that life is often like a locked car—full of problems that seem impossible at first. But with enough effort (and sometimes money), they can be solved.

Tomorrow wasn't guaranteed, but it was waiting. And now, I felt ready to meet it.

OF REGRET & RESOLVE

The morning light filtered through the flimsy hostel curtains; a pale gold that seemed almost too gentle for the chaos it was about to reveal. Dust particles floated lazily in the beam, undisturbed by the muffled sounds of life stirring outside—a distant shout from the hostel corridor and the clatter of buckets in the shared bathrooms. The world moved on, not caring about the mess inside my small, crowded room.

I groaned as sunlight pierced through the thin curtains of my cramped hostel room, stabbing my eyes like needles. The clock on the wall ticked loudly, almost mocking me as it showed 7:00 AM. My head throbbed from last night's revelry—a blur of laughter, loud music, and far too many drinks with Nikhil. I barely remembered stumbling back to my room, collapsing on the bed without a second thought.

Today was important—uncomfortably so. It was the dreaded power systems final exam scheduled for 9 AM. A fact I had conveniently ignored last night, favoring the comfort of "just one more drink" at the local bar over revisiting formulas and theorems.

My phone buzzed violently on the table next to my bed, dragging me from an uneasy sleep. I squinted at the screen through the haze of a pounding headache and blurry vision. My heart sank when I saw the caller ID: Mom.

Groaning inwardly, I picked up the call, clearing my throat in a futile attempt to sound normal.

"Hello?"

"Beta, are you awake?" my mom's familiar voice came through, tinged with concern. "You have your exam today, don't you? You told me yesterday!"

Her words cut through the confusion in my mind like a loud alarm. I rubbed my temples and tried to think of a clear response.

"Uh... yeah, Mom, I'm up," I lied, dragging myself into a sitting position. The sudden movement sent the room into a slow, nauseating spin, a cruel reminder of last night's poor decisions.

"Good. I hope you prepared well. You studied, right?" she pressed, her tone hovering somewhere between encouragement and suspicion.

"Yeah... totally, just revising now," I mumbled, scratching the back of my head. My desk sat in the corner of the room, mockingly untouched, the syllabus buried beneath a pile of junk.

"How many times will you revise? You're going to do well, I know it." Her voice softened a mix of pride and reassurance. It stung, honestly. My mom had always believed in me, even when I didn't deserve it. Engineering had always been my Achilles' heel, a never-ending battle. Yet, somehow, she thought I could conquer it. Or maybe she just needed to believe that I could.

"Yes, Mom, I'll do my best," I assured her, layering my voice with fake confidence.

"Good," she said warmly. "And no skipping breakfast, you need energy to think clearly. I'm praying for you!"

"Thanks, Mom. I'll do great," I replied quickly, ending the call before the weight of her expectations could fully settle in my chest.

Staring at the pile of crumpled notes and unopened books on my desk, I cursed under my breath. I stumbled out of bed, my body aching from the sleepless night before, and splashed cold water on my face in a feeble attempt to awaken my dulled senses. Grabbing my notebook, I flipped through the pages, but the inked formulas and scribbled notes seemed to blur together, mocking me with their incomprehensibility.

My mind raced as I tried to remember everything I had studied. Last semester's tips from my professor, the formulas I wrote down yesterday, and even my classmates' advice felt far away. Nothing was coming to me. Time was running out, and I felt helpless. The exam was getting closer, and panic took over. I wished I could recall what I had learned, but my mind was blank.

My reflection in the mirror told a story I could not ignore—dark circles carved beneath my eyes, and a face etched with the stress of struggling with Power system concepts.

The night before had left its mark on me in more ways than one. My late-night indulgence in convoluted theorems and alcoholic equations had only worsened my state. The equations that once made sense now looked like strange symbols, completely confusing me. My mind was foggy, and I struggled to understand anything I had studied before.

The last night had made it worse and Last moment attempt at revision had made things even worse. I had no idea of what the alphas and betas were trying to tell me at the darkest hour. I was lost in the jungle of integrations and derivations like a wanderer. I was turning blank to blanker.

I even considered dropping out of the exam altogether. The idea lingered until a vision of my mother's smiling face surfaced in my mind. Her unwavering belief in me was enough to push that thought aside. I could not let her down.

This year, despite my strong dislike for formulas, theorems, and equations, I gave extra attention to them to avoid last year's failures. However, I never understood why this subject never clicked with me. I spent months studying Power System, yet I never felt confident about it. The more I studied, the more my confidence dropped instead of growing. Unlike other subjects, Power System always felt out of reach, no matter how hard I tried. I had no idea why it was so difficult for me.

Still, scoring considerably well in Power system - higher than my reach - was my top priority. Nonetheless, it did not seem feasible last night for more than one reasons; one - my natural hatred for the subject, two - my fuzziness when it came to formulas and equations.

My last night's secret hard work was known only to me. It was the kind of thing I should not have committed; a mix of guilt and anxiety had taken over me. I was in deep regret for wasting my time since the morning the day before. Yet, here I was, desperately trying to salvage the situation in a manner I had never thought I would resort to.

I decided to take a different path; one I had never walked before. I thought about cheating, yes, cheating. Just thinking about it made me feel uneasy, but the idea of letting myself and others down felt even worse. My conscience warned me against it, but my fear of failing was stronger. So, I chose to take the risk.

With shaking hands and frightened mind, I spent few time in preparing cheat notes for the formulas and theorem hints. My room was dimly lit, my desk scattered with tiny scraps of paper, an eraser, and a pencil that had grown blunt with overuse. Each letter I wrote demanded precision and focus. My hands had to be as steady as a surgeon's. The tiny letters I scribbled seemed almost too small to read, but that was the point. These notes weren't meant to be seen unless absolutely necessary.

The morning was not so usual either. My restless night of guilt and preparation had left me drained. I had hardly slept for an hour. Even when I tried to close my eyes, thoughts of what lay ahead kept me awake. I woke up & took bath.

After getting dressed, I turned to my wardrobe and focused on my socks. I searched through the drawer, pulling out every pair I owned. One by one, I compared them, looking for the longest ones. The longer the socks, the better they would be for hiding my secret. Finally, I found the perfect pair and put them on.

I felt like I was getting ready for a secret mission, one that needed careful planning and stealth. I folded my cheat notes neatly and slid them into my socks—one note on each side. I made sure they were hidden well and double-checked to be sure nothing was sticking out.

To make absolutely sure everything was in place, I walked around my room as if I were heading to the exam. I wanted to be certain the papers wouldn't move or accidentally show. Each step made me more aware of the notes against my skin, reminding me of the risk I was taking.

As I prepared to leave, a sense of dread and anticipation weighed heavily on me. The day ahead was not just about the test in front of me—it was also a test of my resolve, my ethics, and my ability to handle the choices I had made.

I realized that fate of my commitment was sealed at my ankles. Shivers!

I left all my thoughts behind, picked up my pen and admit card, and took a deep breath. By 8:45 AM, I was already out of the hostel's main door. My head was still pounding from the sleepless night, but my resolve was firm. "Never again," I muttered under my breath, already planning how to make up for this mess in the next exam. But first, I had to survive this one.

The hallway of hostel was eerily quiet as I hurried down towards the exit. The other students were either still sleeping or in their own last-minute prep zones. My steps echoed through the corridor, as if reminding me of the looming battle.

I tried to calm my racing thoughts, but the weight of the situation felt suffocating. My heart was pounding as if it could burst any second. Despite all the doubts swirling in my head, one thing was clear: I had to get through this.

As I neared the main door, Nikhil called out to me from where he stood near the door. He was holding two cups of instant coffee, looking every bit the proud, confident figure, he always seemed to be. His arms were folded across his chest, and there was that familiar smirk on his face, the one he always wore when he was sure he had won something—this time, he thought, it was the battle of nerves

Nikhil, however, was as calm as ever. He walked beside me with a swagger, sipping his coffee like he had everything figured out. I glanced at him, feeling a strange mixture of admiration and frustration. How did he stay so relaxed all the time, even when the pressure was on?

"You know, if you keep worrying like that, you're only going to stress yourself out more," Nikhil said, snapping me out of my thoughts.

I turned my head towards him, eyebrows raised. "I wish I had your confidence. But right now, I can't afford to think about anything but surviving this exam."

Nikhil chuckled. "Surviving? Come on, you're acting like it's a battle to the death. It's just an exam. You know you'll pull through."

I rolled my eyes. "It's not just any exam, Nikhil. It's this exam. The one that's been hanging over my head for weeks. The one that has the potential to ruin everything"

He raised an eyebrow at me. "It's funny how you're always worried before exams. And then you walk out of the hall like you've just aced it. You've got this. Trust me."

I could tell by the way he said it that he meant every word. Nikhil had this strange ability to make everything seem so easy, even when I was drowning in anxiety. But his confidence, no matter how misplaced I thought it might be, had a strange calming effect on me.

"I don't know, Nikhil. I barely studied last night, and I've been stuck on the same topic for days. Every time I try to focus, my mind just...drifts," I confessed, my voice barely above a whisper.

He gave me a knowing smile. "Yeah, I could tell from the look on your face last night. I don't think I've ever seen you that out of it. But you'll be fine. You always pull through, even when you don't think you will."

I shook my head. "You make it sound so easy. But you don't know what it's like to feel like your brain is just...frozen."

Nikhil stopped walking for a moment and turned to face me fully, his expression suddenly serious. "Look, I get it. But you've got to stop doubting yourself. It's the biggest obstacle in your way right now. I mean, how do you expect to do well when you're telling yourself you won't? Have some faith in yourself."

His words surprised me. I had been so focused on all the reasons I would fail that I hadn't stopped to think about the possibility of success. I had been consumed by the fear of failure, and it had paralyzed me. Maybe Nikhil was right. Maybe it was time to let go of all the self-doubt.

"I guess I've been thinking about it all wrong," I admitted, taking a deep breath. "I've been focusing too much on what I'm scared of rather than what I can do."

"Exactly," Nikhil said, his smile returning. "Now, let's go and crack it"

As we continued walking towards the examination hall, the weight on my chest seemed to lighten. For the first time that day, I wasn't thinking about how much I still didn't know. Instead, I was focusing on what I did know and the confidence I was borrowing from Nikhil's unwavering belief in me.

"Thanks, Nikhil," I said quietly. "You really know how to calm me down." I put my hand on his shoulder and we both left for our respective examination hall.

On my way to the examination hall, my mind kept drifting between what was buried near my feet and the last words I had heard. Those words were meant to encourage me, but they wouldn't stop haunting me. "Just do your best. I'm sure you'll succeed this time too, like always," kept echoing in my mind like a drumbeat that wouldn't fade.

As I walked toward the building, my steps slowed down a bit. I couldn't stop thinking about the moral dilemma that had been bothering me. What do I truly want? What should I choose? Should I try my best, knowing I might fail, or should I aim for a perfect score, even if it means cheating and knowing deep down that it wasn't honest?

Each step felt harder, weighed down by my inner struggle.

I tried to push the thoughts away and focus on the task in front of me, but the small pieces of paper hidden in my socks felt heavier with each passing moment. They weren't just notes with quick formulas—they were symbols of my doubt, my desperation, and my shaky confidence.

Last night had been difficult. It wasn't just about the exam; everything seemed to go wrong. My mood was sour, and a series of small, frustrating incidents added up, making me feel like the universe was conspiring against me and by the time morning arrived, I was already exhausted, and my mind felt scattered.

What do I prefer? What should I prefer? A truthful attempt to the best of my ability or a shining score sheet with a hidden cheater-tag which only I would read? All thoughts were creating turbulence in my mind and with that thought came a pang of guilt. I knew deep down that relying on them would rob me of something far more important than a good grade: my integrity.

The weight of that realization hit me like a tidal wave. I found myself standing by a dustbin near the entrance of the building. Looking around to ensure no one was watching, I reached down into my socks and pulled out the chits. My heart raced as I crumpled them in my palm.

With one swift motion, I tossed them into the bin, watching as they disappeared among the trash.

It wasn't easy. My hands trembled as I walked away, feeling the emptiness in my socks where those chits once rested. Yet, as I entered the examination room, I felt a strange sense of relief, as though a heavy burden had been lifted from my shoulders.

ũ

The room was filled with tension. My heart raced as I waited for the question paper. On exam day, I had never felt this strange mix of fear and excitement before. This subject had always been tough for us—a battle where equations defeated students more often than not. Everyone around me looked just as nervous, whispering in low voices. The air felt heavy, filled with worry and hope. I took a deep breath, preparing myself for whatever was coming next.

As the classroom door open, every student's eyes turned towards it. Mr. Dass and Mr. Rishi walked in, their faces giving away no emotion. Mr. Dass held the light brown envelope, sealed tightly, which contained the dreaded exam question papers. Following them, the peon quietly carried a stack of blank answer sheets, his calmness only adding to the serious atmosphere in the room. Just seeing the envelope made everyone feel nervous, and I could almost hear the heavy silence filled with anxious thoughts from all around me.

Mr. Dass, with his trademark no-nonsense attitude, wasted no time. His sharp eyes darted around the room, scanning each of us as though he could see into our very souls. Known for his hawk-like supervision, Mr. Dass had a reputation for catching even the most cunning culprits red-handed. No one dared to test his vigilance. His mere presence was enough to silence even the boldest of us.

"This lot looks nervous today," he remarked quietly to Mr. Rishi as he placed the envelope on the front desk.

"Power system tends to do that," Mr. Rishi replied with a small smile. "It's not the easiest subject for many."

"They should've thought about that before they spent the last month doodling instead of revising," he retorted, her tone laced with mild disapproval.

Mr. Rishi chuckled softly, shaking his head. "You were a student once too, Dass. Surely, you remember the pre-exam jitters."

"I do," he admitted, his lips curving into a rare smile. "But back then, the fear of our teachers kept us focused. These kids, though... they think they can wing it. Let's see how well that goes today."

The classroom itself was a relic of the past, with wooden desks etched by generations of students. Names, hearts, and scribbled equations adorned every surface, a testament to years of boredom and creativity. The walls, once a pristine white, were now a faded cream, dotted with patches where posters had long since been torn away. The symphony of pre-exam hustle and bustle filled the room: the clatter of pencil boxes, the rustle of notes being folded and tucked away, and the low hum of whispered conversations.

Mr. Dass stepped forward, his commanding presence immediately silencing the room. "I will give you exam papers, do not open the seals until I give the signal," he announced, his voice slicing through the noise with surgical precision.

The peon handed him a pair of scissors, which he used to slit open the envelope with a deliberate, almost theatrical motion. He began distributing the question papers, moving methodically through the rows. Mr. Rishi followed, handing out the blank answer sheets.

"I expect absolute silence during the exam," Mr. Dass declared as he walked. "If I catch anyone even thinking about cheating, you'll have more than just this subject to worry about."

Mr. Rishi glanced at him, amused. "You really know how to put the fear of God into them."

"It's a necessary skill," he replied curtly. "Discipline breed's focus. Focus breeds success."

As the question papers started being handed out in the examination hall, my eyes were always glued to the boy sitting at the first desk. He was the first to get the question paper, and to me, he always looked like a sprinter on the starting line, about to take off under watchful eyes. I never missed his reactions.

If he slowly ran his hand over his forehead and held his head in both hands, it was a clear sign of trouble. It was almost as if his neck could no longer handle the weight of his head. But if his face lit up a little, with his cheeks showing the hint of a shy smile, it could mean one of two things: either he had some idea about the answers, or he was completely clueless. It reminded me of a sprinter watching the replay of their race, unsure whether they'd crossed the finish line first or stumbled at the crucial moment.

I always find myself sitting at my desk, ready for the challenges that exams bring. However, it seems that despite all my preparation, I've never truly known what to expect from the exams I've attended.

Each time, it feels as if I've been blindsided by the question paper. I don't know what will come up, and after the exam is over, I'm left wondering what hit me. It's as though the exams exist in a constant state of unpredictability, and no matter how hard I try to prepare, it's never enough.

The moment finally arrived when Ms. Dass, the invigilator, placed the last question paper on the final desk and returned to the front of the room. With an air of authority, he declared, "You may see your exam papers now" His tone was calm and unwavering, but the weight of those words only increased the pressure I felt.

As I approached my desk, I could feel my hands shaking slightly. I picked up the question paper and held the sealed envelope, feeling its unexpected weight. It seemed heavier than it should have, which only added to the anxiety gnawing at me. The paper inside was unknown, and I had no idea what I was about to face.

I put it down on the desk and braced myself for what was coming. The desk, like many others, had marks from years of exams before mine. It was covered with scribbled formulas, random symbols, and bits of advice left by stressed students. But even with all its history, it gave me no comfort. The scribbles on the desk made no sense, just like the challenge waiting for me inside the envelope.

"Wait," said Ms. Dass, glancing at his watch. He exchanged a few hushed words with Mr. Rishi, consulting a notepad he carried. Every second felt like an eternity. I could see the other students, just as nervous as I was, glancing around, trying to decipher the silence. The suspense was excruciating. Finally, the bell rang, signaling the start of the exam.

The exam hall fell silent as Mr. Rishi's voice echoed softly, saying "Okay, you may open the question seals and begin writing. You have two hours." His words seemed to hang in the air, almost as if he was speaking more to himself than to the students.

With those words, the tension in the room suddenly became more palpable. The sound of the paper seals being ripped open filled the room, followed by the rustling noise of students flipping through their exam papers.

There was a faint sound of a pencil box being opened, and someone nervously dropped their metal sharpener onto the floor. The sharp, metallic noise broke the quiet, but it quickly faded as everyone returned their focus to the task at hand.

I adjusted my seat, feeling the nervous energy building up inside me. I wasn't entirely sure how I felt about the exam. My mind was racing, but I couldn't stop myself from scribbling absentmindedly on the corner of my question paper.

The marks from my pen seemed to give me something to focus on, even though I wasn't sure if I was preparing for the exam or just trying to distract myself from the nerves that were bubbling up. In that moment, my thoughts drifted back to the classroom—back to the memories of being a backbencher.

Being a backbencher during those long, tiring classes felt like a kind of blessing in disguise. The lessons were often long and filled with topics that didn't seem to interest me at all. Teachers would drone on about concepts that seemed far from relevant to our daily lives.

As a backbencher, I didn't have to pretend to care about the things being taught. I could let my mind wander without the pressure of appearing overly attentive. I could look out the window and let my thoughts drift, not caring about the lecture that continued in front of me.

There was something oddly comforting about being at the back of the class, especially on days when the classes felt like they were dragging on endlessly. While the students at the front tried their best to stay focused, the backbenchers were often free to daydream, yawn, and let their minds wander

I couldn't help but smile at the thought of those carefree days. The pressure to perform well in exams was nowhere near as intense when we were simply waiting for the bell to ring and the class to end. But now, in the exam hall, it was a different story. The seriousness of the situation was weighing on me. As much as I longed for the days when the biggest concern was whether I could get away with not paying attention in class, the reality of the exam was much more demanding.

I sat there in the exam hall, feeling a growing sense of confusion as I flipped through the exam paper. This was supposed to be power system exam, but then what are physics and mathematics equations doing in the middle. I tried to focus, but my mind was racing, and nothing seemed to fit together. What did these equations have to do with power systems? I kept wondering if I was missing something important or if I had misunderstood the whole subject.

The invigilator, standing at the front of the hall, watched over the room like a warden guarding prisoners. He didn't seem to care about the struggle we were all going through. His gaze was fixed, almost as if he was guarding us from some hidden truth.

Maybe he knew the answer to all the questions, but I doubted it. After all, no one seemed to understand what was written on the paper, and certainly, no one could make sense of the scribbles on the desks.

I search again but to no avail and I fiddle around looking at the boy in the corner, who was furiously scratching his head. Was he struggling to understand the paper, or did he have a dandruff problem greater than mine? The sight offered a brief, absurd moment of camaraderie.

Around me, the rest of the students were working just as hard. They were hunched over their desks, scribbling answers with such urgency as if they believed their pens could summon the right answers out of thin air.

I remember those days in class when the teacher, as usual, spoke in the same boring, monotonous tone. It felt like a never-ending cycle. The students in the front row seemed to be totally absorbed, nodding their heads with every word the teacher said. I often wondered, won't their necks hurt from constantly looking up at the teacher like that? Sitting right under her nose, they seemed like little school kids, paying attention to every detail.

Then there were the students in the middle rows—these were the normal ones. Some were very studious, always writing notes and paying attention, while others were not so bothered. They sat somewhere in between, neither too interested nor too distracted.

And then, of course, there were the backbenchers—people like us. We were the rebels without a cause. We didn't really care about the lecture. We'd sit back, talk, and maybe even doze off occasionally. But we didn't worry much about it.

To be honest, the guys sitting at the back were even worse. They rarely took notes or paid attention. Yet, somehow, they still managed to score decently in exams. It was as if they had some secret to getting by without the stress.

ṽ

The clock ticked loudly. I hadn't written a single word. I looked around the room. Some students were writing quickly. Their pens moved fast, like they couldn't stop. Others looked confused, just like me. Mr. Dass walked up and down the aisles. Her sharp eyes scanned the room, watching every student. She looked like a strict warden. We were trapped in this test, just trying to get through it.

Desperation drove me to examine the desk once more, hoping to find some hidden clue etched into its surface. But the graffiti was as cryptic as ever. I sighed and leaned back in my chair, trying to calm my racing thoughts.

Tick-tock... Tick-tock... The final bell was inching closer, and I had nothing to show for my efforts. I picked up my pen and began scribbling random thoughts on the question paper, trying to jog my memory. My mind wandered again, this time to the countless moments of camaraderie and mischief that had defined my time in this classroom.

I remembered the day we smuggled snacks into class, hiding them under our desks and sneaking bites when the teacher wasn't looking. Or the time we turned a boring lecture into a game of charades, using exaggerated gestures to make each other laugh. Those were the days when the pressure of exams felt like a distant concern, overshadowed by the sheer joy of being young and carefree.

But now, the reality of the present loomed large. The final minutes ticked away, and I knew I had to salvage what little dignity I could. I began writing, cobbling together fragments of knowledge and half-remembered concepts. It wasn't much, but it was something.

When the bell finally rang, signaling the end of the exam, a collective sigh of relief swept through the room. Some students looked triumphant; others defeated. I handed in my answer sheet, feeling a mix of exhaustion and resignation.

The bell's echo still lingered as I shuffled out of the classroom, the weight of the exam clinging to me like a stubborn shadow. My palms were clammy, my mind replaying every scrawled word on the answer sheet. As I reached the corridor, a familiar voice broke through my haze.

"Nikhil" I called out, spotting him leaning casually against the wall, his bag slung over one shoulder. He turned his face lighting up in recognition.

"How was it?" he asked, falling into step beside me.

I sighed, shaking my head. "It was... okay, I guess. Not great, not terrible. Somewhere in between, what about you"

He smirked. "Same here, I mean, I started strong, but then the last few questions? Total blur, it felt like they were testing our survival skills, not our knowledge."

We both chuckled, the tension of the exam momentarily lifting. It felt good to laugh about it, to acknowledge the absurdity of the ordeal we had just endured.

"I couldn't remember any of the stuff from the subject," I admitted. "And for some reason, I spent way too much time on that exam paper. You"

"Oh, same here, I stared at it like it was written in some alien language," he said, rolling his eyes. "Then I just wrote something that *sounded* smart. Fingers crossed the examiner buys it."

We wandered down the corridor, weaving through clusters of students animatedly discussing their answers. Some voices were tinged with panic, others with triumph. The contrast was almost comical.

"Do you think we'll pass?" I asked, half-joking, half-serious.

"Of course," Nikhil said with mock confidence. "We've survived tougher stuff.

I laughed, but the knot in my chest remained. "I don't know. I just... I don't want to fail. I feel like I'll let everyone down if I do."

Nikhil glanced at me, his expression softening. "Hey, it's just one exam. No one's judging you as harshly as you're judging yourself."

"Maybe," I said, though I wasn't sure I believed it. "But I can't believe how fast the time flew in there. One moment, I was staring at the first question, and the next, the bell was ringing."

"That's how exams always are," Nikhil said with a smile. "A mix of stress, not knowing what's going on, and hoping for the best, that's just student life."

As we stepped out into the sunlight, the chill of the exam began to dissipate. The world outside felt alive, vibrant, and full of possibilities, the weight on my chest eased as I realized something: no matter the outcome, this was just one exam, a small chapter in a much larger story.

"Let's grab some coffee," Nikhil suggested. "We deserve it."

I nodded, my spirits lifting. "Yeah, let's do it. And maybe we won't talk about exams for the next hour?"

"Deal," he said, laughing.

And now, the day didn't seem so heavy anymore.

ONE STEP AT A TIME

The evening sun was sinking lower into the sky, casting a warm glow over the football field. The sky turned shades of orange, pink, and purple, with the last light of the day spreading across the green grass. The fading light stretched over the field, casting long shadows that danced as we ran, giving the scene an almost magical quality. It felt like time had slowed down so that we can play for a long.

The sounds of our game filled the air—laughter, the sharp smack of the ball as it was kicked, and the occasional cheer when someone made a good play. The air was warm, but it had a cool breeze, just enough to make the game feel comfortable. The mixture of excitement and calmness in the atmosphere was perfect. Occasionally, you could hear the distant chirp of crickets starting their evening song, adding to the peaceful feeling surrounding us.

Sweat clung to our skin, evidence of the hours spent playing under the sun's waning gaze. Faces flushed and hearts pounding, we moved as one, caught in a rhythm of friendship and shared purpose. In these moments, the looming weight of exams and results faded into the periphery, replaced by the simple, unifying bond of camaraderie.

I was dribbling the ball across the field, weaving around Rohan, who was trying to keep up but was moving with exaggerated movements to make it look like he was playing defense.

"You're terrible at defense, Rohan," I teased, using a quick change of direction to pass him and shoot the ball toward the goal. It sailed through the air and landed in the net with a satisfying swish.

"Yeah, yeah," Rohan muttered, giving me a grin that showed he wasn't taking it too seriously.

"Let's see you do that again." He made a dramatic lunge toward me as I grabbed the ball to start the play again, but his timing was off. With a quick step to the side, I easily dodged him, laughing at his clumsy attempt.

From the sideline, Nikhil shouted, "Rohan, are you even trying? Or are you just here for the exercise?" His comment sparked a wave of laughter from everyone watching.

Rohan threw a playful glance at Nikhil but didn't seem bothered. He was always the one to keep the mood light and never let things get too intense, even during the game.

"You're not getting this one," Rohan said with a look of determination on his face. He was clearly focused now, the easy-going attitude from earlier replaced by a competitive edge. But as I faked a pass and quickly kicked the ball into the net, he groaned loudly. "Okay, that was just luck!" he said, shaking his head in mock frustration.

"Luck has nothing to do with it," I shot back, winking at him as I jogged away in celebration.

Rohan rolled his eyes, still smiling, even as he pretended to be annoyed. "Yeah, yeah," he muttered, but the smile on his face betrayed him. "Let's see you do that again." His words were playful, but his eyes were filled with the spark of competition. He was the type of person who never took anything too seriously. Even when losing, he kept his sense of humor, making it hard to stay upset for long

As I grabbed the ball to start the next play, we both knew the we both would be rival to our upcoming football tournament final next week. Both of our teams had fought hard to reach the final of the college's yearly football tournament, and now it was all coming down to this moment. The championship was within reach, and neither of us was willing to back down.

Rohan and I had always been on rival teams, and this time, the stakes were higher than ever. Our teams were set to face off in the biggest match of the year. Both teams were eager to claim the championship, and we were determined to win.

I couldn't resist bringing it up. "You know, next week's final is going to be intense. I can already feel the pressure.

Your team's good, but you guys don't stand a chance against us."

Rohan raised an eyebrow, his smile widening. "Oh, really? And what makes you think your team's going to win?" he asked, clearly enjoying the back-and-forth. "You guys have no idea what's coming. We've been champions for years, and we'll beat you easily and with a high margin in the finals."

I laughed at his confidence. "Champions? You guys might be fit, but you're still missing the key ingredient—strategy. You might be fast, but you're not going to outsmart us." I paused, trying to think of a good way to tease him further. "Also, your goalie? He's good, but not good enough to stop me."

Rohan's face lit up with mock disbelief. "Oh, please. My goalie's a wall! He's going to stop every shot you make." He paused for a second, pretending to consider my words. "Actually, I'm starting to think you're the one who might need some training, especially after that lucky shot earlier."

I couldn't resist. "Lucky? That was pure skill, my friend. And you'll see that in the final."

Rohan shot me a look of playful challenge. "We'll see about that. But when we win, I expect you to admit that you were wrong." He gave me a quick wink before adding, "And maybe you can buy me dinner as a consolation prize."

"Deal," I said without hesitation. "But don't get your hopes up. You'll be the one buying dinner after we win."

We spent the next few minutes teasing each other about our team's chances. Despite the rivalry, there was an underlying sense of respect between us. We both knew that we were playing against a skilled team, but it was clear that we enjoyed pulling each other's legs more than anything else. It was all in good fun.

"You know," Rohan said after a while, "no matter who wins next week, it's going to be a great game. Both teams have worked hard to get here. But I have to admit, I'm looking forward to beating you guys."

"Same here," I said with a grin. "But I'll be the one walking away with the trophy."

ũ

As we continued to play, a loud shout interrupted the game. "Results are out!" someone called out, their voice cutting through the air with urgency. The words seemed to freeze the moment.

For a second, no one moved. The ball, which had just been kicked toward the goal, hung in the air like it, too, was caught in the tension. The entire field went still, and it felt like the world had shifted. Everyone paused, looking toward the hostel to check the result on laptop. The energy that had been flowing freely moments before was now replaced by a heavy, almost suffocating silence.

The excitement and laughter from the game had vanished in an instant. Players who had been sprinting across the field just seconds before stood motionless, staring at the hostel. It was as though the news of the results had sucked all the air out of the game. And then, without a word, everyone started running toward the hostel, their footsteps pounding against the grass in a synchronized rush. The ball was left forgotten on the ground, abandoned in the sudden chaos.

My heart began to race, not from the adrenaline of the game, but from the sheer anxiety of not knowing what to expect. I wiped my sweaty palms on my shorts, trying to calm my nerves.

Nikhil, sensing my unease, clapped a reassuring hand on my shoulder. "Come on, let's go see how we did," he said, his voice steady. But I couldn't shake the uneasy feeling settling in my stomach as we joined the others, my mind racing with thoughts of the results.

We joined the throng of students streaming toward the hostel, the air filled with the sounds of running footsteps and nervous chatter. It felt like the whole campus was in motion, drawn together by the same uncertainty. As we entered the hostel, the scene that greeted us was a chaotic one.

Students crowded around every available laptop, some with hopeful expressions, others with furrowed brows, unsure of what they would find. The corridors buzzed with tension, punctuated by occasional cries of joy or groans of disappointment as results flashed across the screens.

The results had a way of taking over everything else. Our game, the laughter, the sense of camaraderie—none of it seemed to matter now. It was all about what was on that list, and the waiting felt like it would never end.

In that moment, the bonds formed on the football field seemed to fade into the background, and all that remained was the collective weight of our hopes and fears. The simple joys of the game, the laughter, and the competition were replaced by the anxiety of what the results would hold.

My throat tightened as we approached one of the laptops. "You go first," I whispered to Rohan, my voice barely audible.

He gave me a quick glance, shrugged, and stepped forward. Typing in his roll number, he waited as the screen loaded. Moments later, his results appeared, and I held my breath, unsure of what was to come next.

Then, suddenly, the screen flashed with the results. His face lit up with relief and excitement. "Passed!" he exclaimed, pumping his fist in the air as if he had won a small victory. "Barely scraped through in two subjects, but hey, a pass is a pass." He seemed genuinely happy, even though his results weren't perfect. I managed a weak smile in return, but inside, my stomach churned.

His joy only made me more aware of how much I had to lose.

I forced my hands to relax, but they remained clammy, betraying my nerves. It felt like the ground beneath me was shifting, and I wasn't sure I could hold my balance much longer. I was grateful for Rohan's upbeat attitude, but it didn't do much to quiet the storm brewing in my mind. I had been working so hard these past few months, pouring everything into those sleepless nights of cramming, yet doubts clouded my thoughts. What if it wasn't enough? What if all that time spent reading textbooks, reviewing notes, and practicing problems wasn't enough to secure a passing grade?

"You're up," Nikhil said, his voice pulling me from my spiraling thoughts. He stepped aside, gesturing to the computer as if it were a challenge to be conquered. I stared at the screen, the cursor blinking as though it were mocking me, urging me to make my move. I took a deep breath, trying to steady my nerves. But nothing seemed to help. My hands shook as I typed in my roll number. The screen changed, and the familiar loading icon began to spin. I swallowed hard, my throat tight, and I felt the seconds stretch into what seemed like forever.

Every part of me wanted to look away, to walk out of the room and forget about the results altogether. But that wasn't an option. I had come this far, and there was no going back now. The loading screen felt endless, each passing second intensifying the anxiety that gripped me. I clenched my fists at my sides, hoping it would help steady my racing thoughts. But the truth was, there was nothing I could do now but wait.

"Come on," Rohan urged, his voice gentle but insistent. "The longer you wait, the worse it'll feel." I nodded, forcing myself to keep my eyes on the screen, but the anticipation was nearly unbearable. My mind raced through every possible outcome, from passing with flying colors to failing miserably. I tried to remind myself that I had done my best, but the fear of the unknown kept gnawing at me. Would my hard work pay off, or had I failed to meet the mark?

Finally, the loading stopped. The screen flashed, and my results appeared. I held my breath, bracing myself for whatever came next as my eyes scanned the screen, zeroing in on the numbers next to each subject.

And there it was: Power Systems - 34/100. My heart sank. I needed 35 to pass, just one mark, One. A single mark stood between me and success, and I had failed to get it. My chest tightened, and I felt a wave of frustration rise within me.

"Oh no," I whispered to myself, my voice trembling with a mix of disbelief and sorrow. "I... I failed."

Rohan, who had been sitting beside me, leaned in, his eyes scanning the screen quickly as well. He frowned, clearly disappointed, but his expression softened when he saw the look on my face. He placed a hand on my shoulder, offering a brief moment of comfort.

"Just by one mark, that's ridiculous," Rohan said with his voice full of disbelief. "You were so close, man."

I shook my head slowly, unable to bring myself to speak for a moment. The weight of the failure seemed suffocating. "Close doesn't count," I muttered bitterly, staring blankly at the screen. "I needed it. I studied so hard for it, but it doesn't matter. One mark, just one mark..."

Rohan let out a sigh, his eyes locked onto mine. "I know, it's tough. But... hold on," he said, snapping his fingers as if a sudden idea had struck him. "Have you considered applying for re-evaluation?"

I blinked, momentarily confused. "Re-evaluation" I asked, still a little dazed.

"Yeah, man. Sometimes they miss things when grading. You never know; they could have missed a point or two in your answers," Rohan explained, his tone suddenly more hopeful. "It's worth checking. You could get that extra mark you need. Just imagine—one mark could change everything."

The idea began to form in my mind, but I couldn't help feeling a bit skeptical. "Do you really think that would work? I mean, it's just one mark. They're probably not going to change anything."

Rohan shook his head vigorously. "Don't underestimate it. Trust me, I know people who've had their marks bumped up after a re-evaluation. It's not uncommon. And hey, you're so close already. They might just give it to you."

I rubbed my face with both hands, still processing the suggestion. "I don't know... What if they say no? What if it's just a waste of time?"

"Then you'll know for sure," Rohan countered. "But what if you don't ask and find out later that they missed something? You'll regret not trying, for sure. It's worth the effort."

I hesitated, unsure of what to do next. The uncertainty was almost as frustrating as the failure itself. But the thought of getting that extra mark, of passing, was enough to reignite a spark of hope inside me.

"You really think I should go for it?" I asked, looking up at Rohan, searching for reassurance.

"Of course," he said, grinning. "You have nothing to lose. Besides, it's better to try than to just sit here and wonder what could have been. Just go for it. You've got this."

His confidence was contagious, and for the first time in what felt like ages, I allowed myself to believe that maybe, just maybe, there was a way out of this. The re-evaluation process seemed like a long shot, but it was a shot nonetheless. I could at least try.

I stood there for a while, frozen in place, staring at the screen. Rohan's voice still echoed in my ears, but it felt distant now. "You were so close, man," he had said. "Just one mark" I felt a knot tighten in my stomach, and for a moment, I wanted to shout at the injustice of it all. I had put in hours of study, sacrificed sleep, skipped out on hanging out with friends—all for this one exam, and now I was one mark short of passing.

ॐ

Eventually, I found myself walking back to the room, my steps heavy and slow, as though each one took more energy than I had left to give. The familiar path to my room felt like a journey I didn't want to take, but there I was, heading back to the place where I had spent countless hours studying, stressing, and—more often than I cared to admit—doubting myself.

I reached my room and closed the door behind me with a quiet thud. I sat on the edge of my bed and ran a hand through my hair. The loneliness of the room pressed in on me, and I couldn't stop thinking about what had happened earlier, about the exam, the missed mark, and about the things I hadn't done.

I looked around the room, my eyes settling on the desk where a pile of textbooks sat, untouched. The study sessions that should have been productive had been anything but. Instead, I found myself distracted by everything and anything. I had been reckless, careless even. If only I had put in the hours, I had spent procrastinating, perhaps the result would have been different.

The night before the exam, I chose to meet Ahana instead of studying. We talked about things that didn't even matter and laughed about silly things. It felt nice to forget about the exam for a while, but now I wonder if that was a mistake. I should have been at my desk, going through my notes, solving problems, and making sure I understood everything. But instead, I spent my time enjoying the moment with her. At that time, it felt right, like I needed the break. But now, with the result in front of me, I can't help but regret it. Maybe I should have made a better choice

The regrets kept piling up. If only I hadn't stayed out drinking with Nikhil the night before the exam. If only I had gone to bed early and had prepared myself better. But now, it was too late. I couldn't change the past; couldn't undo the mistakes I had made.

But now, as I sat in my room, the regret hit me like a wave. What if I had spent that time more wisely? What if I had focused on the material instead of the distractions? What if I had just studied, like everyone else? The "what ifs" were suffocating, each one twisting the knife of self-blame deeper into my chest and now I had to face the consequences.

As I leaned back on my bed, staring at the ceiling, my thoughts drifted to another person. My mom, her face flashed in my mind, her smile warm yet filled with expectation. I had always been her pride and joy; her hopes pinned on me like a banner of promise. She had sacrificed so much to get me here, to this point. And I knew that she believed in me, believed that I could achieve anything. But now, Now I had failed, and I could feel the sting of her disappointment before I even told her. How would I face her? How could I look her in the eye and explain why I hadn't succeeded? I could already picture her voice, kind but firm, asking me what had happened.

I closed my eyes, the sting of tears threatening to break free.

I wiped my eyes one last time, taking deep breaths to calm myself. The room was still, except for the quiet hum of the fan. I needed to think, needed to find a way forward, but everything felt so overwhelming. I couldn't keep going like this, couldn't let this one failure define me. I needed to find a way to pick myself up, to move forward, but how?

As I sat there, lost in my thoughts, a sudden knock on the door broke the silence. I wiped my eyes quickly, trying to compose myself before answering. "Come in," I called out hoarsely, my voice still thick with emotion.

The door creaked open, and there stood Rohan, looking at me with a concerned expression. He must have known something was wrong—he had always been able to read me like a book.

"You okay, man?" he asked, his voice softer than usual.

I didn't respond immediately. Instead, I just looked at him, feeling a wave of frustration and helplessness wash over me. What was the point of pretending everything was fine? Rohan knew me too well.

"No, I'm not okay," I admitted, my voice barely above a whisper. "I don't know what to do anymore. I just... I feel like I'm losing everything."

Rohan walked over and sat next to me on the bed, placing a hand on my shoulder. "It's going to be alright," he said quietly. "You've got this. You're not alone in this, okay? We all make mistakes; we all mess up sometimes. But you can still fix it. You've still got time."

I didn't know if he was right, but hearing him say it gave me a small flicker of hope. Maybe I wasn't as lost as I thought. Maybe I could still make something of this, still find a way to turn things around.

"I don't know what to do," I confessed, feeling small and vulnerable. "I don't know how to fix this."

"You don't have to fix everything all at once," Rohan said, giving me a reassuring smile. "Start small. Go for the re-evaluation. See what happens. You never know. And as for Ahana... don't give up on that either. You'll figure it out. One step at a time, man"

As Nikhil finished speaking, a second knock sounded at the door, firmer this time. Before I could say anything, the door swung open, and there stood Nikhil, his ever-serious expression softened with concern.

"You guys didn't wait for me at the hostel," Nikhil said, stepping inside and closing the door behind him. He folded his arms, glancing between me and Rohan. "I figured something was up."

Rohan motioned for Nikhil to sit on the bed. "Yeah, we're here. It's been... rough," Rohan admitted, casting me a brief glance.

Nikhil sat down across from us, his sharp eyes locking on mine. "What happened?"

I sighed, my voice faltering as I explained, "I failed Power Systems... by one mark. Just one mark"

Nikhil's brow furrowed and he let out a low whistle. "One mark, that's brutal." He leaned forward, resting his elbows on his knees. "Have you checked for re-evaluation? Sometimes they—"

"Miss things, yeah," Rohan interjected, finishing the thought. "I told him to go for it, but he's not sure."

Nikhil nodded slowly. "Look, I know how much this sucks, but you need to give it a shot. It's not just about this one mark—it's about trying everything before you decide to give up on it. You've worked too hard to stop now."

I rubbed the back of my neck, feeling the weight of their words. "I don't know. What if it doesn't work? What if I'm just wasting my time?"

"Bro," Nikhil said, his tone firm but not unkind, "do you really want to sit here wondering *what if* for the rest of your life? One mark is nothing. I've seen people get five or even ten marks after a re-evaluation. You're so close; it's worth trying."

"Exactly" Rohan chimed in. "And even if it doesn't work, at least you'll know you gave it everything you had. That's better than sitting here doing nothing."

Their words were starting to sink in, though doubt still lingered. "Okay," I said finally, my voice hesitant. "I'll apply for the re-evaluation. But I can't shake this feeling of failure. It's not just about the mark—it's everything. My decisions, my priorities, everything feels... wrong."

Nikhil exchanged a glance with Rohan before turning back to me. "Look, man," he said, his voice softer, "we all mess up. No one gets everything right, not even those so-called toppers. The important thing is what you do next. You can sit here and watch, or you can stand up, learn from this, and do better. We've all got your back."

I blinked, taken aback by his sincerity.

"Nikhil's right," Rohan added. "We've got your back, man. We'll figure this out together. Besides, it's just one exam. You're way bigger than that. And hey, no one said you have to fix everything overnight."

I nodded slowly, feeling a little better, but still uncertain. The road ahead was unclear, and the weight of everything I had to fix still loomed over me. But for the first time in a while, I allowed myself to believe that maybe, just maybe, things could still get better.

After all, I wasn't alone. And as long as I had people like Rohan & Nikhil by my side, there was still hope.

As I again lay back on my bed, I let out a long, slow breath. There was still a lot of uncertainty ahead, but I knew one thing for sure: I wasn't going to let this failure define me. I was going to keep fighting, one step at a time.

WHISTLE BLOWS

The day before the big match had finally arrived, and the excitement was almost too much to handle. This wasn't just any game—it was the final match, the one that everyone had been waiting for. For weeks, people had been talking about it, building up the rivalry between our teams. The competition had grown stronger with each passing match, and now, we were just hours away from the most important game of the year.

Rohan and I had been preparing in our own ways. I had spent countless hours practicing, running drills, and studying our opponents' gameplay. I had analyzed their defense, their attacks, and their weak spots, hoping to use that knowledge to our advantage. Rohan, on the other hand, was more relaxed. He had been out on the field, showing off his incredible footwork and quick thinking. He played with a confidence that sometimes annoyed me, but I had to admit, it also made him one of the best players on his team.

That evening, I walked around the campus, thinking about the game. My feet moved on their own, leading me to a quiet spot. It was where Rohan and I often rested after practice.

The place was peaceful, away from noise. We would sit there and talk without any disturbance. As I got closer, I saw Rohan sitting on a bench.

He leaned back, looking relaxed. A cigarette rested between his fingers. When he noticed me, a familiar grin spread across his face. It was the same smile he always had, full of confidence and mischief.

"Well, well," he said, exhaling a puff of smoke. "Look who finally decided to show up. Nervous about tomorrow?"

I rolled my eyes but couldn't help smiling. "Nervous? Me? Please. You're the one who should be worried. I've been watching your team, Rohan. You guys are so predictable I could play blindfolded and still win."

Rohan let out a dramatic gasp. "Oh wow, such confidence! Tell me, are you planning to score goals, or are you just hoping we get distracted laughing at your footwork?"

Before I could reply, another voice joined in. "Oh great, you two are at it again," Nikhil said, walking over with his hands in his pockets. He flopped down onto a bench and sighed. "I swear, you two have more chemistry than any other teammates."

"Jealous?" Rohan smirked as he handed a cigarette to Nikhil. "I understand, Nikhil. Not everyone is lucky enough to see our famous rivalry up close."

"Legendary?" I scoffed. "More like a never-ending debate about who has the better team. Spoiler alert: It's obviously mine."

"Oh, is that so?" Rohan leaned forward, resting his elbows. "Because last time I checked, your team couldn't even string together three passes without looking like lost chickens."

I laughed. "At least my team doesn't depend on fake injuries to get free kicks. You should seriously consider a career in acting after this."

Nikhil took a puff of his cigarette and grinned. "He's right, Rohan. In the last match, when you fell, I saw you hold your knee first, then your ankle, and then your shoulder. Come on, pick one injury!"

Rohan threw his hands up. "Hey! That was strategic. Confuse the ref, confuse the opponent. It's all part of the plan."

I shook my head. "Yeah, right. And what's your plan for tomorrow? Hoping we feel bad and let you win?"

Rohan smirked. "Oh no, we've got an actual strategy. We've been running drills, perfecting plays, and let's just say... your defense is in for a shock."

I raised an eyebrow. "Oh please, the only shocking thing about your team is how many times you miss the goal from five feet away."

Nikhil burst out laughing. "That's true! Remember last game when you had a one-on-one with the keeper and still managed to send the ball into the parking lot?"

Rohan groaned. "Okay, that was ONE time! And it was windy!"

"It was a sunny day, Rohan." I grinned.

Rohan waved me off. "Whatever. Just don't cry tomorrow when we destroy you."

I leaned back, crossing my arms. "Oh, I'm looking forward to it. But just so you know, when we win, I'll personally come over and hand you a tissue."

"Ha!" Rohan chuckled. "If you win, I'll not only take the tissue, I'll write you a heartfelt apology letter."

"Oh, I'm holding you to that."

Nikhil shook his head. "You guys are insane. But honestly, I can't wait for the match. It's going to be fun watching you two battle it out."

Rohan smirked. "Oh, it's going to be more than fun. It's going to be a lesson. And I'm the teacher."

I laughed. "In that case, you better be ready for a classroom full of failing students."

We all burst into laughter, the competition still there but mixed with excitement and camaraderie. As much as we wanted to win, we knew that, in the end, the real fun was in moments like these—teasing each other, hyping up the match, and knowing that no matter what happened, we'd still walk away as friends.

"Alright, enough trash talk," Nikhil said, stretching. "Let's go get some food before you two start throwing punches."

Rohan smirked. "Good idea. Let's eat. I need to make sure I have enough energy to celebrate my victory tomorrow."

I grinned. "Or enough energy to chase the ball after we take possession."

With that, we both stood up, clapping each other on the back with a friendly shove. "May the best team win," Rohan said, his voice suddenly softer, the rivalry turning into mutual respect.

"Yeah, may the best team win," I echoed, knowing full well that the next day, we would both be giving it our all.

As I walked away, I couldn't help but think about how much this game meant to both of us. It wasn't just about winning or losing. It was about proving ourselves, about giving everything we had on the field. It was about the friendships, the rivalries, and the memories we had created along the way.

That night, I lay in bed, staring at the ceiling, my mind running through every possible scenario. Would we be able to break through their defense? Would our strategy work? Would I be able to keep up with Rohan's quick plays? I knew that no matter what happened, the next day would be unforgettable.

ॐ

A gentle breeze rustled through the trees, making the perfect setting for an intense match. My teammates and I arrived at the field, our excitement bubbling over as we geared up for the game. The energy in the air was electric—everyone was eager to give their best performance. We tightened our laces, adjusted our shin guards, and huddled together for a quick pep talk, hyping each other up for what was to come.

As we walked toward the center of the field, I spotted Rohan, my longtime rival in game and a best friend, already waiting with his team. He flashed a confident grin, and I couldn't help but smirk back. Despite the competitive tension, we exchanged a few lighthearted jokes, easing some of the nerves.

"Hope you're ready to lose today," I teased.

Rohan chuckled, shaking his head. "You wish! Just try to keep up."

With that, we took our positions in front of the referee. The crowd around the field buzzed with anticipation, eager to witness the clash between two of the finalists in the tournament. The referee raised his whistle to his lips, and in that brief moment of silence, my heartbeat thundered in my chest. Then, with a sharp blow, the match officially began.

Adrenaline surged through my veins as the ball was kicked off. Our team immediately sprang into action, passing swiftly and pushing forward. Rohan's team, two-time defending champions, had a reputation for their rock-solid defense and aggressive gameplay. Their players were well-drilled, disciplined, and in perfect sync. I could see Rohan's towering figure at the back, directing his teammates with authority, his presence commanding the field. He was a natural leader, always knowing when to push, when to hold back, and how to control the tempo of the game.

They had been the top scorers of the tournament, undefeated so far. Breaking through their defense would be no easy task, but we were determined to give it everything we had. This was going to be a challenge—but I wasn't ready to back down.

Our team, though not as physically imposing, had been more organized in their approach. We had a compact formation, focusing on quick passes and breaking through gaps in the opponent's defense. We were smaller, but we had speed and technical skills on our side. I had full faith in our ability to execute the game plan, but I knew we had to be on top of our game. There was no room for error against a team like Rohan's.

The first ten minutes of the match were intense. Both teams were sizing each other up, testing each other's defenses. We kept possession of the ball, moving it swiftly, trying to find the right opportunity to strike. However, Rohan's defense was nearly impenetrable. He had positioned himself perfectly, always in the right place at the right time, blocking passes and intercepting balls with ease. I could see him marking me closely, his eyes never leaving me. It was clear he had a plan—he knew me too well. Today, he was determined to make sure I didn't have a chance to shine.

The intensity on the field was palpable. Our quick passes seemed to have little effect on Rohan's defense. Every time we tried to break through, they were there to shut us down. It was frustrating, but we kept pushing forward. The heat of the match was starting to get to me, but I couldn't afford to lose focus. I could feel the pressure mounting, not just from reaching first time in finals but also form Rohan's team, one of the best team in college, undefeated and champions from last two years.

But then, something unexpected happened. One of our forwards, Amit, made a break down the left wing. He was fast, and his dribbling was impeccable. The defenders tried to close him down, but he managed to slip past them, and with a quick glance up, he spotted me in the perfect position inside the box. Without hesitation, he sent a cross into the air, right into the space where I knew the ball would land. The timing was perfect, and I positioned myself to make the header. My heart raced as I leapt into the air, every muscle straining to reach the ball. But just as I thought I was about to make contact; the ball flew just a bit too high. I stretched my neck and my legs, but it skimmed the top of my head and sailed over the bar.

"Come on, man!" one of my teammates shouted, frustration clear in his voice. He had been counting on me to score. It wasn't just my missed opportunity—it felt like a missed chance for the whole team.

I tried to shake it off, pushing away the negative thoughts. "Focus, guys. We'll get another chance," I said, trying to rally the team. The last thing we needed was to let the missed header get to us.

The match carried on, with both teams now fully engaged. The intensity ratcheted up even higher. Rohan's team, sensing that they had the upper hand, began to dominate possession. It wasn't long before they made a brilliant counter-attack in the 40th minute. Sanjay, their striker, broke past our defense like a freight train. Our defenders were scrambling to keep up, but Sanjay was too fast. With a deft touch, he passed the ball to his teammate, who was perfectly positioned just outside the edge of our penalty box. Before anyone could react, the ball was sent flying into the net. It was a well-timed strike, and our goalkeeper, though he made an effort, had no chance of stopping it.

"1-0 to Civil Engineering!" the referee announced, and the crowd erupted into cheers. The sound of their celebrations was deafening, and I could see the frustration in the eyes of my teammates. We were behind now, and the stakes were higher than ever.

The referee blew the whistle—it was halftime. We walked off the field, breathing heavily. The scoreboard showed 1-0. We were losing, but we knew the match wasn't over yet. There was still another half to play, and we couldn't let our spirits drop.

As we reached the sidelines, bottles of water and energy drinks were passed around. Some of us poured water over our heads to cool down. The sun was beating down, and we were tired, but giving up was not an option. I looked at my teammates—they were exhausted but determined.

We gathered in a tight huddle for a quick team talk. "Listen, guys, we are only one goal down," I said, trying to lift their spirits. "We can turn this around. We need to stay focused and stick to our plan. Keep the formation tight, pass quickly, and look for spaces in their defence. We have to be faster and smarter than them."

The team nodded, understanding the plan. We knew that if we worked together, we could still win. The break was short, and soon, the referee called us back. As we walked onto the field, I could feel the energy rising again.

We weren't going to give up without a fight. The second half was about to begin, and we were ready.

Match started and the next 30 minutes were a blur of energy and effort. We fought for every ball, tracking back when needed and pushing forward with intensity. Every time Rohan's team made a move, we were there to challenge them. It wasn't perfect—we still couldn't break their defense, but we weren't letting up. The tension was building, and with every minute that passed, we knew we had fewer opportunities left to score.

I kept my eyes on the ball, aware that our chances were limited but still very much alive. The clock was ticking, and I could feel the weight of the match bearing down on me. We couldn't afford another mistake. We needed a goal—and fast

It was now or never. The clock was ticking, and the final whistle was fast approaching. Opponent was leading with 1-0 with their strong defense and attack. We had only ten minutes left to make a comeback. My heart pounded in my chest, and my body screamed for energy. The game was slipping through our fingers, and it seemed like fate was cruelly toying with us. But there was no turning back. We had worked too hard, fought too long to give up now.

Amit, once again, broke free on the left and sent a perfect pass toward me. I saw the ball coming, and in a split second, I knew I had to act. The goalkeeper was off his line, and I had a clear shot. I adjusted my position, pulled back my leg, and struck the ball with everything I had. The crowd seemed to go silent as the ball soared toward the goal. It was everything I had dreamed of.

But at the last second, Rohan's goalkeeper, a towering figure in net, managed to dive and make an incredible save, pushing the ball out of bounds. I stared in disbelief, unable to process what had just happened. That was our chance—the one moment where everything could change. And now it was gone. The crowd erupted in cheers for the goalkeeper, their voices rising in appreciation for the remarkable save. I stood there, frozen, unable to comprehend the crushing blow.

"Get ready! We've got one more shot!" I heard one of my teammate's shouts, snapping me out of my stupor. The urgency in his voice fueled a fire in me. There was no time to dwell on the past. We had one more chance, one final play to salvage everything.

The match was almost over, and we were losing by one goal. Our team was attacking with everything we had, trying to score before time ran out. I dribbled the ball down the field, dodging defenders, searching for an opening. Just as I was about to take a shot, a defender rushed in and blocked it. The ball bounced to my teammate, who quickly passed it to another player near the goal. He tried to shoot, but the goalkeeper made a great save, pushing the ball out of bounds. The referee blew his whistle and pointed to the corner flag. It was our last chance—a corner kick.

Everyone hurried into position. We knew this was our final opportunity to score and equalize the game. I stood in the middle of the penalty box, surrounded by defenders, waiting for the perfect moment. Our player placed the ball on the spot, took a deep breath, and stepped back. My heart pounded as he lifted his arm, signaling his move.

The ball floated into the air with precision, the spin carrying it perfectly into the heart of the penalty area. I could feel the tension in the air, the anticipation of the crowd mounting as it made its way toward me. I leaped into the air. The impact was clean, my head connecting with it firmly, sending it toward the goal.

For a brief moment, I thought it was going in. I saw it sailing toward the bottom corner, just past the goalkeeper's outstretched hands. But, as if the universe was conspiring against me, the ball drifted wide, grazing the outside of the post.

It was over.

The final whistle blew, and the stadium erupted in both disappointment and relief. My teammates slumped to the ground; their shoulders heavy with the weight of defeat. I stood there, numb, staring at the empty space where our dreams of victory had just crumbled. Rohan's players celebrated in the center of the field, their cheers echoing in my ears like a cruel reminder of what could have been.

ॐ

We had lost. I stood there on the field, motionless, as Rohan's team celebrated. The cheers of the Civil Engineering department rang in my ears, but all I could hear was the pounding of my heart, a mix of frustration and regret.

I couldn't believe it. We had come so close. Three chances. Three golden opportunities that I had missed. They were the ones that could have changed everything. My mind replayed the moments over and over, each time growing more painful.

Rohan walked over to me, his face a mix of exhaustion and joy. He clapped me on the back. "You played well, man," he said, his voice sincere but tinged with the thrill of victory. "Don't be too hard on yourself."

But how could I not be hard on myself? We had come so far. We had fought tooth and nail to get to this point, and now, standing here, I felt like I had let my team down. I had been the one to make the mistakes, the one who had missed the opportunities. I couldn't shake the feeling that if I had just done things differently, the outcome would have been different too. My heart ached with the knowledge that the victory had slipped through my fingers, and all that remained was the sting of failure.

"I know, man," I said quietly, my voice barely audible above the noise of the celebration around us. "But I had three chances. Three! And I messed up every single one of them."

Rohan's smile faded slightly as he looked at me, his brow furrowing with concern. He placed a hand on my shoulder, trying to offer comfort, but I could feel the weight of my own self-doubt pressing down on me. It felt like the entire world was focused on those three moments, on my mistakes, and no matter how hard I tried to shake it off, it seemed like the only thing that mattered.

"You can't think like that," Rohan said, his voice firm but gentle. "It's not about those three moments. It's about the game as a whole. We win and lose together, you know?"

But how could I not think about those moments? They were there, replaying in my mind like a broken record, each one growing more vivid and painful the more I thought about them. I had been so close to making the difference, to being the one who turned the game around, but instead, I had watched as the ball slipped from my control, as my mistakes led to our defeat.

After a long pause, Rohan spoke again, his voice softer this time. "I know you're feeling bad about it, but you have to let it go, man. One game doesn't define you. Hell, one mistake doesn't either."

I turned to him, meeting his eyes. "But what if it does? What if I can't stop thinking about it? What if it's all I remember from this game?"

Rohan sighed, leaning back against the bench and looking up at the sky. "Look, I get it. You feel like you've failed. But that's not the end of the story. It's part of the story, yeah, but not the whole thing. You know what makes someone strong? Not how they do when they're winning, but how they handle losing. How they bounce back."

I swallowed hard, the lump in my throat threatening to choke me. I had never wanted to learn that lesson again, not like this. I had never wanted to experience the bitterness of failure, especially so frequently. But Rohan was right. The game was over, and the outcome was already set. No amount of regret could change it. The only thing I could control now was how I moved forward.

"I'll try," I said quietly, the words feeling like a promise to myself. "I'll try to let it go."

The next few minutes were a blur. I congratulated Rohan's team, forced a smile, and tried to hide the disappointment. But inside, I felt like a failure. My teammates were supportive, but I couldn't escape the nagging feeling that if I had just done things differently, we would have won.

We sat at the edge of the field, a heavy silence hanging in the air. Everyone was still, too still. My teammates murmured to each other, but their voices felt far away, almost meaningless. They each had their own way of processing the loss, but for me, it was something else entirely. They hadn't missed the opportunities I had. They didn't carry the burden of those mistakes the way I did. They hadn't been so close to victory, only to be dragged back at the last moment by their own hands

As I sat on the bench, staring at the floor, a part of me wanted to lash out. To scream at the unfairness of it all. But I knew that wouldn't change anything. The reality of the loss was already settling in. I had failed, and no amount of frustration could rewrite what had already happened.

Slowly, the others began to gather their things and prepare to leave. Some of them joked around, trying to lighten the mood, while others remained quiet, lost in their own thoughts. I didn't join in the banter. Instead, I kept to myself, thinking about how to move forward. The loss would stay with me for a while, but I couldn't let it define me. I couldn't allow the sting of this defeat to overshadow everything else.

It wasn't just the game that I had to come to terms with; it was the realization that sometimes, despite giving everything, things don't go the way you want. It was a lesson in resilience, one I didn't want to learn but one I had to.

As I left the ground, I took a deep breath, the night air cool against my face. The world hadn't stopped turning, and neither could I. It would take time, but eventually, I'd move on. The loss wouldn't break me. But it would stay with me, a reminder that every victory, every moment, was earned through both success and failure.

THROUGH THE ALLEYWAYS

I locked the door of my room from inside, threw my shoes aside, and collapsed onto my bed. The ceiling fan whirred above me, oblivious to my disappointment. The room felt smaller, suffocating, like the walls were pressing in on me. I had wanted this win so badly. Not just for me, but for my team, for all those nights we had trained under the dim hostel streetlights, for every bruise and scrape we had endured. And now, it was gone.

Hours passed as the hostel buzzed with energy—some juniors were probably still celebrating the thrilling match in their rooms. I just lay there, staring at the ceiling, lost in my thoughts. It wasn't until the clock neared midnight, around 12, that I heard a knock on my door.

"Ishaan, open up," came Nikhil's voice.

I sighed but didn't move.

Then another voice, louder and more insistent. "Bro, don't be a sore loser. Open the damn door!" Rohan said.

I hesitated, my fingers gripping the edge of my bed. The sting of the loss was still raw, like an open wound. We had been so close—so damn close. But in the end, his team had taken the trophy, leaving us with nothing but frustration and regret.

The knocking continued. "Ishaan, come on," Rohan pressed.

I exhaled sharply, forcing myself up from the bed. My legs felt heavy as I walked to the door and unlocked it. The moment I stepped back, they barged in, bringing with them the lingering energy of their celebration.

Rohan still wore his team jersey, the number bold against the fabric, like a taunt. Nikhil followed behind, having a guilty smile on his face, like he felt bad for being part of the winning side's joy.

"Come on, dude, don't sulk like this," Rohan said, dropping onto my chair. "You guys played amazingly. It could've gone either way."

I didn't respond. Instead, I just sat on the bed, running a hand through my messy hair.

Nikhil sighed. "Ishaan, we get it. It hurts. But you can't lock yourself up like this. You gave them a fight till the last second."

"And," Rohan added, grinning, "to make things better, we've decided something huge."

I raised an eyebrow. "What?"

"I've got an idea," he said with a grin. "I'm throwing a party tonight. Everyone from the hostel who played in the final—let's go out and celebrate!"

"You heard me," he said, crossing his arms proudly. "No matter which team, no matter who won or lost—everyone deserves to celebrate. You guys played one of the best matches this hostel has ever seen."

Nikhil nodded. "Yeah, bro. It's not just about the trophy. We all pushed ourselves to the limit. That's worth something."

I hesitated. A part of me wanted to reject the idea outright; to tell them I wasn't in the mood. But another part—the one that knew Nikhil and Rohan wouldn't leave until they dragged me out themselves—considered it.

Rohan smirked. "And besides, if you don't show up, it'll look like you're scared to face me after losing."

I let out a small chuckle despite myself. "You wish. I'm just not in the mood."

"That's exactly why you should come!" Nikhil insisted. "Sulking alone in your room won't change the result. Let's at least end this tournament on a good note."

I sighed, weighing my options. "Fine, what is the plan?"

Rohan clapped me on the back. "That's the spirit! Now let's go make some memories."

"We could sneak out of the hostel tonight," Rohan whispered, his voice low like he was planning some top-secret mission. "Literally sneak out."

I frowned, not sure if I had heard him correctly. "Wait... what?"

"You heard me," he said with a mischievous grin. "We'll escape from here, have some fun outside, and no one will ever know. Come on, no one ever listens to our plans anyway."

I rolled my eyes. "Okay, hold on. You're saying we sneak out of the hostel... and then what? Where will we even go?"

Rohan shrugged like it didn't even matter. "That's the fun part! We'll figure it out on the way. Just imagine—a night without boring hostel life. No rules, no wardens, just us doing something crazy."

I shook my head. "Yeah, great idea. Except the hostel gates are locked. We can't just walk out."

Nikhil, who had been listening quietly, finally laughed. "Who said anything about the gates? We take another route."

I looked at him suspiciously. "Another route? What do you mean?"

Rohan smirked. "The bathroom windows."

I stared at him like he had lost his mind. "You've got to be kidding me. That's insane."

Nikhil grinned. "Come on, Ishaan! Where's your sense of adventure?"

"My sense of adventure wants to stay alive," I shot back. "What if we get caught? The warden will murder us."

Rohan leaned in, lowering his voice. "Not if we do it smartly. First, we gather everyone in the common hall. No shouting, no noise. Just quiet excitement. Then we sneak out one by one. Easy."

I sighed, already regretting being friends with these two.

For the first time since our big loss, I felt something other than disappointment—excitement. The plan was reckless, risky, and maybe even a little stupid. But that was exactly why it felt right.

Within thirty minutes, we had gathered every player in the hostel. Some of them were still upset about losing the match, but as soon as they heard about our secret night out, their mood changed. Even a few juniors joined in, excited to be part of something with the seniors.

There were eight of us in total, sitting together in the common hall, whispering and trying not to laugh too loudly. The thrill of secrecy made everything feel more exciting. Rohan, as always, had somehow managed to sneak in some snacks and soft drinks from his hidden stash.

We sat in a circle, munching on chips and biscuits while cracking jokes. Someone brought up a funny mistake from the match, and soon, we were all laughing, forgetting our rivalry for a while.

"Man, we should have won," one of the juniors said.

"Yeah, but at least we gave them a tough fight," I replied.

"But tonight isn't about that," Rohan added with a grin. "The real adventure starts now."

ũ

We embarked on a covert recon mission around the hostel, moving with cautious excitement. Our target was the washroom window on the ground floor—an old, rusted relic that had clearly been abandoned to time. The metal frame was corroded, the hinges barely holding on, making it the perfect weak spot for our plan.

The objective was simple yet daring: pry the window open, squeeze through, and slip away undetected. Beyond the hostel's boundary lay our escape route—a narrow path winding through the vast farming lands. Under the cover of darkness, we would navigate past swaying crops and uneven terrain, putting as much distance as possible between us and the prying eyes of authority.

"Are you sure this is a good idea?" I asked, my voice barely above a whisper. My eyes darted between the window and the door leading to the hallway, probably checking if our little operation had already been compromised.

Rohan smirked. "Relax, Ishaan. It's just a window. How hard can it be to break it?"

We all stood in front of the washroom, staring up at the window like it was some kind of mythical gateway to freedom. It was a good six feet off the ground—an inconvenient height, but nothing a bit of teamwork couldn't solve.

"Sir, I'll go first," one of the juniors volunteered eagerly. He was the smallest of the group, quick on his feet, and somehow believed himself to be an escape artist. "I'm the lightest, and I've got the skills." He grinned confidently.

"Skills? You mean the ability to make a fool of yourself?" Nikhil scoffed. "Leave it. Rohan, you try."

Rohan rolled his eyes but didn't argue. He grabbed a plastic chair from the washroom corner, dragging it under the window. The chair wobbled slightly as he climbed onto it, his movements about as graceful as a penguin trying to scale a mountain.

He reached up, placing his hands firmly against the rusted window frame. With a grunt, he pushed. Nothing. He tried again, pressing harder this time. Still nothing.

"This thing's tougher than I thought," he admitted, frowning.

"Just smash it, dude," Nikhil suggested impatiently. "It's not like we're sneaking out quietly anyway."

Rohan hesitated for a moment, then took a deep breath. He clenched his fist, pulled back his arm, and with a swift, forceful punch, he struck the glass.

CRASH!

The glass shattered into a thousand pieces, sending shards flying everywhere. For a brief moment, everything went quiet.

"Uh... well, that escalated quickly," Nikhil muttered under his breath.

We all stopped and stared at the broken window, with glass pieces all around us. I sighed, "Well... that didn't go as planned."

Our instincts kicked in. We scrambled to clear the glass from the window frame, each of us working frantically to minimize the mess before anyone noticed. We used our sleeves to pick up the larger shards, tossing them aside as quietly as possible.

"Careful, careful," Nikhil whispered, wrapping a cloth around the jagged edges of the frame to prevent any injuries. "Last thing we need is blood all over the place."

The adrenaline rush made our movements clumsy, but we worked fast. Within minutes, the window was as safe as it was going to get under the circumstances.

"Okay, we're good," Rohan declared, wiping his hands on his jeans. "Now, let's get out of here before someone comes looking."

The first one to climb out was the junior who had volunteered earlier. Despite the earlier ridicule, he moved with surprising agility, swinging himself through the opening with ease and landing in the alley behind the hostel.

"See? Skills," he whispered proudly.

Rohan went next. He made a small noise as he pulled himself up and climbed through the window. He wasn't as smooth as the others, but he still got through without any trouble.

Nikhil followed, pausing momentarily to listen for any signs of approaching footsteps before slipping out.

I was the last to go. As I placed my hands on the frame, the reality of what we were doing truly hit me. We were actually breaking out of the hostel. We had just shattered a window—property damage, potential disciplinary action, maybe even suspension. Was it worth it? Probably not. But in that moment, the thrill of the escape was all that mattered.

Once outside, eight of us were in the back alley, a dark and empty stretch of pavement. The night was still young, and the excitement of breaking out of the hostel made us feel invincible.

"Where to now?" I asked, feeling the adrenaline kick in.

"I say we hit the local Dhaba for some food," Rohan said. "I'm starving."

Nikhil nodded in agreement. "Yeah, and let's avoid the main roads. We don't want to run into anyone."

We walked through a maze of narrow paths in the middle of farming lands, doing our best to stay out of sight. The thrill of escaping filled us with excitement, and our hearts raced with every step.

The journey was not easy. The paths were uneven, with small rocks and patches of mud slowing us down. At times, we had to crouch behind bushes or trees whenever we thought someone might see us. The darkness made it even harder to find our way, and the only sounds were the rustling of leaves and our own footsteps.

There were moments when we felt lost, unsure of which way to go. Our legs grew tired, but we pushed forward, determined to reach our destination. After what felt like endless hours of walking, we finally saw the dim lights of the Dhaba in the distance. A wave of relief washed over us as we realized we had made it.

The small, dimly lit eatery had an undeniable charm. It was a haven for students like us, looking to escape the suffocating confines of hostel life. The scent of sizzling spices and freshly baked naan filled the air, making our mouths water instantly. A few old wooden tables, mismatched plastic chairs, and a single flickering bulb created an atmosphere of rustic comfort. This was the place where legends were made—at least in our college circles.

I stepped forward and called out, "Bhaiya, we need food for everyone! Three plates of mix veg, Four plates of Butter paneer, rotis, and extra rice."

The Dhaba owner, a grumpy old man with a permanent scowl, looked at our group suspiciously. "You kids from the hostel?"

We all froze for a second. Before I could think of a reply, Rohan jumped in. "No, sir. We're... uh... from the nearby college. Just... visiting."

The owner narrowed his eyes but didn't press further. He disappeared into the kitchen, and we let out a collective sigh of relief.

As we settled at a large corner table, Nikhil smirked. "Totally worth the broken window."

One of the juniors, Arjun, grinned. "Best mission ever! We should do this every weekend."

We all burst into laughter, the absurdity of our escape hitting us fully now. The idea of sneaking out just for some decent food was ridiculous, but it was these little acts of rebellion that made hostel life memorable.

"Imagine if warden finds out," I said, leaning back with a smirk. "We'll be scrubbing the hostel floors for weeks."

Rohan scoffed. "If he finds out. But he won't, because we're legends."

"Oh yeah?" Nikhil raised an eyebrow. "Legends don't usually trip over glass window while escaping."

The whole table erupted into laughter again. Rohan rolled his eyes. "That was strategic. I was testing if the path was safe."

"You mean you were testing how loudly a glass can break in the middle of the night," I teased, nudging him with my elbow.

Before Rohan could retort, the first plates of food arrived, and all conversation ceased. The steaming plates of butter paneer and mix veg looked heavenly, the aroma enough to make our hunger intensify tenfold. We wasted no time digging in, and for a few minutes, the only sounds were the clinking of spoons and the satisfied hums of appreciation.

This is amazing," Nikhil said between mouthfuls. "I swear, hostel food has made me forget what real food tastes like."

"No comparison," I agreed, tearing off a piece of soft roti and scooping up a generous amount of paneer gravy. "This is the real deal."

Arjun, chewing happily, wiped his mouth with the back of his hand. "We should bring a tiffin next time and sneak food back to the hostel."

Nikhil laughed. "You really think the warden won't notice the sudden improvement in our diet?"

Rohan, still focused on his plate, grunted. "If we get caught, I'll just say we learned cooking from YouTube."

"That might actually work," I mused. "I mean, I did learn how to make Maggi perfectly through YouTube."

"That's literally just boiling water," Nikhil scoffed.

"Perfection is in the details," I shot back with mock seriousness.

As we continued eating, the conversation shifted to college gossip, professors, and football. One of our team's striker, couldn't resist bragging about our last match against the mechanical engineering team.

As we kept eating, we started talking about college gossip, our professors, and football. One of our team's strikers couldn't stop bragging about our last match against the mechanical engineering team.

Arjun, ever the eager junior, looked at me. "Ishaan sir, do you think we can win the finals next year?"

I hesitated for a second before nodding. "If we play smart and don't let our nerves get to us, we can. But we need to stop overcomplicating our attacks."

Rohan groaned. "There he goes again with his strategy talk."

I chuckled. "Well, someone has to think while you run around like a headless chicken."

The table exploded in laughter, and even Rohan had to grin. The food slowly disappeared from our plates, and the warmth of the meal made us sink into our chairs, content and full.

I leaned back, satisfied. "Best night we've spend all semester."

By the time we finished our meal, it was nearly midnight. The thrill of our night out had begun to wear off, replaced by the creeping awareness of reality. The cool night breeze carried a sense of calm, and for the first time since the football final in the afternoon, I felt at ease. Losing the match had left me with a hollow feeling, but this spontaneous adventure had managed to lift my spirits.

ũ

"We should probably go back," Nikhil said, looking around nervously. "It's getting late, and I don't want to get caught by the hostel warden."

Rohan and Nikhil stood up from their seats. Rohan pulled out a cigarette, placed it between his lips, and flicked his lighter. A small flame appeared, and he lit his cigarette. Nikhil did the same, taking a deep drag and exhaling slowly.

At the table next to them, a group of drunk men was eating dinner. They were loud, laughing and talking in slurred voices. One of them noticed Rohan's lighter and grinned.

"Hey, kid! Come here!" he called out. "Can we borrow your lighter for a second?"

Without thinking much, Rohan stepped forward and handed over his lighter. The man took it, lit his cigarette, and then passed it to his friends. One by one, they all used it, laughing and smoking together.

A few minutes passed, and Rohan extended his hand. "Hey bro, can I have my lighter back?" he asked politely.

The man who had taken it smirked. "What lighter?" he said, pretending not to understand.

Rohan frowned. "Come on, man. That's mine. Just give it back."

Instead of returning it, one of the men suddenly grabbed Rohan by the collar. His grip was tight, and his breath stank of alcohol. His friends chuckled, enjoying the situation.

"You got a problem, kid?" the man growled, his eyes narrowing.

Nikhil stepped closer, his face tense. "Let's just go, Rohan," he whispered.

But Rohan didn't move. He looked straight at the man, his jaw tightening. Things were about to get serious.

"Where are you from? The boys from your college have been acting too proud these days!" he said with a sneer, his breath smelling strongly of alcohol.

We exchanged uneasy glances. "Brother, we're just here for food," Rohan said, keeping his tone calm.

But the man was not in the mood to listen. He suddenly pushed Rohan making him lose his balance and step back. Our group immediately became tense, sensing trouble. Rohan quickly regained his balance and pushed the man back in return. The tension in the air grew stronger as everyone watched to see what would happen next.

"You want to fight?" the man said with a sneer, cracking his knuckles. His two drunk friends stood up, ready to support him. Their eyes were hazy, and they looked like they had been drinking for hours.

Nikhil leaned close to me and whispered, "Come on, guys, let's just leave before this gets out of hand." He grabbed my sleeve, trying to pull me away. But Rohan didn't move. His jaw tightened as he glared at the man.

The drunk man reached out again, gripping Rohan's hand roughly. Before anyone could react, Rohan grabbed the heavy water jug from the table. Without hesitation, he swung it hard—WHAM! —smashing it straight against the man's head. The loud crack echoed through the restaurant. The man stumbled backward, crashing into his chair, which tipped over and sent him to the floor.

For a second, everything froze. The two other drunks stood in shock, staring at their fallen friend. Then, one of them pulled out his phone with a frown.

"Enough! Just watch," he growled, quickly dialling a number. His hands were shaking, but his voice was full of anger.

"Who is he calling?" I asked, feeling my stomach tighten.

"Probably trouble," Nikhil muttered, his face pale.

We knew what that meant. This wasn't just some random drunk guy. These men were locals, and in a place like this, locals had backup.

We exchanged nervous glances. Rohan wiped his wet hands on his jeans, breathing heavily. The unconscious man groaned on the floor.

"Let's go. Let them call whoever they want," Rohan said, his voice cold and steady.

We exchanged glances but didn't argue. It was best to get out before things got worse. We turned towards the Dhaba's exit, stepping over the fallen chair and ignoring the piercing stares of onlookers. The air outside was crisp, the night silent except for the distant chirping of crickets.

We had barely travelled five minutes when we heard the deep, rumbling sound of engines. The noise cut through the quiet like a sharp knife. It wasn't the loud, drunken shouting we had left behind. This was different—calm, steady, and serious. A warning.

Headlights flashed in the darkness, bouncing off the rough road as a group of motorcycles came toward us. They weren't racing like reckless bikers. No, they were moving slowly, closing in like a pack of wolves hunting their prey.

"They brought more people," Nikhil whispered, his voice tense. His hands curled into fists at his sides.

The riders slowed as they got closer. Even in the dim light, we could see they were older, bigger, and completely sober. Their eyes were not clouded by alcohol but focused and serious. This was a different kind of danger.

Our group of eight suddenly didn't seem so big anymore. Fear crept in as we realized we were no match for them.

Then, without any hesitation, someone from our group shouted, "**RUN!**"

That was all we needed to hear. Without wasting a second, we turned around and started running as fast as we could. Our hearts were racing, and adrenaline rushed through our bodies, giving us extra energy to move quickly. The sound of our footsteps echoed on the ground as we bolted forward.

Behind us, the locals were running. Their footsteps grew louder as they chased after us, kicking up dust on the dirt road. We didn't stop to look back—we just focused on running as fast as possible, hoping to escape.

Rohan was ahead, running fast, his feet kicking up dust behind him. He didn't look back, only shouted, "Move faster, damn it!"

My legs hurt, my lungs burned, but I couldn't stop. The angry voices behind us were getting louder, and the sound of our own footsteps was almost lost in the chaos of the chase.

"Shit! The fields!" Arjun yelled, his voice barely reaching over the noise.

Ahead, the dirt path ended, turning into farmland. The land stretched far, covered in tall sugarcane plants. The thick crops looked like both a trap and a chance to escape. We could hide in them, disappear before we got caught. But the uneven ground was dangerous. If we weren't careful, we could fall or get stuck.

Nikhil, panting hard beside me, groaned. "If we get out of this alive, I swear I'll never do this again!"

Rohan didn't slow down. He ran straight into the thick undergrowth, pushing forward with all his strength. And then—

A sudden cry.

I stopped just in time to see Rohan fall. His foot had hit a loose stone, and he crashed down, his arms flailing. His body hit the ground with a heavy thud. Dust rose around him as he groaned, pain clear on his face. His hands were scraped, his knees bleeding.

"Get up!" I shouted, grabbing his arm and pulling him to his feet. He stumbled but didn't argue. We had no time to waste.

The angry voices behind us were still there, though they sounded frustrated. The sugarcane was slowing them down, hiding us, but we couldn't count on that for long.

We ran deeper into the field. The sugarcane stalks hit our faces, their rough leaves cutting into our skin. The ground was uneven, full of hidden roots and sudden dips. Every step felt like a struggle, my muscles screaming for rest.

Suddenly, Nikhil let out a loud grunt. I turned to see him slam into a wooden post, his shoulder hitting it hard. The sound of the impact echoed. He hissed in pain but didn't stop. He shook off the pain and kept running.

"Damn this place!" he muttered, pushing forward.

That was it. I looked at Rohan. Rohan looked at me. We both *nearly* lost it. I felt the laughter bubble up in my chest like soda—my lungs begging to burst.

"Don't laugh. Don't laugh," I whispered, wheezing.

"Bro looked like he hugged the post!" Rohan whispered back, biting his lip.

A voice shouted behind us, closer than before. I glanced back and felt my stomach tighten. The locals had split up, moving through the field from different sides. They were trying to trap us.

"We need to run faster," I gasped, struggling to breathe.

"If we get caught, they'll beat the hell out of us," Arjun said, his voice trembling with fear.

Rohan clenched his fists. His face was set with determination. "Then we don't stop. We run."

I could feel my own heartbeat in my ears, the cold sweat mixing with the dirt on my skin. My shirt was already torn at the sleeve, snagged by the thorny bushes we had just pushed through. A sharp pain burned across my calf, and I realized I had been cut. The juniors weren't faring much better—one of them had a nasty gash across his cheek, another limped from an unseen wound.

Our breathing was heavy, our energy sapped, but the adrenaline kept us moving. I turned back for a brief moment; the locals had stopped at the edge of the field, their torches illuminating their frustrated faces. They were unwilling to chase us further into the treacherous terrain. Relief flooded through me, but we weren't safe yet.

"Don't stop!" Nikhil called out. "Just a little more and we'll reach the hostel!"

We pushed forward, our legs burning, our lungs on fire. The path ahead was barely visible under the faint moonlight, but we recognized the way. Mud splattered our clothes as we ran, the once crisp fabric now clinging to our battered bodies. The hostel wasn't far—just past the next field, through a narrow dirt lane that led directly to the back entrance.

As we reached the final stretch, I risked another glance behind. The locals had disappeared into the night, their shouts fading into the wind.

Finally, the looming structure of our hostel came into sight. I felt a sudden chill go down my back.

"The window!" Rohan gasped, pointing towards the same bathroom window we had used to escape.

One by one, we scrambled through the window, hands slipping on the frame, our clothes drenched in sweat and dirt. Arjun went first, followed by Rohan, then me. I glanced back—Nikhil was still struggling, one leg dangling outside. With a final tug, he made it through. We moved quickly but quietly, trying not to make a sound. The juniors had a tough time, but with a bit of help, they managed to climb in.

My heart raced, half expecting a voice to break the silence, but the hostel remained still. No lights turned on; no footsteps approached. Somehow, luck was on our side tonight. We were back—muddy, breathless, and unseen—our little mission a quiet success.

Once we were all safely inside the thrill of sneaking out and making it back undetected had left us too giddy to go to sleep just yet. We gathered in the corridor, laughing in hushed voices about the night's events.

We were safe. Bruised, battered, and filthy, but safe.

Arjun looked at his torn sleeve and let out a weak laugh. "Well... that was fun."

Nikhil shot him a glare. "Speak for yourself. I'm going to be sore for a week."

Rohan wiped his forehead, his face breaking into a grin despite the pain. "Admit it, though. That was the most excitement we've had in months."

I sighed, leaning against the wall "Next time, let's try to avoid getting nearly killed, yeah?"

We all chuckled, the fear melting into a strange sense of triumph. We had survived. And somehow, despite the bruises and the torn clothes, we felt more alive than ever.

"Bro, we are legends," Rohan said, leaning against the wall with a grin. "Sneaking out, eating food at midnight, and sneaking back in? Not bad."

"Yeah, legends who also broke a window get lucky and don't get beaten up," Nikhil said with a smirk. "So, what's next? Are we going to rob a bank now?"

Rohan chuckled. "Why not? We're on a winning streak."

One of the juniors shook his head. "I don't know about a bank, but we're definitely hitting that place again. That food was something else."

We all burst into laughter—tired, bruised, but alive. Our clothes were covered in dirt, our faces scratched, but we had made it.

The day's stress gradually melted away as laughter filled the air. By the end of the day, I had stopped thinking about losing the football match, the weight of that loss no longer lingered in my mind. Instead, a deep sense of contentment settled over me. Tonight, had been just what I needed—a thrilling, unforgettable adventure with my friends. As we finally tiptoed towards our respective rooms and sank into our beds, exhaustion took over, but a satisfied smile remained.

THE LAST LAP

The last semester of engineering had begun, bringing with it the relentless pressure of projects, placements, and the final attempt to make sense of the past four years. It felt like standing at the edge of a precipice, looking down at everything I had done—every success, every failure, every moment of uncertainty—and realizing that this was my last chance to leave a mark. This was my final opportunity to prove to myself that these years were not wasted.

The air in college was thick with an unspoken urgency. Everyone was running out of time, clutching at whatever opportunities remained. Some were fighting for their dream jobs, others were desperately trying to clear backlogs, and a few were simply hoping to make it through without any more regrets.

I had spent most of my college life wandering through the chaos, searching for meaning, searching for someone who would stand by my side, watching me, appreciating me. I had been lost in distractions, seeking validation in places that never truly mattered.

Connections had come and gone, relationships had flickered and died out, and through it all, I had drifted, unable to anchor myself to anything substantial. But now, the only thing that mattered was survival. It was no longer about what could have been, but about what needed to be done to cross the finish line.

Ever since I failed one subject last year, Rohan and Nikhil had been my backbone, pushing me to focus. They refused to let me sink into self-pity.

"One last chance, Ishaan. We can't afford to mess this up," Nikhil had said, his voice firm but laced with concern. He had always been the pragmatic one, the one who saw life as a series of well-defined steps—study, graduate, get a job, and move forward. For him, there was no space for unnecessary detours or emotional distractions.

Rohan, on the other hand, was my complete opposite. Carefree and light-hearted, he approached life with a reckless optimism that, at times, was infuriating. But he was also fiercely loyal. "We'll make sure you pass, even if I have to teach you myself—which, let's be honest, is a terrible idea," he had joked, grinning at me over a cup of chai in the canteen.

Their constant support worked. I started putting in more effort, attending lectures, solving previous years' question papers, and making notes. It wasn't easy. The habit of casual indifference wasn't easy to break.

There were times I wanted to quit and fall back into the habit of delaying things. But this time, I had to prove something—not to anyone else, but to myself. I wanted to show that I could do it.

Looking back, the past three years had been a series of failures. It wasn't just about academics—I had faced disappointments in almost every aspect of my life. I had loved and lost, tried and failed, started and abandoned countless endeavors.

Football, which once meant everything to me, had become a painful reminder of the matches I had lost and the tournaments I had failed to win. Love, which had once seemed like the ultimate validation, had left me empty and disillusioned. Academics, which should have been my priority from the start, had taken a backseat to distractions that never truly mattered.

My first year in college had started with hope, with dreams of excelling in football, maintaining good grades, and maybe even finding love. I had entered this new phase of life with enthusiasm, believing that I would carve a name for myself, both on the field and in academics. But reality had different plans.

Football had always been my passion. Since childhood, I had spent countless hours on the field, honing my skills, dreaming of the day when I would shine as a star player. College felt like the perfect place to make that dream a reality. I was determined to prove myself, to be the one everyone cheered for. But the competition was fierce. The level of skill among the players was far higher than I had anticipated. I struggled to keep up, making mistakes in crucial moments. My confidence was shattered when

I was benched for an entire season. Sitting on the sidelines, watching others play the game I loved, was one of the hardest things I had ever endured.

I felt useless. I questioned my abilities and wondered if I had been fooling myself all these years. It wasn't just about missing out on playing time; it was the realization that maybe I wasn't as good as I thought I was. The pain of being overlooked, of not being trusted to contribute to the team, ate away at me. I kept pushing myself, training harder, hoping for a chance to prove my worth. Eventually, I managed to break into the team, but fate had another cruel twist in store for me.

When the opportunity finally came, it was in the biggest match of the season—the final. My team had fought hard to reach that stage, and we were determined to win. I stepped onto the field, eager to give my best, to silence my self-doubt once and for all. But in a moment of miscalculation, I made a blunder that cost us the match. The weight of that mistake crushed me. I could see the disappointment in my teammates' eyes, and I felt like I had let everyone down. No matter how hard I tried, I always seemed to fall short.

After that loss, something inside me changed. The fire I once had for football dimmed. I still loved the game, but I could no longer let it dictate my self-worth. Football had taken a backseat now, though I still trained occasionally, using football as an outlet rather than an obsession. It was therapeutic, a way to clear my mind when the weight of academics or personal disappointments became too much. But the fire I once had, the all-consuming passion that made me stay up late practicing shots and strategizing plays, had faded. The game no longer defined me; it was something I cherished, but it wasn't the only thing that mattered.

Love? That had been another disaster. When I had first stepped into college, I was filled with hope—the naive hope of finding love, of experiencing the kind of companionship I had only dreamed about. I imagined finding someone who understood me, who would be my partner through the ups and downs of life. But reality was far from what I had envisioned.

Ahana, chapter I had closed. Or at least, I tried to. She had been one of my closest friends in college, someone I had shared countless memories with. I had developed feelings for this girl. She was everything I wasn't—brilliant, confident, and sure of herself. She walked with an air of self-assurance that I admired, and her presence alone was enough to brighten the dullest of days. I spent months mustering the courage to confess, playing out every possible scenario in my head.

When I finally told her how I felt, she hesitated. Then, with a gentle but firm voice, she told me that she saw me only as a friend. The words stung more than I cared to admit. I had built up so many expectations, so many dreams surrounding her, only for them to shatter in an instant. For a while, I withdrew into myself, letting self-doubt consume me. Was I not good enough? Was there something inherently lacking in me? The questions haunted me, but over time, I learned to let them go

After that, I shut myself off from her. It wasn't that I hated her, but the pain of being 'not good enough' had cut too deep. She had tried to talk to me multiple times, but I always found a way to avoid her. At first, it was out of sheer self-preservation. Seeing her, hearing her voice—it all reminded me of what I couldn't have. So, I distanced myself, physically and emotionally.

Days turned into weeks, weeks into month. I had not spoken to Ahana since that day. Not once. Not even a passing hello in the corridors. Not even eye contact in a crowded campus. It was easier that way. Easier to pretend she didn't exist rather than confront the mess of emotions I still carried.

There were times when I caught glimpses of her in the library or across cafeteria laughing with her friends, completely unaware of the silent storm raging within me. I wondered if she ever thought about me, if she missed our conversations, our shared jokes. But I never found out.

Academically, there also things weren't much better. Despite my initial enthusiasm, I struggled to keep up with the rigorous coursework. Engineering was tough and unforgiving. It was never something I had truly wanted to study, and even now, I knew it was not my dream. I always felt like I was behind everyone else, struggling to understand things that others seemed to grasp easily. The pressure kept increasing, and at times, it felt like I could not breathe. There were moments when I seriously thought about giving up. I wondered if I even belonged in this field.

I had spent years watching others move ahead while I remained stuck in place, paralyzed by my own mistakes. But now, in this final semester, something had shifted. Maybe it was the realization that time was running out, or maybe it was the unwavering support of Rohan and Nikhil.

Either way, I had finally found a sense of purpose, a reason to keep pushing forward.

That was when I made a decision. This last semester would be different. I would not allow any more distractions or regrets. I was tired of feeling like a failure. This was my final chance to prove to myself that I could do better, and I was ready to work for it.

With each passing day, I could feel a change within me. The fear of failure that had once held me back was slowly being replaced by a quiet determination. I no longer cared about proving myself to the world. This was for me. This was my redemption, my last chance to rewrite the narrative of my college years.

The next phase of my life had begun, and with it, the journey toward something more—something greater than just passing exams or securing a job. It was the journey toward proving to myself that I was capable of overcoming my past, of moving forward despite everything. And no matter what happened next, I knew one thing for certain: I wasn't going to give up.

I set up a study schedule, waking up earlier than usual, revising the same topics multiple times until they were engraved in my brain. The evenings that were once spent aimlessly scrolling through my phone or wandering around campus were now dedicated to studying, revising, and understanding concepts I had ignored for years. The library had become my sanctuary, a place where I could detach from the distractions of college life and focus solely on my goal.

The dim glow of study lamps, the rustling of pages, and the quiet determination of other students surrounded me, creating an atmosphere of silent camaraderie. We were all in the same boat, navigating the storm of deadlines, exams, and job interviews.

I started small—attending every lecture, no matter how boring. I forced myself to sit in the front rows, to ask questions, to engage with the subjects I had once ignored. I built a study routine and stuck to it religiously. My days started early, with revision sessions before classes, and ended late at night in the library. I tackled my weaknesses one by one, seeking help from professors and classmates when needed.

The changes weren't instant, and there were days when the weight of everything threatened to crush me. But every time I felt like slipping back into old habits, I reminded myself of why I started. I thought of the disappointment I had felt in the past, the countless nights spent regretting wasted opportunities. I didn't want to go through that again.

Slowly, my efforts started paying off. Topics that once seemed impossible to understand started making sense. My test scores improved, and for the first time in years, I felt like I was in control of my academic life. It was no longer just about passing exams. It was about proving to myself that I was stronger than my past failures. I had finally learned that success was not about being perfect, but about never giving up.

The days passed in a blur of lectures, assignments, and late-night study sessions. The placement season loomed ahead like an inevitable storm, and the pressure was mounting. Companies started visiting the campus, and my classmates were either celebrating their offers or drowning in anxiety. The atmosphere was electric with anticipation. "You applied for any companies yet?" Nikhil asked one evening as we sat in our usual spot near the Football ground. I shook my head. "Not yet. Need to get my grades in order first."

Nikhil chuckled, stretching his arms. "Well, guess what? I got placed."

I looked at him, surprised. "Seriously? Where?"

"A good MNC," he said, his voice carrying a mix of pride and relief. "Decent package too."

I grinned, slapping him on the back. "That's huge, man! Congrats!"

By then, Rohan had joined us, and as soon as he heard the news, he suggested what was inevitable—celebration. "We have to party," he declared. "And there's only one place we can do it right."

We all exchanged knowing looks. The hostel rooftop. The same spot where we had been caught by the warden in our first year, sneaking in with a few drinks and reckless laughter, thinking we ruled the world.

ũ

That night, with bottles in hand, we climbed up once again. The city stretched out before us, a canvas of flickering lights and distant honks, while a cool breeze carried the sounds of life from the streets below. Rohan smirked as he rolled a joint between his fingers, a ritual he had perfected over the years.

"So, remember, guys? This is the same place where we got caught smoking after we broke the lock and sneaked up here?" He chuckled, shaking his head.

I let out a laugh, stretching my legs out in front of me. "How could I forget? Warden acted like we were running an international drug cartel."

Nikhil groaned. "Man, that was the worst. I still remember the look on his face—pure disappointment, like we ruined his faith in students forever."

"Yeah," I said, shaking my head. "We really thought we were invincible back then. First year was just a different vibe."

Nikhil sighed, staring up at the sky. "It was. Everything felt new. That first semester? Struggling to figure out which class was where, getting lost in the admin block, and then pretending we knew what we were doing."

Rohan exhaled and looked at us. "But, dude, somewhere along the way, we changed. Like, think about it. First-year was all about bunking, gaming, and last-minute assignments. Then, slowly, everything started feeling... serious."

I nodded. "Yeah. First-year us wouldn't believe we'd be sitting here, talking about placements, future plans, and how this chapter of life is almost over."

"Forget placements, bro," Nikhil said, stretching. "Football tournaments, heartbreaks.... We've seen everything."

Rohan smirked. "Some of us have seen backlogs too."

"Shut up," I shot back, shaking my head. "But yeah, it's crazy. We've won, we've lost, we've failed... But at the end of the day, we survived."

Nikhil smiled. "And we're still here. On this rooftop. Together."

Rohan leaned back, resting his arms behind his head. "Yeah, we were all idiots back then," he said with a chuckle. "I thought if I just worked hard enough, life would reward me. Turns out, life doesn't owe anyone anything."

I scoffed. "Speak for yourself. I never expected anything. I just wanted... I don't know, things to make sense. But they didn't."

Rohan glanced at me. "You mean love? Or football? Or studies?"

I shrugged. "All of it, I guess. Love was confusing. Football was fun, but it didn't take me anywhere. Studies? Well, I ignored them long enough to know that was a mistake."

Nikhil sighed. "We all got our share of regrets. But what can you do? Life moves forward whether you're ready or not."

Rohan nodded. "Exactly. I went through rejections, misunderstandings, and heartbreaks, which taught me that love isn't something you can force or chase desperately. I used to think finding love would complete me, but I was wrong. People aren't missing pieces that fit perfectly into your life—they have their own dreams, fears, and choices."

I listened, not knowing whether I agreed or just wanted to believe what he said. Rohan had always been the kind of person who could accept things and move on. I wasn't sure if I had that ability.

"So, I stopped looking for approval from others and focused on becoming someone I could respect," Rohan continued. "Life moves on."

I told myself that I had moved on too. Football was no longer my priority, and love didn't seem worth chasing anymore. Instead, I shifted my focus to studies, something I had ignored before. I spent my time reading textbooks and doing assignments, trying to make up for the past.

But no matter how much I tried to move on, there were moments—late at night, in the quiet of my room—when the past would come back. The thoughts of "what if" and "could have been" played in my mind like an old, broken song.

I had changed. I wasn't the same person I was when I started college. The boy who once dreamed of love, football, and success had learned that life doesn't always go as planned.

And maybe, that's okay.

There was a brief silence as we all just stared at the skyline, lost in our own thoughts. The city never stopped moving, but for us, in that moment, time stood still. The distant hum of traffic, the occasional shout from the street vendors below, and the sound of the wind brushing against the rooftop railing felt oddly calming.

Rohan broke the silence. "You know, sometimes I wonder what happens next. Like, when we step out of here, into the real world. Will we still have these conversations? Or will we be too busy running after money, promotions, and responsibilities?"

"That's the scary part," Nikhil admitted. "Right now, we have each other. But life? It moves fast. People get jobs, move to different cities, get married, start families. What if we just become names in each other's contact lists?"

"I don't know, man. I'd like to believe we'll stay in touch. That we'll still meet up, have these stupid deep conversations, laugh about old times. But reality? It's unpredictable." I said, taking a sip and leaning back against the wall.

"Maybe that's why this moment feels so important," Rohan said. "Because we don't know what's next."

We sat there for what felt like hours, reminiscing, sharing our fears about the future, and realizing how much we had all grown. The sky above us stretched endlessly, mirroring the uncertainty of our lives ahead.

But for now, at least, we had this night, this rooftop, and each other.

The world outside awaited, full of uncertainties. But for the first time in a long time, I wasn't afraid. I was ready. Because this was just the beginning.

THE LAST ROLL CALL

The final days of engineering had arrived. Four years of assignments, sleepless nights, coffee-fueled study sessions, and last-minute submissions were coming to an end. It felt surreal, almost as if time had accelerated in the last few months. The anticipation of the end was mixed with nostalgia, excitement, and a tinge of anxiety about what lay ahead.

All the written exams were over, and the relief of being done with them was immense. The late-night revisions, endless discussions, and frantic flipping through notes had finally come to an end. However, one final challenge remained—our project viva. Unlike theory exams, this was different. It wasn't just about memorizing formulas or writing lengthy answers. It was about defending months of hard work, proving that we had actually learned something beyond textbooks.

The project viva carried a great weightage in our final year marks. A good performance here could make all the difference. I stood outside the academic hall, taking a deep breath, trying to calm my nerves. This was it—the last hurdle.

The classroom was abuzz with hushed whispers and last-minute revisions. Some of my classmates were flipping through project files, their eyes darting across pages in a desperate attempt to soak in every last bit of information. Others sat in silence, lost in thought, perhaps reflecting on the years gone by. The atmosphere was thick with tension, a mixture of nervous energy and quiet determination.

Kumar Manu, who was in my project group, looked very confident. He sat back calmly, as if he already knew all the answers. While the rest of us were busy reading notes in a panic, he seemed completely relaxed. I was sitting right next to him, feeling nervous. I kept repeating the project details to myself, my fingers tapping anxiously on the desk. My eyes showed my worry, just like many others in the room. The tension was high, but Kumar Manu's calmness made him stand out.

The clock ticked steadily, each passing second drawing us closer to our moment of reckoning. My palms felt slightly damp as I clutched my project file, stealing a glance at the door to the examination room.

"Group 6, Next".

The professor's voice silenced the chatter, making me nervous. I took a deep breath and stood up, trying to smile. Feeling both careful and anxious, the four of us walked toward the Viva room. My heart was beating fast, filled with both fear and excitement about what would happen next.

Inside, a panel of professors sat across a long table, their expressions unreadable. The head examiner, an elderly man with sharp glasses that seemed to pierce into the depths of our understanding, leaned forward slightly. He started with me, studied me for a moment before offering a small smile.

"Tell us about the project you've worked on."

I exhaled slowly, gripping the file a little tighter. This was my moment to prove myself.

I cleared my throat, reminding myself to stay composed. "Our project is a smart energy management system designed to optimize power consumption in residential and commercial spaces..." I launched into an explanation, detailing the motivation behind the project, the methodology, and the potential impact it could have on energy efficiency.

My words flowed smoothly, and with each passing second, my confidence grew. The panel of professors and examiners listened intently, occasionally nodding in understanding.

I explained how our system used real-time monitoring, machine learning algorithms, and IoT integration to regulate energy consumption efficiently. We had tested the system in a simulated environment and observed a significant reduction in energy wastage. Encouraged by their engagement, I elaborated on the cost-effectiveness and scalability of our design. For a moment, I felt completely in control.

But then came the moment I had been dreading—the external examiner decided to test my depth of knowledge with a tough electrical engineering question.

"Can you explain in detail the impact of harmonics on power quality and how you would mitigate them in a three-phase system?" he asked, his gaze sharp and expectant.

The question hit me like a sudden voltage surge. I had studied harmonics, written about them in our report, and even solved problems related to them. Yet, at that moment, my mind went completely blank. I could feel the weight of silence stretching longer than it should.

Panic threatened to take over as I tried to recall the technical specifics, but nothing came to me. My heart pounded. My teammates glanced at me, sensing my hesitation. One of them subtly shifted in his chair, as if ready to step in, but I knew I had to answer this myself. Taking a deep breath, I willed my mind to focus, hoping to regain my composure before it was too late.

The examiner smirked slightly, then leaned back in his chair. His gaze was sharp yet unreadable, as if he were assessing not just my answers but my very thought process. I shifted in my seat, gripping the edge slightly, my mind racing to anticipate his next move. The viva had been relentless so far—technical question after technical question, some of which I had fumbled through, others where I had barely managed to hold my ground. My nerves were fraying, and I could feel the sweat forming at my temples.

He tapped his pen against the desk, a slow and deliberate motion. "You seem tense, Ishaan," he noted, almost amused. "Let's take a different approach."

I held my breath, unsure of what that meant. Was he about to increase the difficulty? Throw in an unexpected twist? His tone, however, had softened—less like a strict examiner and more like a curious observer.

"You know," he continued, "engineering isn't just about solving numerical problems. It's about vision, about innovation. It's about people who change the way we live."

I blinked, absorbing his words.

"Tell me, "He said, his voice now lighter, almost conversational, "You know the well-known engineer, also known as the 'Metro Man of India'?"

For a moment, I was caught off guard. A non-technical question in the middle of a viva? But then, relief washed over me—I knew this answer. Gathering myself, I responded with confidence.

Engineer E. Sreedharan, popularly known as the 'Metro Man of India,' is an exemplary figure in the field of engineering and urban infrastructure development.

The examiner smiled and nodded approvingly. "Good. I am impressed how you added Engineer before his name, ok, and what lessons can an engineer take from his work?"

I took a deep breath and continued, "His career teaches us the importance of discipline, integrity, and innovation in engineering. Engineer Sreedharan believed in meticulous planning and execution without compromising on quality. He demonstrated that even the most complex engineering challenges could be overcome with determination and efficient leadership. For us as aspiring engineers, his legacy is a reminder that technical knowledge must be complemented by strong ethical values and problem-solving skills."

The panel looked at each other, their faces hard to understand. For a moment, I thought I had said something wrong. But then, I saw a few of them smiling a little. That's when I knew my words had made an impact and caught their attention.

A brief silence followed, stretching longer than I was comfortable with. My heartbeat quickened. Had I impressed them, or was this just the calm before the storm? Finally, the head examiner leaned forward, tapping his pen on the table.

"Well, Ishaan," he said, his lips curving into a smirk. "That was... something." He paused, letting the weight of his words sink in before exchanging another knowing glance with his colleagues. "You may go now. And somehow, despite everything, congratulations on completing your bachelor's degree."

I couldn't tell if that was a compliment or an insult, but at that moment, I didn't care. I had made it through

As I stepped out of the examination room, I exhaled deeply, a mix of relief and satisfaction washing over me. Despite stumbling on the technical question, I had managed to leave a positive impression. Maybe engineering wasn't just about knowing every formula and theorem—it was also about staying composed under pressure and demonstrating a keen understanding of the world beyond textbooks. And in that moment, I felt one step closer to becoming an engineer in the true sense of the word.

Relief washed over me as I stepped out of the room. It was over. My last viva. My last exam. The realization settled in like a quiet wave—my degree was now just a formality away.

Outside, my classmates had gathered, discussing their experiences animatedly. Some looked relieved, others exhausted. A few were still nervously awaiting their turn. The air was thick with emotions—relief, joy, nostalgia. The day scholars, the friends with whom I had shared countless Class bunks, chai breaks, and group study sessions, were preparing to leave. There was a sense of finality in the air.

"So, this is it, huh?" Kumar Manu said, patting my back. "No more waking up at 7 AM for lectures."

"No more fighting with the assignments before submission deadlines," added by another classmate, laughing.

We chuckled, reminiscing about the countless hurdles we had faced together—the 11th-hour assignments, the all-nighters before exams, the nerve-wracking practical's where we barely understood what we were doing but somehow made it through. The bunked lectures, the hostel pranks, the endless discussions about career plans and uncertain futures. Every single moment had shaped us in ways we couldn't fully grasp yet.

We wandered through the campus one last time, visiting every familiar spot—the canteen where we had spent hours debating over trivial topics, the library that had witnessed our desperate attempts to cram before exams, the football ground where rivalries were forged and friendships deepened. Every corner held a memory, a story, a piece of our journey.

As the sun dipped below the horizon, casting a golden glow over the campus, reality set in. This chapter of our lives was closing. Some of us had secured jobs, ready to dive into the corporate world. Some were preparing for higher studies, chasing bigger academic dreams. Others, like me, were still contemplating the next step, uncertain but hopeful.

"We'll stay in touch, right?" someone asked. We all nodded, promising to meet again, to not let distance and responsibilities erase the bond we had built. But deep down, we knew that life had a way of pulling people in different directions.

The final goodbyes were the hardest. One by one, friends departed, each farewell leaving an ache in my chest. Watching them leave, I felt a mix of emotions—happiness for the journey we had shared, sadness for its inevitable end, and excitement for the road ahead.

As I took one last glance at the campus, I felt a quiet sense of accomplishment. Four years ago, I had walked in as a nervous freshman, unsure of what lay ahead. Now, I was walking out as an engineer, ready to face the world.

The journey was ending, but a new one was about to begin.

THE LAST WALK

The sun had barely risen, casting its gentle orange glow over the sprawling campus, as I stood on the balcony of my hostel room for what felt like the thousandth time. This time, however, it felt different. Today was the last day of college—the end of four years that had slipped through my fingers like sand, leaving behind a bittersweet blend of memories, regrets, and unfulfilled dreams.

I took a deep breath, letting the chilly morning air fill my lungs. My eyes scanned the horizon, a view i had taken for granted over the years. The football field stretched out like an eternal promise of potential i had never quite grasped. The thought stung a little. I had spent countless afternoons there, watching friends practice, my own jersey remaining pristine and unused for a while.

My phone buzzed on the rickety study table behind me. I glanced at the screen; it was a message from Rohan, my roommate and closest friend. "Breakfast in 10 minutes, let's make it count today, bro."

I smiled faintly, typing a quick "Sure" in response. Rohan's cheerful optimism had been a constant in my otherwise tumultuous college life. I turned back to the room, my gaze lingering on the walls covered with posters, exam schedules, and half-torn reminders of assignments i had meant to submit on time but never did. The room was a collage of my almost—almost passed every semester without a retake, almost achieved what others expected of me.

By the time I reached the mess, the place was buzzing with chatter. Groups of students, many of whom I barely knew beyond casual greetings, were savoring their last meal together. The air was thick with nostalgia, laughter, and the bittersweet feeling of impending goodbyes.

Rohan waved me over, grinning as always. Seated at their usual table was the rest of our hostel gang, including a bunch of juniors who had become like younger brothers over the years. As I pulled up a chair, Nikhil smirked.

"Finally decided to grace us with your presence, huh?" he teased, nudging my arm.

"Overslept, as usual," Rohan added with a chuckle. "Classic Ishaan."

"Hey, at least I made it," I shot back, grinning.

The conversation flowed effortlessly, just like it always had. Jokes were exchanged, stories retold for what felt like the hundredth time, yet still bringing the same bursts of laughter. We talked about everything—the ridiculous pranks we had pulled, the hostel warden's exasperated scolding's, the terrifying yet hilarious encounters with our professors. The juniors sat wide-eyed, soaking in every detail, already dreading the void our departure would leave behind.

One of them, Aman, piped up, "Bhaiya, you guys are leaving, and we're going to be left with all the boring seniors! Who's going to sneak us out for late-night chai now?"

I chuckled, ruffling his hair. "You'll find a way, Bro. We did. And remember, if you ever get caught, just say you were on a 'mission to relieve stress.' No one argues with mental health."

The table erupted into laughter.

As plates were being emptied and glasses of tea made their rounds, a silence settled in. For a moment, nobody spoke. The reality was finally sinking in. This was it. The last time we would all be together like this. I wanted to freeze the moment, to stretch it out forever.

"Man, it's crazy how four years flew by," Nikhil said, breaking the silence. "Feels like just yesterday we were clueless freshers, scared of every senior who walked by."

Rohan sighed dramatically. "And look at us now—legends of this hostel."

I rolled my eyes. "Legends? More like infamous troublemakers."

We all laughed, but there was a weight behind it, a collective acknowledgment that this chapter of our lives was coming to an end.

After breakfast, we wandered back to our rooms, the reality of impending goodbyes settling in. My packing was only half done. I threw clothes, books, and random knick-knacks into the suitcase without much thought. Every item I picked up seemed to have a memory attached to it—a quiz I had flunked, a ticket stub from a movie night, a birthday card signed by all of my friends. Each object felt like a piece of my soul being packed away.

As the day wore on, the hostel corridors buzzed with activity. Friends hugged, exchanged promises to stay in touch, and took endless selfies. I participated half-heartedly, my mind elsewhere. I felt like a spectator watching everyone else's lives move forward while I remained stuck in the same loop of unfulfilled potential.

My mind was in last farewell to my love. It wasn't something that could be defined with a single word. I had been silently in conversations with Ahana for months, watching her from a distance, wondering what it would be like to hold her hand, to be the one she turned to for comfort. But i had always kept my feelings locked inside. And now, with graduation just hours away, i knew i couldn't leave without bidding farewell to her.

I took a deep breath and pulled out my phone, scrolling to Ahana's contact. My finger hovered over the call button for a moment before i pressed it. The phone rang twice before Ahana's voice echoed through the speaker.

"Hello?"

My heart skipped a beat. I had not imagined this moment like this, but now that it was here, I didn't know what to do.

"Hey, Ahana, it's... it's Ishaan," I said, my voice wavering slightly.

There was a brief pause on the other end, and then she spoke, her voice as calm and familiar as always. "Ishaan! How are you? It feels strange, doesn't it? Our last day of college."

I could hear the bittersweetness in her tone, and it made my heart ache even more. "Yeah, strange. Listen, I... I was wondering if you could meet me at the cafeteria for a bit. Just for a final goodbye."

Ahana replied quickly, "Sure! I just finished submitting my book at the library. I'll be there in a minute."

A silence settled for a moment before she spoke again, her voice softer. "Ishaan... you sound different today. Is something wrong?"

I exhaled slowly. "Not wrong, just... I guess I didn't realize how hard this would be. Leaving everything behind, leaving... you behind."

Her breath hitched slightly, and when she spoke again, her voice was quieter. "I know. It's been such a journey, hasn't it? And now, suddenly, it's all coming to an end."

"Yeah," I murmured. "I just don't want to regret anything, you know? I don't want to leave things unsaid."

There was another pause. "What do you mean?" she asked gently.

I hesitated before responding. "I mean... I just wanted to thank you, Ahana. For everything. For being there, even when you didn't realize it. For making college bearable, for making it memorable."

A soft chuckle came from the other end. "You're making this sound like a farewell speech."

"Maybe it is," I admitted. "Or maybe it's just me finally saying what I should've said a long time ago."

Ahana sighed, and for the first time, I detected a hint of emotion in her voice. "You don't have to say everything over the phone, Ishaan. I'm on my way. Just wait for me."

I smiled slightly. "I will."

The phone call ended, and I couldn't help but feel a surge of nervousness. I had spent so many years beside Ahana, yet today, the thought of speaking to her one last time, without the familiar comfort of the next day or the day after, felt like the weight of the world on his shoulders.

"Hey," she said softly as I waited in the cafeteria, her voice carrying an undertone of familiarity I had almost forgotten.

I turned and saw Ahana standing there, her hair tousled slightly by the wind, the faint glow of the cityscape behind her giving her an ethereal presence. For a moment, I thought she was a figment of my imagination, a fragment of memories I had tried so hard to suppress.

"I thought you'd still be here," she added, her lips curving into a small, tentative smile.

My heart skipped a beat, and I straightened up, trying to mask the chaos of emotions inside me. "Couldn't leave without one last look," I said, my voice tinged with a forced casualness.

Ahana walked closer, her presence warming the space around me. She stood so close that our shoulders almost brushed. There was a silence that fell between us, but it wasn't heavy. It was the kind of silence that carried weight—a silence brimming with things left unsaid, emotions too delicate to voice. Together, we gazed out at the city lights, the quiet amplifying the unspoken tension between us.

Finally, she broke the silence, her voice firmer now. "Why, Ishaan? Why did you stop talking to me?"

Her question caught me off guard. I glanced at her, unsure of how to respond. She wasn't done.

"Months, Ishaan. You didn't reply to my texts, didn't answer my calls. You wouldn't even look at me when we crossed paths. What did I do? Was it something I said, something I did?" Her voice cracked slightly, and she looked away, biting her lip. "Do you have any idea how that made me feel?"

I inhaled deeply, the weight of her words pressing on me. I had dreaded this conversation, yet here it was, staring me in the face.

"It wasn't you," I said finally, my voice low. "It was never about you, Ahana."

She turned to face me fully, her eyes narrowing in frustration. "Then what was it about? Because it sure felt like it was about me. Like I wasn't worth your time anymore"

Her words stung, but they were fair. "I... I was a mess," I admitted, running a hand through my hair. "I didn't know how to handle everything. Life felt like it was spiraling out of control, and I couldn't bring myself to face anyone. Especially you"

"Why especially me?" she asked, her voice softer now but still laced with hurt.

"Because you saw through me," I said, meeting her gaze. "You always have. And I was scared—scared of what you'd see if you looked too closely. I didn't want you to see how much I was falling apart."

Ahana's expression softened, and for a moment, she seemed to be processing my words. "So instead, you just shut me out?"

I nodded, shame washing over me. "It was easier than admitting I needed help. Easier than being vulnerable"

She shook her head slowly, her eyes glistening with unshed tears. "You idiot," she said, but there was no anger in her voice. "If you are going through any tough time. I would've been there for you, no matter what."

"I know that now," I said, my voice barely above a whisper. "And I'm sorry, Ahana. I'm sorry for pushing you away when I needed you the most. You didn't deserve that."

My eyes filled with tears, and a lump formed in my throat. I wanted to cry, but I didn't let the tears fall. I blinked quickly, trying to push them back, but my vision blurred for a moment. I took a deep breath, forcing myself to stay strong, even though the pain inside me was hard to ignore.

Finally, she broke the silence. "You're going to be okay, Ishaan. You know that, right?"

I glanced at her, surprised. Her voice held a certainty that I'd never felt about myself. "What makes you so sure?" i asked, my tone more vulnerable than i intended.

She turned to face me, her gaze unwavering and charged with an intensity that made my heart tighten. I've seen you, the real you, you're stronger than you realize. You just don't give yourself enough credit.

Her words hit me like a wave, washing over years of self-doubt and insecurity. I wanted to believe her, to let her confidence in me replace the voice in my head that always told me it wasn't enough. But doubt was a stubborn adversary. "Thanks, Ahana. That means a lot," i said finally, my voice barely above a whisper.

She smiled, but it didn't reach her eyes. There was something bittersweet in her expression, a hint of sadness that mirrored my own. "I'll miss you, Ishaan," she said, her voice soft but resolute.

I swallowed hard, the lump in my throat threatening to choke me. "I'll miss you too," i replied, the words feeling inadequate to express the depth of my feelings. And then, before i could stop myself, i added, "More than you know."

For a fleeting moment, our eyes met. In her gaze, I thought i saw a flicker of understanding, a glimpse of something that made my heart ache with both hope and despair. But just as quickly, she looked away, and the moment passed, slipping through my fingers like sand.

Ahana stepped closer and gave me a quick hug. I closed my eyes, memorizing the feel of her arms around me, knowing it would be the last time. When she pulled away, she lingered for a heartbeat, as if she wanted to say something more. But instead, she turned and walked away, her figure gradually fading into the shadows of the memories.

I stood there, rooted to the spot, as the weight of her absence settled over me.

My heartfelt heavy, but a part of me knew this was how it had to be. Love, i realized, wasn't always about declarations and happy endings. Sometimes, it was about quiet acceptance and letting go. And so, with one last glance at the campus where so much had been left unsaid, i walked away, ready to face whatever came next.

ũ

The evening settled over the campus, casting long shadows as I walked slowly down the path leading to the parking lot. The once-bustling corridors and green lawns now seemed eerily quiet, as if the world itself was holding its breath, mirroring the bittersweet knot tightening in my chest. This was it – the last day of college. Four years of laughter, struggles, and growth had come to an end.

My bag was slung over my shoulder, lighter than I'd imagined it would be. All the physical belongings were packed, but the memories, they were impossible to box up. I stopped by the oak tree near the library, my gaze drifting to the bench beneath it. That bench had witnessed countless late-night study sessions, heated debates about life and dreams, and even my first awkward attempt at confessing my feelings to someone special. Now it was just another piece of the campus i would leave behind.

In the parking lot, I saw a familiar group of faces waiting for me. Rohan was the first one I noticed, his perpetually messy hair sticking out in every direction, and that lopsided grin of his—it was both reassuring and bittersweet. Standing close to him was Nikhil, whose eyes were unmistakably red and puffy, clear signs he had been crying. Yet, in typical Nikhil fashion, he was trying to mask his emotions by cracking jokes, even though his forced laughter didn't quite reach his eyes. Nearby, a group of juniors from our hostel lingered awkwardly, their presence a quiet reminder of how far our little circle had grown.

As I approached, the chatter died down. One by one, their gazes turned to me, and the atmosphere shifted into something heavier, more solemn. No one said a word. It wasn't that we didn't have anything to say—it was just that words felt inadequate, too small to carry the weight of what we were feeling.

And then, as if we had rehearsed it, we all moved toward each other at the same time. No one hesitated. We fell into a tight, almost chaotic group hug, our arms tangling and shoulders bumping as we held on like we never wanted to let go. It was messy and awkward, a tangle of limbs and sniffles, but it felt just right. That hug was us—imperfect, unpolished, and full of unspoken understanding. It captured everything our friendship had always been: complicated, raw, and absolutely perfect in its own way.

"So, this is it," Nikhil said, his voice breaking as he pulled away. "No more last-minute study marathons, no more late-night chai runs, no more... us."

"It's not the end," Rohan said, his grin faltering for the first time. "We'll stay in touch. Video calls, group chats, reunions. We'll make it work."

"Yeah, like you're going to have time for all that when you're touring the world with your girlfriends," Nikhil teased, his voice shaky but still carrying its usual sass. "Don't forget us little people when you're famous, okay?"

"Never," Rohan promised, his voice unusually serious.

The conversations turned to laughter, even as tears threatened to spill. We reminisced about our favorite moments: the disastrous cooking experiments in the hostel, the time we got locked out on the hostel terrace, and the endless pranks we'd pulled on each other. Each memory was a reminder of how much we'd grown together, how much we'd meant to one another.

Just as we were lost in our nostalgia, a group of juniors approached us hesitantly. One of them, Ravi, cleared his throat and said, "Bhaiya, it's hard to imagine this place without you guys. You've been the heart of our hostel. Who's going to set the rules now?"

We chuckled, and Nikhil dramatically placed a hand on his chest. "The torch must be passed," he said, wiping an imaginary tear. "You guys must carry forward the legacy of midnight Maggi, proxy attendance, and acing exams on pure luck and desperation."

The juniors laughed, but there was a hint of sadness in their eyes. One of them, Ankit, added, "And what about football? Without you guys, it won't be the same."

Rohan clapped a hand on his shoulder. "It's your time now. You take the team forward. And if you ever need motivation, just remember how we crushed them in the finals."

I nodded, feeling the weight of our departure settle in. "You'll make new memories, form your own traditions. We did our part, and now it's your turn."

For a moment, silence stretched between us. Then, Ravi asked softly, "Are you guys scared?"

That question hung in the air. Were we? Of course, we were. Leaving behind the comfort of these walls, the friendships that had become family, stepping into the unknown—it was terrifying.

Rohan exhaled. "Yeah," he admitted. "A little. Maybe a lot. But that's how life works, right? You don't get to stay in the same place forever."

I looked around at my friends and then back at the juniors. "But fear isn't a bad thing. It means you care about what you're leaving behind. It means this place mattered."

Nikhil smirked, nudging me. "Deep as always, Ishaan."

I shrugged. "It's true, though."

One by one, the goodbyes came swiftly and painfully. Hugs were exchanged, tears were shed, and promises to stay in touch were made. As I watched my friends bidding me farewell one by one, I felt a hollow ache in my chest. This was it. End of an era.

I turned around to take one final look at the campus. The buildings stood quietly, their walls echoing with countless stories that would endure long after my departure. I reflected on the lessons I'd gained here - not only from textbooks but from life itself. The near-victories that shaped my resilience, the near-failures that instilled humility, and the almost-love that gave me courage.

Sliding into the driver's seat of my car, I took a deep breath. As the engine roared to life and the car pulled away, i made a silent promise to myself.

"I'll take the lessons of my almost and turn them into victories."

The road stretched ahead, unknown and full of possibilities. My story wasn't over yet. It was only just beginning.

www.ingramcontent.com/pod-product-compliance
Lightning Source LLC
LaVergne TN
LVHW091711070526
838199LV00050B/2350